D1523955

A House for Keeping

MATTESON WYNN

For Moira
without whom this book wouldn't be here

Chapter One

Magic fingers, my ass.

I heaved myself upright and gave the vibrating hotel bed the sleepy version of a death glare. After a groggy moment wondering when and why I'd decided to turn on the "magic fingers" in the first place, I concluded it must've seemed like a good idea to my road-weary self. Now, not so much.

I shook my head in an attempt to knock my sleepy thoughts into some kind of order, and memories of the previous night floated to the surface.

I'd been driving cross-country, and I'd stubbornly stayed on the road longer than I should have. When my head thunked into my steering wheel, it was clear that my choice was either to take a catnap or take a dirt nap, so I'd pulled over, gotten a room, and totally passed out. Fully clothed. I hadn't even taken my shoes off.

Classy.

That put me…

…Um…

I felt like that kid in *Sleepless in Seattle*. I knew I was "somewhere in the middle"—not the desert I'd left, not the East Coast I was heading for—but that was as close as my bleary brain cells could come to a location at the moment.

So, right. No-tell motel. Lots of vibrating.

How the hell was I supposed to be Finn the Fearless Traveler if I couldn't get any sleep?

Having had my fill of magic for the evening, I looked for the box by the bed to try and turn it off and…huh. No box. So why did my bed sound like a cat with the hiccups trying to purr?

I wondered if maybe it was the people in the next room getting creative. While part of me applauded my mystery neighbors for their innovative sexy times, I had a lot more driving to do, which wasn't gonna happen unless I got some shut-eye. Even at 22, a girl needs her rest.

I considered trying to just sleep through it, but then the hum got louder, so I gave up on that idea and decided to call the front desk. As I leaned over to grab the room phone, the bed wobbled, I lost my balance, and I found myself making friends with the floor.

It was vibrating, too.

With a groan, I staggered to my feet. Realizing sleep was not likely to happen in this room, I grabbed my purse off the nightstand with one hand and my rolling suitcase handle with the other, and started for the door. I wasn't in the mood to negotiate, so I was going to march down to the lobby, and they could just move me to another room ASAP.

I'd only taken a couple of steps when the floor lurched, sending me stumbling forward. Heart skipping, I scrambled for the door while my suddenly alert brain tried to recall which parts of "somewhere in the middle" had earthquakes.

I turned the door knob and pulled, did a double-take, then pulled again.

The door wouldn't open.

I leaned back, pulling with all my strength, but the sucker wouldn't budge. While I was wondering whether kicking it would help, the humming changed to a low roaring sound. Suddenly, the floor heaved, sending me slamming into the door, head first.

Eyes watering, I stood there, momentarily stunned, face plastered against the door as my necklace swung back and forth, knocking on the door. I had a sudden understanding of how mosquitoes must feel about windshields.

Peeling myself off the door, I pulled on the doorknob again. This time, the door opened halfway, but then it stuck.

I shoved my suitcase and purse through the opening, and

got one foot in the doorway when an earsplitting crunching sound came from behind me. The door shuddered, slammed partway closed, and then stuck again, trapping me half in and half out, facing into the room. When what I was seeing finally registered through my panic, I froze, gaping.

The floor was eating the bed.

It started by sucking down a leg, then moved on to inhale a corner. Within seconds, the whole bed had disappeared.

I gasped as I realized the rest of the room was sliding toward the growing hole that had just snarfed down my bed. It was like my own special Pit of Sarlacc had opened and was devouring the room.

Like any good prey, I kept my eye on the thing about to eat me, but I tried like hell to escape. I exhaled all my air, sucked in my gut, and tried to push myself through the door. It didn't budge, and neither did I.

The pit, however, was having great success. As I struggled, the nightstand disappeared down the hole, accompanied by a horrible grinding sound.

Saying a prayer to the skinny-bitch gods to temporarily make me thinner, I pushed and wiggled harder. From the amount of sweat pouring down me, I was amazed I couldn't just slide through the door.

A loud crack reverberated through me. Under my feet, I felt a slipping sensation, and then the section of the floor I was standing on tilted downward and began to separate from the wall.

The door picked that moment to swing open. Arms pinwheeling, I teetered and slid forward.

A hand clamped down on my shoulder, yanking me backwards, and I landed on my ass in the hallway, with a thud just as—

The noise was deafening.

The whole floor fell in, taking everything in the room with it. All that was left was a gaping hole.

Well, not quite.

The damn door still hung drunkenly from one hinge.

Chapter Two

Adrenaline: Nature's way of lettin' ya know that now is not a good time to take a nap.

For years, I'd listened to the truck drivers who frequented our diner trade tips for staying awake while driving. "Nearly getting sucked down a sink hole" never made the list somehow. Well, it was certainly working for me, and I was putting my newly acquired wide-awakeness to good use by speeding down the highway.

As I put miles between me and the Hotel Room of Doom, my thoughts turned to my rescuer. When I'd landed in the hallway, I found myself staring at a pair of worn cowboy boots. When I panned up, the face peering down at me looked to be made of the same cracked leather as the boots. It'd occurred to me that I might be in shock when I found myself starting to count the man's wrinkles to figure out his age, like you do with the rings on a tree. I was guessing he was a redwood of some sort.

"That's it. Focus on me," he said. "Well, you're not bleeding, missy, so that's good. Can you move everything okay?"

While I wiggled my bits and pieces, people began pouring into the hallway. A teenager had squeezed his way to the doorway of my room and peered in. He said, "Wow! Look at that sink hole!" and then proceeded to take a selfie with the room as his backdrop.

Boots rolled his eyes and put himself between the kid and me, keeping me out of the photo shoot. Small favors.

I looked at Boots and asked, "Sink hole?"

"Did your floor sink into a big hole?"

I nodded.

He shrugged, "Sink hole."

I must have looked as confused as I felt, because he added, "Not your regular old sink hole, either. That's a doozie." He patted my shoulder, checked to make sure the budding photographer had moved on, and retreated down the hallway himself.

I must've still been dazed because it had taken me a full thirty seconds to yell, "Uh, thanks!" after him. He'd waved as he kept on going.

A huge yawn refocused my attention on the highway. Alas, adrenaline only takes you so far. Plus, my mom's car Babs was muttering at me, and I'd learned to pay attention to her when she says she needs a rest. Babs and I had a deal. We both just had to hold it together till I got cross-country. After I attended my family's reunion, I'd be boarding a ship, and she could rest in peace.

I pulled over at a truck stop just as the fatigue came roaring back to bitch slap me into submission.

As I sat in the truck stop diner snarfing down a breakfast burrito and working my way through a pot of coffee, I noted the energy level in the diner. The truckers were buzzing like a bunch of teenagers, which meant something juicy had happened. I eavesdropped on the truckers closest to me, but only heard a few snatches of the conversation.

"Did I hear something about a storm coming?" I asked Sue, my waitress. "I checked my phone, but I didn't see anything in the forecast."

"They're talking about that freak ice storm," she said. "Turned the freeway into a slip-and-slide over near the state line. Caused a huge pile-up involving something like a hundred cars." She topped off my coffee without me even having to ask and added, "You might be in for a little rain, though," and headed off down the counter.

Jeez, if I hadn't left my hotel when I did, I would have been skating across the freeway like everyone else. So the sink hole was kind of a blessing in disguise, I guessed—and who would've thought those words would ever cross my mind?

The waitress was right. Back on the road again, oh boy did it rain. Coming from a place where the forecast had mainly to do with whether the sun was going to bake, roast, or fry you, I'd been looking forward to actual weather, particularly some rain. I had rain all right. All day long, I had types of rain that I'd never even known existed.

The morning started out okay, with the usual kinds of civilized rain I'd expected: dashing, dancing, and prancing across my windshield. I really enjoyed how the soft tapping soothed my sink-hole-induced anxiety.

Then the rain got vexing. It seemed like it couldn't decide if it actually wanted to be rain or some kind of weird drool that confused my windshield wipers so much they emitted disgruntled squeaks as they swiped at it.

I guess the drool was a warning because I got vomit rain next, arriving in chunky waves. I also had polluted rain, which somehow made my car dirtier. And, then came the blitzing rain, which appeared out of nowhere.

I frowned at the distressed noises Babs was making as the blitzing rain got heavier. I decided to call this new stuff Gandalf rain—so heavy, you shall not pass!—and I pulled over at another truck stop to wait until it let up. As I was slowing to pull off the highway, I noticed cars around me starting to hydroplane. I patted Babs and thanked her for insisting I pull over before I had to use her as a surfboard. My thanks turned into a growl of protest when she refused to open her door against the wind and rain pushing at her. I sighed. I could wait a little longer to pee. This would be a good time to try to reach the reunion again.

You'd think that in this day and age, there'd at least be a reunion website set up, but no. The invitation had come with just a phone number.

On the day I found the invitation, I'd been dismantling Dad's office. The sale of the diner had gone through, and I'd had no choice if I didn't want strangers going through all of our things.

I squeezed into the office, automatically checking for any

critters milling about underfoot. Of course, they'd all been given homes, but it was an old habit. Dad had always brought home strays, but after Mom died, he went from a random rescue or two to a rotating herd.

As I moved past, the pages on the overtaxed bulletin board waved hello to me. I decided to start there and get the "this was your life" portion of the day over with. On the top layer, there were the schedules I'd constructed, the manifests for goods that I'd ordered, the running tally of things we needed. Beneath that, I knew I'd find art projects I'd made and papers I'd written, which Dad'd refused to take down. I sighed, pulled on my big-girl panties, and began ruthlessly trashing or recycling everything.

By the time I trudged upstairs to our apartment, I looked like I'd been attacked by a crazed paper fairy and lost. My hair made it clear that the fairy had spent some quality time dive bombing it. My clothing was equally disheveled, sporting a nice new hole where I'd gotten stuck on the rough edge of the file cabinet. And to top it off, I was covered with a light coating of pixie paper dust. Why the hell hadn't Dad gone digital? As the paper cuts on my hands taunted me with their endless stinging, I lamented my dad's lack of tech savvy. Guys were supposed to be obsessed with gizmos and gadgets, right? Well, someone had forgotten to whack my dad with the technology stick, and now I was paying the price.

I stood in the living room debating the urgency of my needs: beer or shower? Priding myself on being an effective multitasker, I took the beer with me into the shower. Newly refreshed, I tackled the pile of mail I'd been ignoring. I already had a zillion paper cuts, what were a few more?

The invitation was buried near the bottom of the stack. Oddly, it was addressed just to me.

It looked like a wedding invitation, all cream-colored thick paper, hand-lettered in a fancy calligraphy style. It said:

Foster Family Gathering

It gave a date, a state, and an RSVP phone number.

At the bottom there was a note that said: *Directions to come.

Perhaps the invitation caught me at a weak moment, but I sat sipping my beer and thought, *Why the hell not?* I'd never met most of my mom's family. I was heading to the East Coast anyway to start my oceanography degree by doing a year at sea. The timing worked out. But I hesitated. Mom and Dad had had little contact with their families, and there must've been a reason for that. But the fact that they were gone made the idea of making connections with my remaining family impossible for me to resist.

I'd called the number and gotten a standard mechanized recording, not even a personalized message. I RSVP'd and received another letter confirming my attendance and giving the address of where to attend along with directions. Not just local directions, either. They'd mapped a route all the way cross-country, which I found both sweet and weird. But the overkill in the directions department just emphasized the lack of other info. No list of activities. No ideas about what kind of dress code this involved. No idea how many people were attending. I knew from my parents that the Fosters were a huge, old family, spread out all over the globe. But did that mean this was an international thing, or just for the U.S. branch of the family? I didn't know whether we'd be doing champagne and formal dresses, or if it'd be burgers and dogs in the backyard. Since I didn't own anything super formal, I was kind of banking on the latter. I'd been dialing periodically, trying to reach an actual person to pump them for info, but so far, I'd only gotten voicemail.

So I took my momentary rain break there in the car to try calling. Again. And was momentarily speechless when a woman actually answered the phone.

"Hello?" she asked again. "If this is a crank call, the least you could do is make an effort and throw in some heavy breathing."

"Uh, hi," I said. "I'm, uh, calling about the reunion?"

"Oh sure," she said. "I'm Meg. I live at the house. How can I help you?"

"Meg? As in Cousin Meg?" I couldn't believe my good luck.

"Probably. Who is this?"

"Oh, sorry, hi, I don't know if you remember me, it's been a while—a long while—I mean, I'm twenty-two now and I was, like, eight then—but we spent a summer vacation together, and oh my God I had such an awesome time!" Oh my God was right. I'd idolized Meg that summer, following her around, hanging on her every word and deed. Here it was, years later, and I was still gushing like an idiot. What was wrong with me?

There was a brief pause. "Finn?" she asked.

"Oh hey! You remember me!" I winced. Dogs for miles would be howling from the high-pitched perkiness in my voice. Ew.

"...Hello. It's been a while..."

"Yeah. I can't wait to catch up."

"You're coming here? For the reunion?"

"You betcha." You betcha? I supposed I should be happy I hadn't thrown in a "by golly" for good measure. I desperately needed to get off the phone and get a freakin' grip.

"Sorry I seemed so surprised. I'm not in charge of the RSVPs so I haven't seen the list," she said. "So Finn, what can I do for you?"

"Oh, I just wanted to check to make sure everything was still on and to get the details," I said.

"Yes, we're still on. I'm not sure what you mean about the details. The reunions are always the same. Didn't your parents fill you in?"

I floundered for a minute, trying to come up with an answer other than "How can they, they're dead?" and finally settled on, "Nope."

There was a pause. "Well, you'll get the complete rundown when you get here, but it's basically what you'd expect."

I had no idea what she thought I expected, but I didn't want to sound any more clueless than I already did, so put a lid on the pile of questions bubbling in my brain, and said, "Okay."

"When do you think you'll be arriving?" she asked.

"Well, I'm driving cross-country as we speak. Oh, and you won't believe what happened to me!" and I told her about my sink hole.

"That sounds frightening," said Meg. "Are you calling from the hotel?"

"No. The hotel manager was, of course, upset about the whole thing and insisted I take a new room. I said yes to make her happy, but no way was I staying. It was only a matter of time before the insurance guys and lawyers came swarming in." I shuddered. "I've had all the lawyers and insurance guys I can take for one lifetime, thank you very much. So, I washed up and snuck out, and now I'm back on the road."

"Well, you've still got plenty of time to get here."

"Yeah, about that. The invitation says to show up at five on Friday. I can't check in at my hotel until after three, so I'll check in and then head over," I said.

"Hotel? You're not staying in a hotel!" Meg said. "All of the reunion guests stay at the house. Didn't anyone tell you?" She didn't give me time to interject. "Of course they didn't," she muttered. "Well look, we've got tons of room, so reunion guests always stay here."

"Uh, sure," I said. "Thank you so much." I figured if the reunion was super awkward, I could always bail and find a hotel later. In the meantime, it'd be a good idea to save my pennies. My textbooks were going to cost an arm and a leg and who knew what kind of mad money I'd need while sailing around the world.

"Great," Meg said. "I'll see you soon."

After I hung up, I was torn between bouncing up and down in excitement and shaking my head at what a total goober I'd just made of myself. It was a small miracle that I hadn't said something cringe-worthy about slumber parties or pillow fights.

Then I thought, *Oh the hell with it,* and I bounced up and down anyway. Babs squeaked along with me. This reunion whim of mine was already working out great. I'd get to see Meg and meet some new relatives, too. All in all, I suddenly felt a whole lot less alone than I had in a long time.

Chapter Three

Road Trip Hokey Pokey! You take a left turn in. You take a right turn out. You detour to see a 200-year-old tree. And you drive it all about!

The directions in the invitation had mapped out the straightest, quickest route to the reunion. It was a nice thought. But I'd spent years cooped up in the desert—"straight and quick" were not on the menu. For me, this trip was an all-you-can-see buffet, and I was determined to squeeze every bit of adventure sauce out of it that I could. I picked most of my destinations, but Babs added the hokey to my pokey. She'd start shuddering or huffing, and I'd have to improvise and find something neat to see nearby so she could rest. It was awesome: I never knew what I'd see next.

By the time I reached the East Coast, I'd zigzagged my way across the country. Along the way, I'd encountered enough wacky weather to quench even my parched desert heart. I'd seen fog, hail, and freezing rain. And, if Babs hadn't been wheezing and made me pull over, I might have had a Dorothy moment and experienced my first tornado up close and personal. As it was, seeing it from a distance was plenty impressive. I also got to indulge my inner road warrior by madly dodging road hazards, including pot holes, fallen trees, a rock slide, and what looked like a very cranky moose.

But now, I was ready for the reunion. I'd stayed in a hotel the night before because I'd been starting to look like an extra in *Mad Max*. Once I'd showered the road off of me, I'd tried to get some sleep. But every time the motel bed creaked, I'd snapped awake. Eventually I'd given it up and gotten back on the road.

Unfortunately, leaving in the wee hours of the morning meant that I motored into town super early for the reunion. It was only lunch time, and the invitation said not to arrive till 5 p.m. I figured I could amuse myself for a few hours, but first I should do a flyby and locate the reunion spot. Good thing, too. It wasn't easy to find in full daylight, never mind in the five o'clock twilight.

The directions had said the driveway was surrounded by "some trees," so I thought I'd be looking for a yard with a couple of oaks fronting it. Instead, I found myself in the middle of a small forest. If I hadn't been going so slow, I'd have missed the mailbox and the driveway. Both were tastefully blended into the trees so that they looked like they were part of the surrounding forest. I pulled up and read the number on the mailbox. 55. Yup, this was the place. I couldn't see anything but more trees down the driveway, so I figured that the house must be set back from the road.

Destination successfully located, I decided to kill some time exploring. Further down the road, the forest gave way to a small strip mall. There was a convenience store, a salon, and some kind of a restaurant. Babs was starting to grumble, and so was my stomach, so I parked and went in search of food and caffeine.

When I opened the door to the restaurant, a strong gust of wind shoved me so hard that I stumbled through the door and went skidding across the hardwood floor. The draft I'd created swept into the room, hit the fireplace, and caused the fire to flare with a roar. I blushed, righted myself, and tried to look casual as I walked forward.

Two more steps into the dimly lit room and one deep breath told me this wasn't a restaurant so much as a pub. I had the place to myself, except for a pair of older gentlemen perched at the far end of the bar, and a bartender, all of whom were staring at me after my graceful entrance. Something about the old guys said "regulars" to me. I had the feeling that when they stood up, their barstools would bear their butt prints.

I sat at the other end of the bar from them, ordered a burger and fries, and asked for a cup of coffee while I waited.

The bartender brought my coffee. He leaned on the bar near me and asked, "You new around here?" The regulars swiveled to listen in on the conversation.

"No! Just passing through," I said.

"Our neck of the woods not to your tastes?" he asked with a grin.

I smiled back. "No, it's not that. I'm just here visiting family."

"Family, huh? Sure you don't want me to add something stronger to your coffee?"

I laughed. "No thanks. But if it goes badly, I may come back here and take you up on it."

"Who's your family, if you don't mind my asking?" he said.

"The Fosters—they're just up the road that way," I said, turning to gesture vaguely in the direction I'd come from. I turned back to see the bartender had straightened up and was trading a look with the two regulars.

"You know them?" I asked.

"Just by reputation," said the bartender as he stepped back from me and began drying a glass.

I said, "Oh," and took a slow sip of my coffee. Whatever that reputation was, I was guessing it wasn't good. I surveyed the situation over the rim of my cup. The bartender had shifted his weight to the balls of his feet and put distance between us, something I did at the diner when I thought there might be an issue, and I'd have to move fast. The old guys were so rigid they reminded me of hunting dogs on point. I could practically see their ears standing at attention. I really wanted to yell "Squirrel!" and see what happened.

Instead, I set my cup down gently, gave the bartender my best disarming smile, and said, "I'm from a distant branch of the family, so I've never met most of them, either." The three of them just stared at me. I held onto my smile and said, "I'm Finn." I waved at the regulars and then held out my hand to the bartender to shake.

For a moment, I thought he wasn't going to take it. The fire filled the silence, popping and hissing, and I glanced over to see it sending a shower of flaming sparks into the air. I shifted my gaze back, as the bartender gave my hand a quick, firm shake.

"And you are…?" I asked.

"Iggy," he said.

I looked over at the regulars. Old guy number one said, "Pete." He pointed to old guy number two and said, "He's Lou." Lou nodded at me. I nodded back.

Iggy said, "I'll just go check on that burger," and he went through a door behind the bar.

Pete and Lou were still staring at me. I smiled at them again but that seemed to make them more tense. I considered leaving, but then Iggy reappeared and plunked my burger and fries in front of me. And the check. Subtle. I nearly walked right then, but the scent of burger and fries wafted up, and my stomach whined at me. I took a bite of the burger, and my eyes closed in bliss. Okay fine, I would eat fast and then go.

As I set about inhaling my burger, Iggy drifted down to the other end of the bar, where he, Lou, and Pete commenced talking in low voices. What, did they run out of mean girls, so they went and formed a mean men club?

Tuning them out, I focused on deciding what to do with myself until it was time to go to the reunion. Well, I wasn't that far from the water. I wondered if I could sneak in my inaugural visit to the ocean a little early. I brightened at the thought and found myself smiling. The more I thought about it, the more excited I got.

I was finishing my burger when I saw Lou and Pete approaching me. They stopped a few feet away. I quashed the impulse to sniff my armpits and see if I smelled.

I just looked at them as I chewed on a fry. The burger was gone, and they had until I finished the few fries on my plate to say whatever they had to say, then I was outta there. The ocean awaited.

Pete shifted back and forth for a moment, then said, "Let's say for a moment we believe this whole 'distant branch' thing. What *do* you know about your family?"

"Nothing really," I said.

Lou snorted. Pete said, "Nothing?"

"Er, well, it's a big family," I said.

"That's it?"

"Uh, really big," I clarified.

Lou crossed his arms and looked at Pete.

They could glance meaningfully at each other like divas in a telenovela all they wanted. I only had three more fries to go. I ate another one and began digging out my wallet.

"Are you here about the house?" Pete asked.

I looked up. "What house?" Was that why they were being so weird? Some kind of property dispute going on between the Fosters and their neighbors? Great.

Pete looked at Lou, who shrugged and said, "I can't tell if she's lying or just ignorant."

I looked askance at him. "Hello! Sitting. Right. Here!"

Pete eyed me. "Well, she doesn't look like the sharpest tool in the shed…"

Gaping, I said, "Jeez, I've heard about New England reserve, but you guys," I pointed at them, "are just rude." I thumped my money on the bar. Generally, I speak old guy—a necessary survival skill working in a diner. Maybe they spoke a different dialect in the Northeast because something was definitely getting lost in translation here.

I crammed the last two fries in my mouth, grabbed my purse, and hopped off the stool.

Lou and Pete got very still. Iggy stepped up so he was flanking them from the other side of the bar. I shook my head and headed for the door.

"That's it?" Lou called after me.

"What do you mean 'that's it'? Yeah, that's it." I didn't know what information they thought I had, but I didn't really care. I waved goodbye over my shoulder and stomped out the door.

Chapter Four

I marched back to Babs. Grumpy old men, indeed. Well, at least I had plenty of time for my ocean adventure. I could practically hear the waves already. When I reached Babs, her door was stuck again. As I began tugging and begging, a kind of crying noise distracted me. Head cocked, I stopped and listened, trying to figure out what I'd heard. The noise came again, seemingly from behind the convenience store. I crossed to the building and made my way around the side.

And stopped short as I slammed into a wall of stench. Either a bunch of fish had decided to commit mass suicide nearby, or I was headed for a dumpster. Sure enough, rounding the corner from the side to the back of the store, I encountered the pair of dumpsters emitting a set of smells so spectacular I swear I could see them wavering in the air like in a cartoon.

Clamping my shirt over my nose, I looked around, trying to see what had attracted my attention. Peering between the two dumpsters, I found the culprit.

Oh no. I should've known.

With a sigh, I crouched down and surveyed the ball of fuzz, peering up at me with a combination of hope and terror in its eyes.

"Hello wee beastie," I said.

It squeaked at me.

I sighed. "This is so not fair! I'm supposed to be on vacation."

It looked at me with big eyes and squeaked again.

"No, I can't take you home with me. I don't even *have* a home. So don't start with the whole 'Oh I'm so cute and pathetic' thing. I'm not falling for it."

Of course, I'd already totally fallen for it, no matter what I said. I was my animal-rescuing father's daughter, after all. And the animals all seemed to know it somehow.

And this poor thing! The fuzzy ball was tiny, just a baby, and painfully thin. It was sitting among a bunch of styrofoam containers that had fallen over the side of the dumpster. I could see bits of fish sticking to its fur, which told me it had been scavenging for something to eat. My heart broke a little as I realized it had been trying to survive on rotting fish.

I inched forward, trying to get a better look at the fuzzy, watching for signs of distress.

As I moved forward, it backed up under the dumpster against the wall. Its fur was filthy and matted, but from what I could tell it was some kind of kitten. It looked as though some asshole had dumped it with the trash. I tamped down on my anger lest the kitten pick up on it.

"Okay little Fuzzy—can I call you that?—I'm just gonna reach in there and get you, and then we'll have a proper look at you." Unfortunately, my arm didn't reach all the way back, so I couldn't quite grab it. Muttering, I got down on my hands and knees and squeezed myself between the two dumpsters. Well, on the bright side, at least the dumpsters were in the back of the store so the customers wouldn't be subjected to the sight of my ass sticking out. Inching forward as far as I could, I kept up a steady cooing stream of "Who's a handsome boo boo?" as I reached again for Fuzzy.

The dumpsters were doing their part to make this as fun as possible. My eyes were watering from the smell. Fuzzy started squeaking pitifully, obviously alarmed at my approach, so I stopped again. The squeaking stopped, and Fuzzy's gaze locked on my chest. I looked down to see my necklace had popped out of my shirt and was swinging. I wiggled it a bit. Fuzzy crouched down and started to creep forward. I wiggled it some more. Fuzzy got close enough to bat at it, and I snagged the scruff of Fuzzy's neck.

"Okay Fuzzy, it's okay," I kept muttering nonsense words as

soothingly as possible as I scooted back. I felt something squish and looked down to see I'd just crawled through a puddle of some kind of goo. Perfect.

As I wriggled the rest of the way out, I said, "I'm so sorry to tell you this, but we both need a bath—" and looked up into the unsmiling face of a cop.

"Uh, Officer." He just looked at me. "Not you! Uh, I wasn't saying you need to take a bath. With me."

"Convenience store clerk said some lady was out here digging in the garbage, talking to herself," he looked me over. "I take it that's you?

"I was talking to this," I held up the wiggling Fuzzy, who'd started with the pitiful squeaking again.

The officer peered down at the furball. "Whatcha got there?" he asked in a gentle voice that immediately raised my opinion of him.

"Some kind of kitten." I took a quick look at it. "A male, I think. Poor thing's a mess. I saw it behind the dumpster here and decided to fetch it out."

The officer nodded. "It's starting to get too cold at night for a little guy like that to be out and about on his own." He frowned, looking around. "Don't suppose you've seen any sign of his mother?"

I shook my head. "I'm thinking some jerk probably just left him here."

The cop made a disapproving noise. "What are you going to do with him?" he asked.

I held up Fuzzy. "Maybe you could take him? I'm just visiting relatives, so I'm not staying in town for long."

The cop took a step back, raising his hand. "Oh no. If I bring home one more stray, my wife'll kill me. I'll tell you what though. The vet's just a mile or so down the road. Maybe you could drop by with the kitten? I'll give him a call and let him know you're coming."

While I didn't really want to incur a massive vet bill, there was no way I was going to leave Fuzzy literally out in the cold. I sighed. There went my side trip to the ocean. Well, I'd waited this long to see the ocean, I could wait a little longer. I said, "Sure. Where's the vet at?"

The cop gave me directions, then went to his car to call the vet. When he came back, he had a hand-drawn map to help guide me. He handed it over and said, "They're expecting you and will fit you in."

I took the map, thanked the officer, and headed toward Babs with Fuzzy. He had stopped squeaking, but now he was shivering. I tucked him down the front of my sweater to keep him warm and continued to talk softly to him. Two men in the parking lot looked at me strangely. I realized that to them it looked like I was cooing at my breasts. Crazy dumpster lady who talks to her boobs. A few hours in town, and I was already making quite an impression.

Babs helpfully opened her door on the first try. I grabbed my blanket from the back and used it to cover my seat to protect Babs from the bits of the dumpster that came with me. Then Fuzzy and I climbed in and headed for the vet.

As soon as I turned the engine on, Fuzzy explained that he had very definite opinions about cars. Like most felines, he disapproved. Loudly. Then with claws. Then he peed on me. In the brief amount of time it took me to get to the vet's office, I acquired a whole new appreciation for carry cases.

We pulled up, and I stumbled out of the car. Fuzzy stopped yowling and popped his head out of my sweater to check out his surroundings. I hurried inside before he got wiggly and tried to make a run for it.

Chapter Five

One step into the vet's office, and Fuzzy decided that it fell into the "to be avoided at all costs" category. As I struggled across the waiting room to the reception desk, the people and even the pets shrank back. It was a toss-up whether it was from Fuzzy's caterwauling or the eau de Fuzzy wafting in my wake.

I reached the receptionist. "Uh, I'm here to see the vet? The uh—dammit, Fuzzy, will you quit it? Ow!—cop guy said he called ahead?"

She didn't even bat an eye as Fuzzy did his best *Aliens* impression and tried to claw his way through my sweater. "Yup. Why don't you have a seat, and he'll be with you soon." She gave me a brief smile and turned to answer the phone.

Grateful she hadn't given me a pile of forms to fill out, I turned around to look for a seat.

A vet tech in scrubs appeared, calling, "Mr. Sherman?"

A woman sitting next to the only open seat in the waiting room said, "Why don't you let the young lady go next? You don't mind waiting, do you Ron?"

A man holding a terrier said, "Sure, go ahead."

The terrier and everyone else in the room looked relieved as I turned and followed the tech.

"I see we're doing the 'but I don't want to see the vet' dance," said the vet tech with a smirk as she led us to an exam room.

Once she closed the door, I reached down into my sweater and extricated the squeaking troublemaker. The vet tech weighed him, then handed him back, and was out the door in record time, with a "The vet will be in soon," before she closed the door behind her.

To my surprise, the vet appeared almost immediately. My guess was the closed door hadn't done enough to muffle the smell or the noise, and we were upsetting the other patients.

Fuzzy took one look at the vet and decided he needed to get down. Now. I grappled with his wriggling body and said, "Jeez, from the fit he's pitching, I'd swear he already knew what a vet was. No offense."

"None taken," he said. Waving his hand in front of his nose, he said, "Wow. That is truly impressive. And that's more than just cat pee. What did you do?"

"He was in between a couple of dumpsters—what was I supposed to do, leave him there?" I said. Normally, I'd be flapping my arms in indignation. But since Fuzzy was a two-hand job at the moment, I settled for pulling myself up to my full height and giving the vet the stink eye.

Now that I was looking at him fully, it just made me give him the stink eye even more. I was covered in dumpster drippings, so of course he was handsome. He was all scruffy and rugged, with hair that I bet was tousled from actually being outside, not from a ton of hair gel. His eyes sparked with laughter. At me. I considered "accidentally" bumping into him and wiping my sweater on him.

My thoughts must've been showing because he raised his hands in surrender. "Hey, no harm, no foul. Believe me, I've been covered in worse." He started to grin again, "But not recently."

I was about to suggest what he could do with his sweet smelling self when Fuzzy let out a particularly pitiful squeak.

The vet's demeanor changed immediately. "Hey buddy," he said, voice soft. He looked at me and asked, "May I?" When I nodded, he gently pried Fuzzy off my sweater. When the vet had Fuzzy cupped in his hands, Fuzzy quieted immediately. As the vet talked to him in a soft, low voice, Fuzzy looked up, head cocked.

My dad used to do that. Just touch an animal and talk to it, and it'd sort of melt under his touch, no matter how panicked it had been. He'd have loved my Fuzzy adventure. Realizing my eyes were filling with tears, I stepped away and checked out the exam room. Like the waiting room, it was pristine, but somehow very welcoming. Rather than the usual blinding white I associated with vet offices, this room had warm wooden paneling.

"By the way, I'm Dr. Meriwether—Hugh," the vet said.

"Oh, yeah, hi, I'm Finn," I said, turning back to him. His hands were full of Fuzzy, so I just sort of waved at him instead of trying to shake his hand.

"Well, he's a boy," Dr. Meriwether said, as he examined Fuzzy. "He's obviously underfed, and I'd say he's not quite eight weeks." He looked at Fuzzy. "Too soon for you to be off gallivanting on your own there, boyo." He stroked Fuzzy between the ears, and Fuzzy leaned into his touch.

Dr. Meriwether made some notes in a chart, and then he scooped Fuzzy up. "We'll do a quick blood test, deworm him, and clean him up. You want to come back in a couple of hours and pick him up?"

"Um, hang on, didn't that cop tell you? This is a drop off. I'm just visiting relatives here in town—I can't take on a kitten."

Dr. Meriwether didn't look happy. "Listen, normally that wouldn't be a problem, but the timing couldn't be worse. We're actually closing tonight for the whole weekend, which is weird for a vet, I know, but I'm going out of town." A calculating look appeared in his eyes. "You seem like you're awfully good with animals. I'm betting this isn't your first dumpster-diving rescue?"

What, did I have "sucker for strays" written in glitter on my forehead? "First dumpster, actually yes. First stray?" I looked down at my feet, scuffing the floor with my shoe. "No," I muttered.

"So you've got some experience fostering?"

I grinned at the "fostering," not that he'd get the joke. Unfortunately, he mistook my grin.

"Well good. Since you've done this before, can you keep him for the weekend? We can find him a real foster when we reopen on Monday."

I nearly said "You've got your real Foster right here," but given the reaction of the other locals, I said instead, "Uh, well, I don't know."

"Are you staying in a hotel?" he said.

"No. I'll be at my relatives' house." I must've looked as unconvinced as I felt, because he resorted to bribery.

"Tell you what," Dr. Meriwether said. "Check with your relatives while I'm cleaning him up. If you guys can take him for the weekend, then this whole visit is free. I'll even send you home with a goodie bag to get you through the weekend. Hey, trust me, one look at this cute face, and they'll be goners. In fact, they may decide to keep him after you go."

I really did want Fuzzy to find a good home. "Fine," I said. "If they're okay with it, I can look after him for the weekend." At the very least, he'd give me an excuse to escape the festivities if I needed one.

Dr. Meriwether whisked Fuzzy away and reappeared with a bulging bag of supplies.

I glared at him. "That is way too many supplies for one weekend."

He was all innocence. "You know, it's just in case. Better to be prepared, than not have enough."

It wasn't worth arguing with him. "Wait, there are bottles in here. He's not fully weaned?"

Dr. Meriwether said, "Hard to tell. Like I said, better to be safe than sorry."

Awesome. I'd be on bottle duty in the wee hours of the morning. I snagged the bag and headed for the door, "Thanks for the loaner. I'll return whatever's left over when you take him back on Monday."

Chapter Six

By the time I left the vet's, I was running late. When I arrived at the stretch of woods, the combination of the tree shadows and the fading sunlight made the driveway all but invisible. Even knowing where it was, I still drove by it once and had to double back.

Babs and I bumped down the driveway, which was more like a private road that wound through the woods. I drove with the windows down in the hope that I'd wind up smelling more like pine than dumpster. Nothing short of a shower—or a fire hose—was truly going to deskunk me at this point, but I'd take what I could get.

Between running late and feeling like a hot mess, I was a ball of teeth-clenching, steering-wheel-strangling stress. But the farther I drove, the more the twilight calm of the forest started sinking into me. My jaw relaxed, my hands loosened on the steering wheel, and I started to chuckle. Well, at least I'd make a big entrance. Hopefully I wasn't the only one in the family with a sense of humor.

My first sign of civilization came when I crossed a small wooden bridge that arched over a tinkling creek. On the other side of the bridge, the driveway straightened out, and I could see to the end of the road.

Standing sentinel on either side of the entrance to a clearing, two enormous oak trees dominated the landscape. The oaks' branches reached over the driveway so that it looked like they were hugging each other over the road. I'd read about these kinds of really old, massive trees, but the descriptions didn't come near to describing the age and strength radiating from them. It's like they *knew*. I wasn't sure *what* they knew, but I found myself sitting up straight and wanting to mind my manners. As I drove beneath their canopies, I got the oddest sense that they were scrutinizing me as closely as I was them.

My attention was yanked away from the trees when I rolled into the clearing and slowed Babs to a stop.

I was at the edge of a grove that formed an open, round area. While part of the grove was still grassy, some of it had been converted into a circular driveway with a parking area off to the right.

But I couldn't really focus on any of that because I was too busy staring at the house.

It looked like an old-fashioned farmhouse had strolled out of the past and plunked itself down in the middle of the clearing. Made entirely of aged, darkened wood, the house looked as though it could have sprung right out of the forest floor with the rest of the trees. Something about the way the house anchored into the land had me picturing an old man in a frayed cardigan, settled into his favorite chair in a dark study.

I nudged Babs forward and parked next to the other cars off to the right. There weren't very many cars, so maybe I wasn't the only one who was late.

Babs and I both sighed as I shut her off. I patted her dashboard. Later it'd hit me that we'd completed the first part of our journey, but I didn't have time for deep reflection just now. So, I did a little "Woohoo, we made it!" wiggle dance and promised Babs we'd celebrate later. Then I climbed out, snagged my suitcase, and headed for the house.

The stairs grunted a greeting as I climbed onto the drooping porch. I raised my hand to knock on the door, but my nerves were back, and my hand was shaking. I put my suitcase down and took a moment to get a grip. Turning to look across the grove, I saw the big oaks stretching toward me, the breeze making them look as though they were waving at me. I grinned at my fanciful thoughts, but that didn't stop me from doing a little finger wave back. Taking a slow, deep breath I let the leafy scent of the forest, the rustle of the wind in the trees, and the soft twi-light wrap around me. The hostility of the men in the bar made more sense to me now. I could see why someone would start a fight over this property. It was enchanting.

The ticking from Babs's cooling engine prodded me to stop stalling. I faced the house and knocked. While I waited, I stud-ied the worn wooden door. The woodgrain was so beautiful that I reached out to trace the patterns with a fingertip.

Apparently the door didn't like being felt up by a stranger because it gave me a huge splinter. Worse, my finger bled on the door. The wood was so dark, I doubted anyone would notice, but I tried to wipe off the blood with a clean spot on the edge of my sleeve. I was wiping at the door when it opened.

And there was Meg. Pristine. That's what popped into my head. She looked like she'd walked off the pages of a Chanel ad, model pretty, perfect makeup, dark hair gleaming. Dressed in a blouse and flowy trousers, she looked expensive. I, on the other hand, well I didn't want to think about what I looked like, but I was guessing it was in the neighborhood of "homeless chic."

Her perfume wafted by me about the same time my own special scent must've hit her because she took a breath to speak, choked, and took a step back.

"Finn? You're Finn, right? God, what happened to you?"

"Meg! Hey, you recognize me after all this time!"

"Well, no…not really. It was just process of elimination—you're the last to arrive." As she waved a hand in front of her face, she looked me over with a blend of amusement and dis-taste. "Really, what happened?"

"Well, I found a stray kitten in a dumpster, and I couldn't just leave him there, but he turned out to be harder to get than it looked, and then he freaked out and peed on me when I took him to the vet, and I don't have a hotel room to go change in cuz I'm staying here, so now I'm kind of a mess…sorry." Oh no. I was doing it again.

Meg laughed and shook her head. "I see you haven't changed a bit. Well, come on in, and we'll see what we can do about—" she gestured at me, "—this."

"Well, wait, there's more. The vet asked me if I could look after Fuzzy—the kitten—while he finds a foster for it." I smiled when I said "foster," since she'd obviously get the joke. She didn't smile back.

I started shifting from foot to foot as I talked. "But the vet's office is closed this weekend—apparently he's going out of town—and, anyway, would it be a problem for me to keep him with me in my room? The kitten, not the vet," I added with a grin and an eyebrow waggle. Still no smile.

I plowed on. "Uh, no pressure though. Honest. I can bunk at a hotel, like I planned, and keep the little guy there." I stepped back a little. "Actually, now that I'm thinking about it, that might be a better idea anyway, because I could have a chance to wash up before I have to meet anyone else." Hell, that was a great idea. I was just sorry that I'd been so distracted by Fuzzy and focused on not being late that it hadn't occurred to me sooner. I took another step back.

As I soon as I started backing away, Meg's look changed to concern. She held up her hand in the "stop" gesture. "That's ridiculous. You're already here, and of course you'll stay. Kitten included. In fact, we've got some rooms with their own bathrooms. I'll just put you in one of those."

Some with their own bathrooms? I looked up at the house. How big was this thing?

"Uh, okay, great. I mean if you're sure," I said. "I promise we won't be any trouble."

Meg shrugged. "It's just a kitten, and you'll take care of him. Come on in. You can grab a shower. Oh, and you should definitely take advantage of the laundry room. Speaking of which, do you need to borrow something to wear? We wouldn't want you to feel awkward when you meet the other guests," she said as she yanked the door open as wide as it would go and stood as far away from me as possible.

Like I could feel more awkward than I did already. I stepped over the threshold and into the house.

Chapter Seven

Meg shut the door behind me, and I stopped short to let my eyes adjust to the dimness.

I felt like I'd walked into some dude's man cave from the 70s. The walls were wood. The floors were wood. Even the ceiling was wood. And they were so dark. No airy, golden wood here. Just deep, dark wooden planks, slats, and panels as far as the eye could see. Which wasn't very far. A single light fixture hung from the ceiling, providing a gentle, diffused yellow light that blurred and smudged the edges of things, like it was dusk inside the house.

It should have been creepy, or at the very least depressing. Instead it felt comforting and inviting, with a side order of mysterious. The house was playing coy with all its half-revealed spaces, enticing me to come peek behind the shadows. I loved it.

From where I stood in the entryway, I could see open doorways to my left and right, but with no lights on, I wasn't sure what kind of rooms they were. The hallway I was standing in ran straight back, past a staircase on the right that led upstairs. At the end of the hallway, I could see a window that I was pretty sure was part of a back door. Voices drifted from the back of the house, so I was betting there was a kitchen back there. People always seem to gather in the kitchen.

I was so excited to go explore that I was bouncing on my toes a little. I stroked the wall next to me and sighed, "Ooh Meg. You have a lovely home!"

Meg's head snapped around, and her eyes narrowed. I dropped my hand from the wall. I couldn't blame her. In her place, I wouldn't want my grubby hands touching stuff, either.

She said, "We can do the grand tour later. Come on."

Meg headed up the stairs, and I followed her. I nearly started giggling at the racket the stairs made. My climb was accompanied by a truly spectacular stair symphony composed of squeaks, grunts, and groans. If I'd been alone, I'd have made up a song to go along with it. I swallowed a laugh as I imagined the look on Meg's face if I started singing along with the stairs.

The lighting upstairs wasn't any better than downstairs. There was another long, straight hallway with a bunch of closed doors on either side. Oh and wood. Lots and lots of wood. Nary a fleck of paint or wallpaper in sight.

Meg walked to the middle of the hallway, opened a door on the left, and waved me into a room.

She hovered in the doorway while I went in the room and plunked my suitcase down. There was a door in the left corner that Meg pointed to. "Bathroom is in there." She pointed to another door to the left. "Closet there. Towels and stuff are in the bathroom. Do you need anything else?"

I shook my head, "Nope, I've got everything I need in my bag."

"Great, I'll leave you to it. I'll be back to check on you in a bit," and she closed the door.

I prowled around my new space. The room was small, containing a bed, a nightstand with a lamp, and a dresser. It was the perfect size for Fuzzy to explore without getting into trouble.

There was a window, but the view was blocked by a big tree. I didn't mind. Staring into the limbs of the tree made me feel a bit like I was in a treehouse.

I checked out the bathroom. It had enough room for me and would be a good place to sequester Fuzzy if needed. There was even room for his litterbox under the pedestal sink.

Thinking of Fuzzy reminded me how badly I needed a shower. I stripped and looked around for a place to put my necklace. There were hooks for towels on the back of the door, so I hung it there, then climbed into the shower. After some chugging and sputtering, the water came on steadily.

"Oh thank you," I told the shower as the hot water poured over me. "For an old house, you sure know how to treat a girl right!"

I might have lingered in the shower, but my cell phone rang. I wrapped a towel around myself and ran to dig my phone out of my purse. A quick glance at the number told me it was the vet.

"This is Finn."

"Hi, it's Dr. Meriwether."

"Changed your mind and decided to keep him after all?"

He laughed. "Nope."

I sighed. "Okay, well, they said yes, so I can hang onto him for the weekend. How late are you open? I'm just getting out of the shower, but I can pop right back over as soon as I get dressed."

"Where are you staying?"

"I'm over on Old Postal Road."

"Post, Old Post Road. You're in luck. I might be driving right by you, depending on which end of the road you're on, in which case I can drop him off. What number?"

"Seriously? A vet that makes house calls?"

He laughed again and said, "Shocking, I know. And, I really do appreciate you guys going to the extra effort and keeping an eye on the little guy for the weekend, so I don't mind making the effort. What's the address?"

"It's 55. It's kind of in the middle of the woods that are by the convenience store where I found Fuzzy."

There was a pause and when he spoke again, all the laughter had gone out of his voice. "You're a Foster?"

Oh jeez. Not him too. I guess he hadn't looked at the name on Fuzzy's chart too closely. I said, "From a distant branch of the family, but yeah."

There was a brief pause. "Okay."

"If it's a problem, really, I'll just come and get him."

"No…no, that's fine. I'm going right by there. I'll drop him off."

"Uh, alright, if you're sure?"

"I'm sure."

"Okay, well, just a heads up, though. The house is kind of hard to find."

"I know where it is. I'll come by soon."

I thanked him again, and we hung up. I really needed to talk to Meg about whatever was going on with her and the people around here. Maybe she was in a territorial dispute with some local conservationists. Given how pretty it was here, that'd make sense.

A knock on the door interrupted my thoughts. "Finn?" It was Meg. Jeez, it hadn't even been a half hour.

I clutched my towel closer and called, "Not dressed yet!"

"Do you need anything?"

"Nope, I'm fine."

"Okay. I'll be back to collect you in a few minutes."

"Okay." It occurred to me that I might be holding up dinner, and I scrambled to dig some clothes out of my suitcase. I didn't have anything in Meg's league, so I just grabbed my dark-blue jeans and a knit top. Once dressed, I hung my towel and retrieved my necklace. I never went anywhere without it, but since it was a family heirloom, I felt especially proud to wear it at dinner. I took a quick peek in the mirror. I'd inherited my mom's thick, wavy blond hair, and I kept it short so it was easy to manage. A quick finger comb, and I was good to go. I put my shoes on and headed out to find Meg.

As soon as I took one step into the hallway, the warped wooden floor tripped me. I got to see the lovely flooring up close and personal and hear how nicely the wooden acoustics amplified the thud I made.

"Ow, that looked painful," a male voice said.

"Could be worse," I said. When I got a look at the source of the voice, I thought, *It's worse.*

Somehow, it hadn't occurred to me that if Meg was here, her brother Doug would be, too. I glanced up at all six foot something of him and did my best not to sigh like an idiot. Son of a bitch, he'd gotten even better looking with age. What was it with their family anyway? If Meg looked like a model from a Chanel ad, Doug looked like he'd strutted off the Abercrombie and Fitch ad on the adjacent page.

Thinking of Doug half naked in an Abercrombie ad was not a good idea. I'd met him during the same summer vacation I'd met Meg. Images of me following him around like a puppy flashed through my head. Not an experience I was anxious to repeat.

Normally, the idea of crushing on your cousin would have grossed me out so much that all of Doug's hotness would've been neutralized by my disgust. But in this case, we were so far removed that "cousin" was really stretching it. My mom had said our great-, great-, great-, great-something-er-others had been related back in the day. That connection was so distant that I'd asked my mom she knew we were related at all. She'd muttered something about having had a genealogy hobby back before "an impertinent child" took up all her time. Then, she'd just shaken her head and gotten what my dad called her "give it up, I'm not gonna budge" look and informed me that we were family, no matter how far removed, and I'd be calling them cousins to be polite. The "or else" was implied.

I was trying to peel myself off the floor when my "cousin" Doug leaned down, grabbed my hand, and hoisted me up. He held onto my hand a little longer than he needed to, giving me that teasing smile I'd absolutely not been thinking of over the intervening years.

Well, maybe him being here wasn't so bad. Maybe he had fond memories of me, too.

He asked, "And who might you be?"

Or not.

"She's Finn," Meg called, striding down the hallway.

"Really?" he said, giving me a slow once over.

He still hadn't let go of my hand, so I was kind of at a loss. I gave him a brisk handshake. "Uh, yeah. Hi. Nice to see you again." I took my hand back.

Doug slipped into big brother mode and started razzing Meg. "Did you trip her?"

I jumped to Meg's defense. "Of course she didn't. She wasn't anywhere near me, you boob. You just saw her coming down the hall yourself."

He broke off giving Meg an amused look to give me one. "Did you just call me a boob?"

"I did."

He barked out a laugh. "You really are Finn."

I didn't know how to respond to that, so I turned to Meg. "I was just coming to find you. Where's the party?"

Chapter Eight

"Party?" said Doug. "Oh boy."

Meg gave him a look, then turned her attention to me. "It's really more of an intimate soiree than a big party. Feeling better? You look like you feel better."

I barely had a chance to nod in response before Meg said, "Good," and hooked her arm through mine. As she talked, she slowly walked me down the hallway toward the back of the house. Doug trailed after us.

"About the reunion. Help me out—I'm kind of at a loss here. After you called, I checked in with the reunion organizers, and they told me all about your family—"

"Wait, what? How do they know anything about my family?" Because that wasn't creepy at all.

"The reunion invitations are sent out by a...there's a family—it's kind of like a historical society—they're big into the whole Foster genealogy thing, and they keep track of the family tree. *All* of the family tree. Your mom was a Foster, as are you, so of course your family is on their radar. Speaking of your mom, she never mentioned the reunions to you at all?"

I shook my head. "Nope."

"But you know all about the Fosters, our history...our traditions?"

I shook my head again.

Meg huffed. "My guess is they just assumed she taught you all about being a Foster from the time you were small, so they didn't bother to give you any info on the reunion when they invited you. Ridiculous. I mean really, not everyone in the family gets the Foster lore drilled into them from birth."

"Cretins," said Doug.

"Lazy," said Meg. "They dropped the ball." She looked exasperated.

I smiled and shrugged. "Well, my mom did say we were just a tiny twig on a distant branch of the family tree—"

"Doesn't matter. A Foster is a Foster, no matter how thin the blood. They should have reached out." Meg sighed, shook her head. When she spoke again, her voice had softened. "And well, they said you lost your dad just recently—our side of the family really should have made an effort, offered some kind of support." She glanced at Doug, paused a bit, then said, "We lost our mom recently, too, so I know it's tough." She gave my arm a little squeeze.

I felt a wave of empathy for her and squeezed her arm back, saying, "I'm so sorry to hear that." Meg gave me a sad smile, but Doug didn't make eye contact when I looked back at him. He just looked at the floor.

We reached the end of the hallway and stopped at a staircase at the back of the house.

Meg turned to face me, her hand on my arm. "I have the feeling that this reunion isn't going to be what you expected. But I hope you'll stay here the whole weekend anyway. Give us a chance to get to know you better, even if this isn't what you had in mind…. Having family to support you is important. Especially now."

"Of course I'll stay, Meg." She looked so relieved that it occurred to me she must have been really lonely. She'd said on the phone that she lived here. Thinking of her in this big old house, trying to cope with her grief, had me stepping forward and hugging her as I said, "And I really am sorry about your mom."

She did the stiff hug with the awkward pat on the back thing, ending the hug quickly. Doug was hanging back a few feet so I didn't try to hug him, but I sent a sympathetic look his way.

"Let's go join the others," she said. As we descended the stairs, she added, "Everyone is in the kitchen."

"Oh good, is there food? I'm starving!"

Doug snickered behind me. I shot him a questioning glance over my shoulder. He said, "Meg doesn't cook."

"True," said Meg. "But I can order in just fine."

At the foot of the stairs, there was a sort of mudroom area that doubled as a laundry room. Meg pointed to the washer and dryer and said, "Finn, feel free to use these. Raid the cupboards for any laundry stuff you need."

"Thanks so much," I said. I'd left my nasty clothes soaking in the tub, but I really needed a proper washing machine.

Crossing the hallway, we walked past the back door and into the kitchen.

After the dimness of the rest of the house, I had to fight the urge to shrink back into the shadows like a vampire confronted with sunlight. Someone had actually used a light-colored wood in the room. Not only that, but they'd turned on the lights. Like, all the lights. The effect was super bright and in a minute or so, when I could see again, I'd probably find it cheery.

As my eyes adjusted, I scoped out the space. To my right, flanked on both sides by cupboards and counters, the sink stood under a window in the back wall. It was dark now, but during the day I bet it looked out on the woods. My mom would've called it a bribe window. It enticed you with a gorgeous view, and then while you were standing there, you wound up doing the dishes.

Of course there were no dishes in sight. The kitchen's butcher block island didn't even have a bowl of fruit on it. The room was so spotless that it reminded me of a magazine photo. With its miles of empty counter space, the kitchen was begging for someone to come on in and cook up a storm. But there wasn't an ounce of culinary activity in sight.

My attention was drawn to a big rectangular table occupying the left side of the room. Sitting at the table was an Asian woman and a black man. To my relief, they were both dressed casually. The Asian woman had her shoulder-length hair down and wore a blouse and jeans. The black man had glasses and wore a button-down shirt and slacks. Both were on laptops, and the Asian woman was texting as well. They looked up when we walked in, and both of them stood up as we approached.

Meg said, "Well, we're all here now. This is Finn. Finn, this is Noriko—"

"You can call me Nor."

"And Wil."

"You can call me Wil," he said with a cheeky little smile. Nor rolled her eyes and grinned.

While I shook hands with them both, and we exchanged "hi's" all around, I was thinking, *This is it?* Meg had said it was intimate, but this wasn't even enough people to qualify for a decent orgy.

Meg looked at me and said, "Not what you expected, right?"

I gave her a small smile. "Not exactly, no."

Meg looked at Nor and Wil. "Finn never learned about the reunions—she doesn't know *anything* about our family." They both looked startled, and Wil looked like he was about to say something, but Meg held up her hand. "I know you're the history expert, Wil, but there's no need to drown her with the full annals of the Fosters. Let's start with the short version." Meg turned to me. "Basically, the reunions are a, I guess you'd say it's a 'getting to know you' kind of thing. The family is huge—spread out all over the world. So, you can imagine it's hard to keep a sense of Foster family pride intact."

I nodded and glanced at Wil and Nor, who were also nodding. They were watching Meg intently, like they were hearing this for the first time, too. Maybe they didn't know as much about the Foster family as Meg thought they did. It made me feel a bit better to know that I wasn't the only one out of the loop.

Meg continued. "That Foster historical council I told you about? They decided that a way to, uh, foster, connections within the family was to invite people 'home' to the original Foster lands and to this house that's been in the family since, I don't remember the year, but let's just say it's been here forever."

"That's cool of them, to make an effort to share this place. From what I've seen so far, it's really beautiful," I said.

Meg said, "We take great pains to keep it that way. Which

is why we don't do huge reunion parties. We want to share, yes. But the house is old and kind of fragile, so it'd be unwise to throw a big party and have a ton of people running around. Not to mention, that'd be counterproductive, since the idea is to actually get to know one another. So instead of one big reunion, we do a series of small gatherings."

Ohhkay. To me, that just raised a whole bunch of questions. How often did they do this? Was it a one-and-done kind of deal, where you only got to visit once? How did they pick who got invited? It sounded kind of odd. From the look Nor was giving Meg, she thought so too, but she didn't say anything, so I didn't either. I just nodded.

"Your group is the last one for this round of reunions," said Meg. "Sorry if you're disappointed."

My manners shouldered their way past my sinking enthusiasm, and I smiled. "No, not at all. I mean, it's not what I expected, but I'm thinking about it, and I guess it makes sense. Big parties can definitely get out of hand." I patted the kitchen island. "And we wouldn't want to damage you, sweetie, now would we?"

Nor's eyebrows shot up, and Wil looked a little alarmed. "Are you talking to the house?" he asked.

Doug laughed. "Oh man. That brings back memories. When we were kids she would talk to everything. And I mean everything—the trees, the rocks, the dishes. You still do that?" he asked with an incredulous smile.

I shrugged. "Well, yeah." At the diner, people were used to me talking to everything like it was a person. And it was such a habit I didn't even think about it as unusual.

Nor and Wil seemed to take it in stride, Doug seemed to think it was funny, and Meg said, "That's...cute."

There was an awkward pause, and my stomach decided to fill the silence by growling loudly. I rubbed my belly and said, "Well clearly, I'm hungry. What's the deal with dinner?" Food would help make this more festive. Food made everything better.

"As I said, I don't cook," said Meg. "But the refrigerator and pantry are fully stocked. You're welcome to help yourself. And now that we're all here, I'll order some pizza. It should be here in half an hour or so."

First there were no people, now it was fend-for-yourself food? This was the weirdest family reunion, get-together, whatever you wanted to call it, ever. Although how would I know? Maybe this is what some families did. But my parents would have passed out in shame if guests showed up, and we didn't have something to eat and drink laid out for them. Maybe that was just a diner people thing?

Thinking of the diner had me looking around the kitchen again while Meg texted for pizza, and the others made small talk. Something about the place seemed off, and it was bugging me that I couldn't put my finger on it. Well, there was no food, sure. And it didn't really smell like a kitchen to me. With dawning horror, I rescanned the room. There were no appliances. There were no appliances? WHERE WAS THE COFFEEMAKER? No food was one thing. But no coffee? What kind of freaks of nature were these relatives of mine?

I was about to ask Meg, as calmly as possible, if there was a coffeemaker hiding somewhere, when knocking at the front door derailed me.

I said, "Oh I think that's for me—that's the vet with Fuzzy. I'll just go let him in," and headed for the door. Would it be too much to hope that he came bearing a side order of coffee along with the kitty?

Chapter Nine

I dashed down the hallway and opened the front door. Sure enough, Dr. Meriwether stood on the porch. He was holding a cardboard kitty carrier. No coffee, though.

"Hi Dr. Meriwether, thanks so much for coming by," I said. "Would you like to come in?"

Meg pushed her way in next to me and gripped the edge of the door, effectively body blocking the entrance. She said, "No."

"What?"

"Finn, where are your manners? The man's out making house calls after business hours—he's obviously busy." She said to him, "I'm sure you've got loads on your plate. We don't want to be rude and take up any more of your time than necessary."

Don't want to be rude? I gaped at her. In what way was this not rude? I turned back to Dr. Meriwether, ready to offer an apology, but he was smirking at Meg. I looked back at Meg who stood perfectly straight, chin up, staring him down.

"Uh," I said.

Dr. Meriwether broke eye contact first and shifted to look at me. The porch board he was standing on wobbled and let out a groan so loud that for a moment I was worried he was going to fall through. He took a careful step back off the complaining plank and said, "It's okay, Finn. Thanks for the invitation, but she's right, I've got to get going." He slid his gaze to Meg. "Maybe another time, though."

Well, since he wasn't coming in, I decided to step out onto the porch, which fortunately held steady under my feet. Meg took my place in the doorway, closing the door slightly so she filled the entire space.

Dr. Meriwether and I wandered over to the porch stairs, where he handed me Fuzzy, who stuck a paw through one of the holes in the carrier to try to bat at me. I poked a finger into his carrier, and he nuzzled it.

"Um, thanks again for coming by to drop him off. I really appreciate it," I said. I lowered my voice and said, "I hope you don't think we're being rude. Meg's, uh…" *a total weirdo control freak* "just trying to be, um…polite…"

"No problem," he said, and from the grin on his face, it looked he meant it. Maybe Meg's antisocial behavior was the norm and that was why people around here didn't like the Fosters. Well, at least he found it amusing—he certainly seemed more unfazed than I was.

We started walking to his car, and Dr. Meriwether pointed to Fuzzy. "So, we tried him on some food, and I'm sorry to tell you that, while he'll eat some wet food, he's going to need bottle supplementation. He just inhaled a whole bottle, so he should be good to go for a while."

"Okay. I know the drill."

"I figured you did. And you're good with diarrhea?"

"Is this a trick question?"

He laughed. "Just in case he has any issues, I left you some instructions in the bag I gave you earlier."

I sighed. "Great. I'll deal."

"I'll be back on Monday, and we'll talk then." He looked at Meg over my shoulder and gave her a little salute, calling, "Bye, Meg." He gave me a little wave, looked like he was about to say something, then just shook his head and said, "Have fun, Finn," and left.

As he drove off, I walked over to Babs to retrieve the bag of vet supplies. I patted Babs with longing. I had the strongest urge to put Fuzzy in the back, hop in, and drive away. But then I'd be the one being rude, not to mention that my clothes were upstairs. And hadn't I just promised Meg that I'd stay the whole weekend? Fine, but that didn't mean I was going to be meekly following Meg's every command like I did as a kid. With the bag in one hand and Fuzzy in the other, I strode back to the house.

As I approached, Meg stepped out of my way and then closed the door behind me. I set Fuzzy down carefully on the staircase. He squeaked at me.

"Hey buddy, you doing alright? Just hang on a minute okay?" I said.

I swung around and faced Meg. "What was that? That nice man went out of his way to be helpful, and you didn't even invite him in for a minute? I get that I'm a guest here and all, but that was…" I sputtered for moment, threw up my hands and said, "Ugh…I don't even know what that was. I mean, what *was* that?"

Meg looked amused and shrugged. "Weren't you listening in the kitchen? This is an old house. We can't have just anyone traipsing in and out of here. It's really important to limit foot traffic as much as possible."

Doug was leaning against the wall, watching with his arms crossed. Nor and Wil were standing in the hallway. I looked to them for some help, but they were nodding along with Meg.

I glared at Meg. "I get that we need to treat the place with respect and care, but it's not like it's some kind of cloistered convent or something. I mean, you live here, right?"

"I'm the Foster in residence, yes. There's always one of us here to be a caretaker to the house."

My response was interrupted by another knock at the door.

"That'll be dinner," Meg said, as she answered the door. Sure enough, a pizza guy stood on the porch.

"Hey Meg," he said, handing her a receipt and a pen.

"You can put it in the kitchen," she said.

My mouth dropped open. The pizza guy strolled by me, right on down the hallway to the back of house. Obviously, he'd been here enough times to know where the kitchen was. "So, wait, it's okay for the pizza guy to come in, but not the vet?"

"That's different," Meg said, as she signed the receipt.

"How different?"

Pizza guy came back up the hallway, and Meg gestured at him. "He's a distant cousin." He gave me a quick wave, took the receipt, and left.

I shook my head. "I don't get it. What's being a cousin have to do with anything?"

"Family is family," said Meg.

"And?"

"This is a family home, so all Fosters are welcome here. In limited numbers, of course."

I mulled that over for a second. "Wait, do you mean all Fosters or only Fosters?"

"Both."

"Oh." Banjo music started playing in my head. We weren't in some remote community deep in the Ozarks, so I didn't understand the isolationism I was seeing.

It was becoming increasingly clear to me why my mom had avoided this part of the family.

A loud meow from Fuzzy saved me from having to respond any further. I picked up his carry case and made some cooing noises.

Turning to Meg and the others, I said, "Um. Yeah. Okay. Well, I'll just get the kitty settled. Don't hold dinner on my account. I'll catch up in a few minutes. C'mon, Fuzzy, let's go get you comfy." I escaped up the stairs before Meg said anything else.

Chapter Ten

The stairs didn't seem quite as vocal this time, maybe because there was just me and Fuzzy. But their muted tones matched my muted enthusiasm, and in my head, they sang "weird, weird, weird, weird" as I trudged upstairs. As soon as I closed the door to my room, I let out a big sigh.

Placing Fuzzy's carrier on the bed, I opened it to find him peering up at me. My shoulders dropped from around my ears, and I smiled.

"Hello handsome. Don't you look lovely since your bath." Without all the mats, his coat was shiny and fluffy, colored a tawny-brown-tinged, grayish tabby with darker gray markings. His chin, belly, and ruff were a grayish white. I could see now that his ears had little tufts at the end, which made me wonder if there was some bobcat in his family tree, despite his long tail.

I stroked his head, and he started purring. "Well, Fuzzy, welcome to crazy town. Don't get me wrong, the house and property are really pretty, but the people who own it might be a little nuts. Don't worry, though—I'll protect you. And, fortunately, neither of us has to stay here that long."

Fuzzy started batting at my necklace, so I stopped petting him and stood back to see what he would do. I wasn't sure if he'd want to leave his carrier right away or if he'd need to hunker down for a bit.

Fuzzy hopped right out, padded across the bed, and leapt down to the floor. The floorboard hummed a bit when Fuzzy landed, and Fuzzy froze, his head cocked. I thought maybe the noise had scared him, but then he leaned down and nuzzled the floor, scent-marking it with the side of his jaw. Huh. That was a first. I'd seen kitties scent-mark the corners of things, but I'd never seen one go right for the floor. Maybe the vibration and noise from the floorboard reminded him of a purr. Well, whatever fluffed his fur was fine by me.

I took the bag of vet goodies into the bathroom, and Fuzzy followed me in.

"I doubt you're litterbox trained," I said to him as I knelt and set up the litterbox, "but let's see how you do. Just to be clear, you should go to the bathroom here. Not on the floor." The floor groaned as I stood up. I looked at it and said, "I hear you, pal. On Fuzzy's behalf, I apologize for any unfortunate incidents that are about to occur. And don't worry, I'll fix it, whatever happens."

Placing a bowl of water for Fuzzy, I told him, "Please try to drink this, rather than licking the faucet. I've also got some formula to help out while you get used to eating big boy food, but your next bottle isn't until later. I'm not going to put out wet food for you just yet until we see how your tummy is doing with your last feeding."

Fuzzy explored the bathroom. He jumped up on the toilet seat—I made a note to myself to keep it closed—and then he leapt up on the sink. He headbutted me to remind me it'd been a whole five minutes since I'd petted him. I laughed and obliged by scritching him under the chin, then went and let the water out of the tub so he wouldn't try drinking it. I looked at my poor clothes. I didn't have many outfits, so I was really hoping they were salvageable. Soaking my clothes had helped the smell, and hopefully they wouldn't stink up the place while I went to eat.

Grabbing a clean towel, I made Fuzzy a little bed on the floor. "There you go. In case you want to nap."

I wiggled the towel to get Fuzzy to look at it, and he took a flying leap and attacked it. The floor let out a squeak when Fuzzy pounced, which just encouraged him to scoot back and pounce again. I spent a few minutes giggling as I watched the scoot-pounce-squeak sequence. Given that the floor was behaving like a giant squeaky toy, I felt pretty sure it'd keep him entertained for a while.

After stalling as long as I could, I said, "I've got to go for a bit." Fuzzy stopped playing to look at me. "You hang out in here while I'm gone. Don't look at me like that. I'm thinking you've got the better deal here. Sure, I get pizza, but it comes with people who might be wackadoodles—I'll introduce you later, and you can see for yourself. Anyway, I'll be back in a little while to check on you, and I'll bring you a bottle." I looked around at all the wood. "Uh, hey, do me a favor. Don't use this place as one big scratching post, okay?" As I shifted my weight to leave, the floor underneath me let out a sigh, and I whispered "Good luck" and scooted out, shutting the door behind me.

I listened for signs of distress, but all was quiet on the other side. Then, I heard a thud and a squeak as Fuzzy started playing again.

Well, he was fine. That meant it was time to go for dinner. My stomach growled again. At least there'd be food, and I could try and find the coffee so I'd know if I needed to go find a coffee shop first thing in the morning. I put the kitten-formula canister and a bottle in my messenger bag and headed downstairs.

Chapter Eleven

As I started down the back stairs to the kitchen, I heard muffled voices and what sounded like heated whispering. But then the stairs announced my approach, and the voices hushed further. By the time I walked into the kitchen, no one was saying anything. From the flush on Nor's face, the stiffness of Wil's shoulders, and the grim set of Meg's mouth, I was pretty sure I'd interrupted a fight. Doug was the only one who looked amused, which pretty much confirmed my suspicion. He was Doug—if there'd been an argument, it was likely he'd been enjoying the fireworks.

I cleared my throat. "Hey guys, sorry to interrupt," I said.

"You're not interrupting," said Meg. "Help yourself to some pizza. How's the kitten?"

As I wandered to the counter where the pizza waited, I said, "Fuzzy's good, actually. Settling right in. I've got him stashed in the bathroom for the moment. Plates?"

Meg said, "In the cupboard."

I looked at the host of cupboards and tried to guess which one she was referring to. The one all the way to my left drifted open just slightly, like someone had recently closed it, and it hadn't shut properly. I walked over and tried that one first. Score! I grabbed a plate, snagged my pizza, and turned to face the others.

They were all staring at me.

Meg gave me a big smile. She was showing so many teeth that I was caught between wanting to back away slowly and wanting to ask her how she kept them so white.

It took me a moment, but I suddenly realized they were all staring because they were politely waiting for me to join them. "Oh, jeez, sorry, don't wait on me! Please keep eating," I said, and I hurried over to the table.

Meg was sitting at the head of the table with Nor and Wil on either side of her. Doug was at the foot. I grabbed the closest empty seat, which was next to Wil.

Hanging my messenger bag over the back of the chair, I sat down, and said, "So what did I miss?" and began inhaling my dinner.

Meg smiled. "We were just having a spirited discussion about one of our Foster family traditions. Wil here is quite the family history buff, so he's full of all sorts of fascinating information." She smiled at Wil. "You know, you really should consider joining the family council—" she looked at me "—that's our little historical society I was telling you about." She looked back at Wil. "In fact, I'd be happy to put in a good word for you at the end of the weekend."

From Nor's raised eyebrows, I took it that Meg's offer was kind of a big deal.

Wil seemed overwhelmed, fiddling with his glasses while he said, "Thanks."

Meg turned to me. "Speaking of which, Finn, I just realized you don't know that one of the benefits of the reunion is that you get to meet with one of the members of the historical society," Meg said.

Doug snorted.

Meg shot a look at Doug, then said to me, "To keep up with this big clan of ours, the council tries to meet as many branches of the family tree as they can. It's nice to have a face to go with a name, to make a personal connection."

As he shoveled a slice of pizza into his mouth, Doug said, "Nice for *them*."

Meg folded her hands. "I'll concede that their... inquisitiveness—"

Doug said, "Nosiness."

"—can feel a bit like an interrogation."

Doug snorted again.

"In their defense, they're just really into their jobs," said Wil.

"So they can be a bit overenthusiastic," added Meg. "It's actually kind of sweet that they're so interested. And besides, you want to meet more of the family, don't you Finn?"

My mouth was full so I just nodded.

Nor looked like she was going to add something, but a look from Meg had her taking another bite of pizza instead. I was guessing she was like Doug and wasn't into the whole genealogy thing. While I had some curiosity about the Fosters, I'd never been into genealogy either. I had no idea what I could possibly have to say that would interest these historical council people, but I had come here to meet family members, so the more the merrier. And maybe I could gently broach the whole "keeping tabs on my family" topic and see if it was as stalkery as it sounded.

I was about to ask Meg for more info, but got waylaid by the pepperoni lodged in my throat. Looking around the table, I saw that everyone was drinking iced tea or water. Aw jeez. At least a beer or a little wine might've loosened things up a bit.

"Mind if I grab some iced tea?" I said.

"Help yourself," Meg said. As I walked over to the cupboards, she said, "Glasses are in the cabinet next to the plates… So, Nor, tell us a bit about your work."

As Nor described life as a lawyer specializing in international corporate law, I grabbed a glass and located the iced tea in the fridge. My stomach did a sigh of relief when I saw the fridge was crammed with food. Well, I might go into coffee withdrawal, but at least I wouldn't starve this weekend.

Since I was up, I slipped into diner mode and walked around offering to refill everyone's glasses while Nor talked.

When she paused for a breath, I asked, "Anyone want more pizza?" As Nor finished giving us an overview of her globe-trotting adventures negotiating high-stakes deals, I dished out slices, then returned to my seat.

"Well aren't you handy," Meg said to me.

I smiled. "Force of habit."

"Oh?" Nor said. "What do you do?"

"Well, I used to work in a diner. Now, I'm going to school!" I did a little victory wiggle in my chair. "I'm doing a year at sea. At least a year. But a year for starters. I'm getting an oceanography degree! I ship out next week and I. Can't. Waaaaaait." I sang the "wait."

Nor furrowed her brows a bit. "That's a bold choice."

I shrugged. "Not really. I had to postpone college for a bit, but we, my parents and I, had planned on me going. And actually, I think being a few years older than the average college student will come in handy."

Doug said, "Don't you live in the desert? Have you ever even been to the ocean?"

"I did, and nope, not yet."

He laughed. "Awesome. Fearless Finn. You're not even a little worried you might not like it, are you?"

"Nah. It's the sea. Who doesn't love the ocean?"

Meg said, "Me. Too much sand, the humidity and wind mess with my hair. And, it smells. Like fish." She shuddered.

I laughed. "It's like when we were kids, and you didn't want to get your dress dirty."

Doug snickered. Meg gave him an unperturbed smile and said to me, "One is never too young to have good style. Or to want to travel, apparently. Even as a kid, you were so excited to see new places—you'd have thought that little vacation we were on was in Paris or something, you were so excited. It's really wonderful that you're finally getting to travel now."

I was grinning so hard my face hurt. "I know, right? I've never been anywhere, well except that vacation, and now here, so I've got this huge list of places I'm dying to see, and now I'm finally going to start checking stuff off the list! And, I get to earn a degree at the same time."

"Well, I may be biased, but I highly recommend academia," Wil said, adding, "I'm a history professor."

"Oh! That sounds fun," I said. "Is that why you're such an expert on the Foster family's history?"

"Actually, it was my passion for the Foster history that got me interested in history in general. Now I'm a bit of a menace with the random historical trivia," he said, his mouth quirking up at the corner. He flicked a glance at Meg then looked back at me, "Don't worry though, I won't launch into a history lecture, I promise."

"You know, Finn," Meg said, "when you talk to the council rep tomorrow, make sure to mention your plans."

"That's right," said Wil. "The family has a scholarship program."

"Wow, cool, thanks," I said.

Nor stood up. "I'm going to heat some water for tea. Anyone else want some?"

"Would you mind boiling the water in a pot instead of a kettle? After you make your tea, I can use the leftover water to make Fuzzy a bottle," I said.

"No problem." Nor got some water going on the stove, and while Meg was talking to Wil about his job, I puttered around making Fuzzy his bottle. Nor went into the pantry, and I followed her, hoping I would find—

"Oh thank the coffee bean fairies! Coffee!" I said.

Nor smiled. "I found the tea in here earlier this afternoon. I think they're stocked up on the essentials, despite the sparse appearance."

"That must mean there's a coffeemaker around here somewhere."

"Probably...this house, it has all sorts of unexpected stuff."

Meg appeared in the doorway. "Find what you need?"

Nor held up the box of tea, "Yes."

"Is there a coffeemaker somewhere?" I asked, shaking the coffee can at Meg.

"The appliances are under the kitchen island. It should be in there."

"Great!"

Meg stepped to the side so we could leave the pantry. "After you."

I put the coffee back and went back to the stove to check the water. I looked behind me for Nor and caught Meg glaring at her. Was Nor drinking Meg's private stash of tea? Nor gave her a blank look, went to get a mug, and came to stand next to me. The water was boiling, so I poured some for her, then put the pot on a cool burner and set Fuzzy's bottle to soak.

"Does anyone want more pizza?" I asked.

Everyone shook their heads.

"I'm going to feed Fuzzy, but I can help with the dishes when I get back," I said.

"It's taken care of," said Meg.

"I'm on dish duty," said Doug. When I raised my eyebrows, he laughed and said, "She bribed me."

Meg stood, and so did Wil and Doug. "Well, thank you all for a lovely dinner. Wil, Nor, I know you both have work you need to do." She turned to me. "Nor has an overseas conference call," she looked at Nor, "starting soon, right?" At Nor's nod, she turned back to me. "Wil is on a tight deadline for the papers he's grading. And of course, Doug and I will be attending to the last minute arrangements for the weekend. So you get a chance to rest up, Finn. There's no TV in your room, but the house has Wi-Fi if you need it. The password is Foster." Meg folded her hands in front of her and stood there waiting.

I hid my surprise by fiddling with Fuzzy's bottle, testing to see if it was warm enough. Given her earlier weird overprotectiveness of the house, it didn't surprise me all that much that Meg was basically sending us all to our rooms. But this early and before even offering dessert? I'd just been in the pantry so I knew damn well that there were cookies and chocolate in there. Not to mention that my plans to make some after-dinner coffee when I was finished feeding Fuzzy just got canceled. I supposed I could always sneak back down and get some later if I was desperate.

With her back turned to Meg, Nor sent me a look that I couldn't quite read. It looked kind of like sympathy, but it seemed like I should be feeling bad for her, not the other way around. At least I got to spend my night playing with a kitten— she was about to be stuck on a conference call. Ick.

Nor finished making her tea, then she and Wil grabbed

their stuff.

Fuzzy's bottle was warm enough, so I put his formula canister in the fridge, grabbed my messenger bag, and prepared to leave, too. Everyone else was kind of milling about, and I wasn't sure what we were waiting for. It turned out we were waiting for Marshal Meg to dismiss us.

"Alright, see you all in the morning," said Meg. "Breakfast is at nine." She made a sweeping motion with her hand, and Wil and Nor headed out. I followed them up the back stairs, and Meg took up the rear.

"What happens tomorrow?" I asked.

"The council rep arrives at breakfast," Meg said. "We'll be spending the day with her."

Well, that was as clear as mud, but I decided to let it go. I was more worried about feeding Fuzzy while his bottle was warm enough than dragging details out of Meg.

Nor and Wil had rooms down the hall from me, nearer the back stairs. They stood in the hallway with Meg, watching as I walked to my room. I felt the itch between my shoulder blades that meant they were staring at me, and it made me both self-conscious and irritated. I suddenly couldn't wait to get away from them all.

As I opened my door, I gave them a little wave. "'Night guys. See you tomorrow morning," I said, then shut the door on the lot of them.

Chapter Twelve

Fuzzy was curled up on my pillow. He picked his head up and started purring as I approached him.

"Hey Houdini, how'd you get out of the bathroom?" The bathroom door was wide open. I did a quick survey and was relieved to find the bathroom was claw-mark free, and the litterbox had been used.

I walked back to the bed. "Good job, Fuzzy. Thanks for not making a mess. How about something to eat?" When I pulled the bottle out of my bag, Fuzzy ratcheted his purr up to 11. I laughed. "I see that you recognize the good stuff already. Okay, let's eat." I climbed onto the bed, back against the headboard. To my surprise, Fuzzy climbed right into my lap. He sure didn't behave like a feral kitten. "Hungry, huh?"

While he guzzled his bottle, I said, "Well, Doug was right—and don't you dare tell him I said that—but that was SO not a party." I sighed. "At least the pizza was good. Mind you, Meg didn't bother to ask anyone what kind they wanted. And get this: she didn't offer us anything to drink, either. Or dessert!" Fuzzy flicked a glance at me. "I know, right? Who doesn't offer dessert?" I wiped away a drop of formula that was sliding down his chin. "At least there's coffee. Not that she offered us any of that, either. I suppose I can go and make some on my own. But I think I'm actually gonna have to sneak, because you know what? She sent us to our rooms for the night! Like we're five years old or something!"

Fuzzy kneaded me as he ate, and I smiled at him. "You're the nicest thing about this reunion by far, Fuzzy. How sad is it that I'm relieved to spend the night in here with you instead of having to socialize with the people I came here to meet? It wasn't that anyone was mean, exactly. But…I don't know…I feel like I don't fit in." And then I added in a softer voice, "It makes me want to go home." Fuzzy looked up at me. "I know, not happening. But still…" I sighed again. "Anyway, thanks for listening."

Fuzzy finished his bottle, and I leaned forward and kissed the top of his head. I put my cheery voice on and said, "Good job on the bottle. It's great to see you eating. No offense, but you're gonna start looking like a Shar-Pei if that skin under your armpits gets any looser—we've got to put some weight on you and fill you out."

I snuck downstairs to the kitchen so I could give his bottle a good wash. When I found the kitchen was empty, I took the opportunity to quickly brew myself some after-dinner coffee to take with me back upstairs. Nor appeared while I was in there. To my surprise, she made herself some tea and lingered in the kitchen with me, until we heard Meg coming. We decided to slip back upstairs before she caught us and had a fit.

Back in my room, Fuzzy was waiting for me on my bed. "Sorry I took so long. I just ran into Nor in the kitchen." I sighed. "I can see that she was trying to show interest in me— she even asked about my road trip here—but the more I talked with her, the more I felt like the distant cousin. Which I am, so I don't know why it's surprising to me that I feel that way."

When I leaned over to pet him, Fuzzy's focus shifted to my necklace, and he started batting at it. "Well at least you appreciate my necklace. You know, I didn't even get one compliment on it tonight?" I let him swipe at it for another minute, but when he went to chew on it, I tucked it safely into my shirt.

I hopped off the bed and changed into my sleeping outfit of yoga pants and a t-shirt. Fuzzy helped me by attacking my clothing as I pulled it out of my suitcase. I washed up for bed—trying to floss with Fuzzy in the room was a special experience—then I pulled a shoelace out of one of my sneakers, and we played with that for a while. By the time Fuzzy was tuckered out, I was too, so I climbed into bed early and called it a night.

Fuzzy clambered onto the pillow and formed himself into a vibrating cat hat. As his purr lulled me, I wrapped my hand around my necklace.

It was round and thick, the weight somehow comforting. The surface had a five-petal star-shaped flower etched into it. Each petal was concave. It reminded me of the star you saw when you cut an apple sideways—the one with the little divots that held the apple seeds—especially since on the pendant, the concave petal that was the top arm in the star shape had a seed glued in it. When I was little, I liked to sit on my mom's lap and run my fingers over the bump of the seed.

I almost never took the necklace off these days, except to bathe. Wearing it constantly was kind of the adult version of carrying a woobie around, but I didn't care. I fell asleep clinging to my last bit of home.

By 3:30 a.m., both Fuzzy and I were wide awake. He needed another bottle, and my internal alarm clock was set to somewhere between "Morning Talk-Show Host" and "Time to Make the Donuts." Plus, I never slept much. Just a few consecutive hours, and I was good to go. I usually got a lot done in the wee hours of the morning. Like laundry! I realized I could do laundry while I fed Fuzzy.

I put on my shoes before I went wandering around, just in case the house decided to object to my late-night jaunt by stabbing me in the foot with another splinter. Fuzzy watched me for a moment and then trotted ahead of me to the door. "Meow," he said, pawing at the door.

"Tell you what, let me put the water on and grab the laundry basket I saw by the washer. You can ride in the basket when I take the laundry down. Okay?" Fuzzy sat back on his haunches, which I decided to take for agreement. I opened the door and slipped out before he could change his mind.

The hallway had the deep quiet that I associate with the middle of the night. Someone had left the hallway light on, but I didn't hear anyone else moving around, so I assumed everyone was asleep. I was worried about the creaky floorboards waking everyone up, but I managed to make it downstairs without the house squawking at me. I got the water going, grabbed the laundry basket, and was back to my room in record time.

Fuzzy was sitting in the same spot by the door. I fetched him, his bottle, and my laundry and went downstairs. I started the wash, and returned to the kitchen with Fuzzy now riding in the empty laundry basket. In the time it took me to make his bottle, Fuzzy figured out how to get out of the basket. I snatched him up just as he was calculating whether he could jump from the table to the kitchen island.

"Not just Houdini but a daredevil as well, huh? You're your own little variety act aren't you?" I plunked him on my lap where he attacked his bottle.

As he ate, I surveyed the kitchen. I'd only needed to turn on the light above the stove. The lighter wood in the kitchen reflected the moonlight that was streaming in through the window over the sink, filling the kitchen with a soft glow that made the kitchen seem romantic.

While Fuzzy chugged, I started mentally remodeling the kitchen. I couldn't help it—years of making the best of our cramped, cranky diner kitchen had turned my family into kitchen junkies. Anytime we'd seen a kitchen on TV, we'd play a game of date/marry/kill, kitchen edition. As I looked around me, I decided I'd date the stove, because old didn't necessarily mean useless; I'd marry the kitchen island, because we'd always wanted one but never had the space for it; and I'd kill a huge chunk of the far wall and put in a bunch of windows. Seriously, what were they thinking, not having a view of the woods in here?

I shook my head. Forget them, what was I thinking? Hell, what was I doing? This wasn't my kitchen, and I was willing to bet Meg wouldn't want decorating advice from me. I was cuddling a critter that I was already becoming attached to and couldn't possibly keep. And the more I thought about dinner last night, the more I had the sinking feeling that relatives or not, these weren't my people.

I had one of those late night moments of clarity: I was in a strange kitchen, with a strange cat, surrounded by strangers, playing a mental game with dead people.

I was wrong, the moonlight wasn't romantic, it was ghostly, and it made the kitchen seem alien.

I tried to take comfort in the sounds of the house sighing around me, tried to pretend that it was whispering in consolation and commiseration. But the house had an echoing emptiness that made it seem as lonely as I was, and it just reinforced my sense of isolation.

A loud creak had both me and Fuzzy swiveling our heads to the door.

Doug strolled into the kitchen, all tousled and sleepy. He looked at us, blinked and ran a hand through his hair, making it stand up even more. He looked like he'd been rolling around in bed. I thought, *Oh no, don't think about Doug in bed. Don't think about Doug in bed. Too late.*

"Hey, Finn." His voice was sleep-edged, deep and slightly raspy.

"Hey. That's some fabulous bed head you've got going there."

He gave me a slow smile. "Must've been wrestling my sheets. What are you doing up?"

I looked down at Fuzzy and nodded at the bottle. "Feeding time. You?" I asked.

"I'm also having a snack attack." He dropped his voice and said, "You feeling hungry, too?"

I nearly rolled my eyes. "Nope."

"Why are you sitting in the dark?" Doug asked as he walked over, opened the fridge, and surveyed its contents.

Because I'm having a private pity party, which you're interrupting, thank you very much, I thought. I shrugged and said, "No sense in turning all the lights on when we're just going back to bed." As if he'd timed it, Fuzzy picked that moment to finish his bottle and start squirming. "See, there, all done," I said, gently putting Fuzzy back in his basket with a "Stay." To my relief, he plopped down and started grooming. I took the bottle to the sink. "I'll just rinse this out, and we'll be off."

Doug closed the fridge and sauntered over behind me. I could feel his warmth radiating against my back. I ignored him and went about rinsing the bottle.

He stepped even closer, placing his arms on either side of me on the edge of the sink. He just rested his hands there, loosely, so I could easily step away if I wanted to. My heart sped up. He smelled good, warm and sleepy and Doug-like. I closed my eyes, trying not to breathe him in, but I couldn't help it with him all wrapped around me.

He leaned his chin on top of my head. "Feeling lonesome?" he said.

"Just tired," I lied.

He tipped his head down so his lips were next to my ear. "I can keep you company, if you like."

"Thanks, I've got Fuzzy." His breath on my ear and in my hair made me break out in goosebumps. I shivered.

"Cold?" he whispered, his lips just barely grazing my ear, and before I could answer, he slipped his arms around me, in a loose hug.

All that warm, solid male felt really good wrapped around me. I almost went for it. I was so damn lonely. One-night stands were my relationship type of choice, and he had "booty call bandit" written all over him. In theory, I had no problem doing a Doug drive by.

Then Doug said, "Aw c'mon, Finn. We could open a bottle of wine, go find a quiet corner and stay up the rest of the night telling each other secrets, like we did when we were kids." He paused, and I heard the grin in his voice. "I'll show you mine if you show me yours."

The reminder of us being kids made up my mind. We did spend one glorious night staying up till dawn and trading secrets. But in the morning, he'd told everything to Meg, and the two of them had teased me mercilessly for the rest of the vacation. And the thing was, I had the distinct feeling that he and Meg were still a team, and anything I said could and would be used against me.

"You're sweet," I said, patting his hand like he was a child. I pulled away and retrieved the laundry basket from the table. Miraculously, Fuzzy had stayed put. "But, I've got to get Fuzzy to bed." I held Fuzzy's basket between me and Doug like a shield. Fuzzy started bounding around the basket, burning off the energy his feeding had given him.

Doug smiled. "He doesn't look sleepy to me."

I snorted. "Just give him five minutes. He'll be ready for a nap."

Doug stepped closer. He stopped just a few inches from the basket. "Want some help getting all tucked in?"

"Thanks, I'm good," I said.

"I'll bet."

I shot him a grin and a wink that brought a speculative gleam to his eyes. Then I headed around him for the door, before I changed my mind and did something stupid. "Enjoy your snack."

I headed up the stairs to my room, trying to get away as quickly as possible without looking like I was actually fleeing.

Chapter Thirteen

Safely back in my room, I distracted Fuzzy and myself by playing "attack the shoelace" some more. I didn't want to think about Doug, I didn't want to think about being lonely, I didn't want to think about how much this weekend was sucking, so I focused on Fuzzy and wiggling the string. At least he seemed happy.

Once we'd killed enough time, I said, "How about you take a nap while I go put my laundry in the dryer?" But as soon as I moved to leave, Fuzzy went and sat in front of the door. I laughed. "I take it you want to come along? Okay, come on." I picked him up and carried him with me.

As we traipsed back downstairs, the house seemed even darker than before. At first I thought maybe the moon had set, but then I realized the light was off in the hallway. I guessed Doug had turned it off. I made my way carefully down the steps, and breathed a sigh of relief when they didn't squeak even once as I descended. When I reached the mudroom, I tried to turn on the light, but it wasn't working. Still, there was just enough dim moonlight spilling in from the hallway for me to make my way over to the washer and dryer.

Just as I reached them, I heard muffled voices approaching from the front of the house. I paused. It was a weird hour of the morning for people to be up. I started to call out to them when Fuzzy put his paw on my mouth, startling me into silence.

Fuzzy and I swiveled to look at the doorway as the voices approached. I recognized Meg and Doug, but they were with at least one other man and woman whose voices I didn't recognize.

Fuzzy let out a deep, soft, nearly subsonic growl. His fur stood up. I wasn't sure why, but Fuzzy felt threatened. I hugged him closer to comfort him, but he was rigid, eyes fixed on the door to the hallway where the people would be any second. Fuzzy's reaction had me tensing up. Telling myself we were both being ridiculous, I stepped forward and took a deep breath to call out to the approaching people.

Somehow I misstepped in a way that made it feel like the floor lurched. I fell back on my ass, Fuzzy clutched in one arm as I braced my fall with the other. The floor seemed to swallow most of the sound of my impact, but I still made a dull thud.

The voices paused.

"Did you hear something?" whispered Doug.

"Check it out." That sounded like Meg.

There was no way this wasn't going to look bad if they found us now. They'd think I'd been spying on them. Maybe if I kept quiet, they would head for the kitchen and wouldn't see us.

I'd landed near the shelves next to the washer. Fuzzy pushed at me, and it occurred to me I should move. I scooted back until I was leaning against the wall under the shelves, where the shadows deepened around us. I clung to Fuzzy, who for once was statue still. My heart was thumping.

Two tall silhouettes appeared in the doorway, and I froze. One of them was Doug, but I had no idea who the other guy was. His face was in shadow, so I couldn't see him clearly.

I heard a clicking sound as Doug tried the light switch by the mudroom door. The two men retreated into the hallway.

"Light's out," said Doug.

There was a pause. Meg said, "It shouldn't be."

Not-Doug said, "You still have that flashlight app on your cell phone?"

Well the game was over now. They'd surely see me, and I didn't really have a good excuse for hiding on the floor in the dark. I was pretty sure "my kitten told me to" wouldn't make sense to anyone but me.

I was trying to figure out how to explain myself, when, without making a sound, the wooden planks in the wall behind me separated, the floor slid me and Fuzzy through the opening, and then the wall closed in front of us. I found myself in a crawl space between the walls.

If I'd thought my heart was racing before, it was about to explode out of my chest now. What the hell had just happened?

A beam of light swept the wall where I'd just been leaning, interrupting my thoughts and redirecting my attention back to the mudroom. The wall's paneling had closed up tightly, and only a little light leaked through. Still, I flinched. I tried to breathe quietly and clung to Fuzzy, whose attention was riveted on what the people were doing. I heard someone walk over to the wall right in front of us. There was a scraping sound as they picked something up off the floor.

"Box of dryer sheets," said Doug. "It must've thumped when it fell off the shelf."

Not-Doug made a "hmm" sound. I could hear him walking around the laundry room. It looked like he was panning the light around the room. "Someone's got laundry in the washer."

"Finn," said Meg, and the way she said it made me feel cold. "Damn house. It was supposed to keep her in her room."

"You told her she should do her laundry," said Doug.

"I did, didn't I. And the house took advantage of the loophole so it could try to please her," she said.

Not-Meg said, "The house is trying to please her?"

"No, no, no, of course not," said Doug. "It's more...just showing an interest in her."

There was a pause and then Not-Meg said, "You were right. It was worth the risk to come here tonight."

Not-Doug said, "Let's get this done."

They all retreated to the hallway.

I tried to wrap my brain around what they just said. The house was interested in me? They were talking about it like it was alive. I looked around my cozy hiding spot, and goosebumps rose on my arms. I decided to try something. I leaned forward, so that my lips were nearly touching the wall, and whispered, "I need to see what's happening."

I jerked back as the boards in the wall in front of me

separated just enough so that I could see into the mudroom. They'd opened at just the right angle that I had a view across the room, out the door, and into the hallway.

My heart was discoing around my chest. I swallowed a couple of times and tried to process. I hadn't actually expected that to work, and I wasn't sure what to do. Well, when all else fails, I was taught to fall back on good manners and be polite. In a shaky whisper I said, "Thanks. Uh, good house," and patted the wall. The house sighed a little in a way that I thought sounded happy, so I gave it an extra pat.

"Let's do this," said Meg.

Fuzzy and I peered out. Meg, Doug, and their guests were standing in the hallway, facing the wall next to the mudroom. From where they were standing, I was pretty sure they were facing a door that was on the same wall as the stairs. It was closed when I'd walked past it earlier, but I'd guessed it was a closet or maybe the entrance to the basement.

Doug stepped back and leaned against the kitchen wall. Meg stepped forward and Not-Doug and Not-Meg flanked her, standing back a bit on either side of her. Meg put her arm out. I couldn't see what she was touching, but I guessed it was the door. She just stood there. Several minutes ticked by, and then she opened the door.

"See what I mean—nothing." Meg shut the door quietly.

"Even though her position is provisional, she's the current housekeeper, so she should have full access," said Doug.

Meg said, "They've been keeping it a secret, but it's been getting worse over time, and now it's been weeks since it worked at all. I don't care what they say, I think the house is out of juice. For this to work, we have to compensate for the missing energy."

Not-Doug and Not-Meg came forward next to Meg and all three reached out their hands. From the way they were leaning, I was pretty sure they were all touching the door.

A low vibration thrummed through the wood around me. It was so quiet that I don't think I'd have noticed if I wasn't sitting on the floor. The vibration remained low and steady—it didn't build like the sink-hole noise did—but I still broke out in a nervous sweat. A weird energy was building in the air, like the electricity that builds before a big thunderstorm.

Fuzzy strained toward the hallway, scrambling desperately to get down. I had to wrap both arms around him to hold him in place.

"Now. Try it now," whispered Not-Doug. His voice sounded strained.

Meg pulled hard on the door. It made no sense to me because she'd just opened it. But she was obviously straining. Suddenly, she slipped back very slightly, and a wind swept into the hallway, along with some leaves and dust. There was a thump, the wind cut off, and Meg let go.

Fuzzy meowed, but it was drowned out by the thump.

They stepped back, all three of the them panting.

Doug had straightened from the opposite wall. "You did it!"

"We only got it open a crack," said Not-Meg.

"Yes, but the fact that we opened it at all—now, before I'm even officially in charge..." Meg gave a low laugh that made me shiver. "Just imagine what we're going to be able to do."

"Agreed," said Not-Doug.

Groaning hinges signaled a door opening upstairs.

"We woke someone up," said Doug.

The floorboards creaked as someone walked along the upstairs hallway.

Not-Doug and Not-Meg moved quickly and silently to the back door. Not-Meg slipped out, but Not-Doug paused. "Make it through this weekend, and we have a deal," he said. "We'll be nearby if you need us," and then he left.

The stairs squeaked out the approaching person's descent down the back stairs. Meg stole away toward the front of the house, making no noise as she went, and Doug moved into the kitchen and started banging around, opening and slamming cupboards.

Nor walked through the mudroom. By the time she got to the kitchen, it sounded like Doug was digging around in the refrigerator, talking to himself. From my vantage point, I could only see a little ways into the kitchen. Nor was standing in the doorway with her back to me. Doug hadn't turned a light on, but the refrigerator light silhouetted Nor.

"Doug?" she said.

I heard a thud.

"Ow. Shit, Nor—you scared me half to death," Doug said.

"Sorry, didn't mean to make you hit your head. What are you doing?"

"Snack attack. I'm having a craving." There was a pause. Doug's voice dropped. "You feeling hungry, too?"

Holy crap, that was exactly the same thing he'd said to me. And he'd used the same deep tone of voice too. Ew. I felt like patting myself on the back for good judgment in not jumping him. I wondered what Nor would do.

"You trying to refrigerate the whole house?" she said.

Doug chuckled and shut the fridge door, plunging the room into shadow. "So, you up cuz you want something?" He kept his voice low and added a little purr in it.

Nor turned on the light.

"Ow, Jesus, bright," he said. "Way to ruin the mood."

I grinned. Nor could clearly take care of herself. I heard Doug moving around in the kitchen. Nor stayed in the doorway.

She said, "I thought I heard voices and a door slam. Was someone here?"

"Huh. I was talking to myself while I was trying to find stuff in the cupboards. Sorry if I woke you." His voice took on a teasing, flirty tone again. "Though not really, if I'm honest… that short little robe you've got on is really working for you."

Nor shifted in the doorway, and I could see her looking around the kitchen and up and down the hallway as she said, "Mmm. So, two things. One, that wasn't a no. And, two, seems like you're trying awfully hard to distract me, Doug." She looked back at him. "Do I look like someone who loses focus easily?" Her voice sounded casual, but I could see a tension in her shoulders. I'd have bet money she was giving him some kind of terrifying lawyer look.

"You know you're not allowed to bring random people here, particularly now. It's against the rules."

"Look around you, Nor. Do you see anyone else? It's just lonely little me down here."

Nor went to the back door and looked out the window into the night. She must not have seen anything because she said, "I'm going back to bed."

"Sure there isn't anything I can do for you? Since you're up and all," Doug said.

"'Night, Doug." Nor padded past me and up the back stairs. The house creaked and moaned as she went, so it was easy to hear her progress. I knew she was in her room when her door groaned as she opened and closed it.

Doug waited a moment, then shut off the kitchen light and exited the kitchen. No creaking accompanied him, but I could hear his footfalls as he walked down the hallway and then went up the front stairs.

I was sure he was gone because the wall in front of me opened up, and the floor slid me and Fuzzy forward into the mudroom. When I looked behind me, the wall had closed up already and looked normal.

Competing thoughts battled it out in my head. Little Monty Python men were yelling "Run away!" in one corner of my mind, while another corner had the *Poltergeist* chick shrieking, "What's happening?" In the middle, Mister Spock stood with one eyebrow raised saying, "Fascinating" and thinking we should investigate.

So I sat frozen, clutching Fuzzy to my chest, occasionally blinking and swiveling my head to make sure no one was sneaking up on me.

Then Fuzzy started purring. I looked down at him, and he chirped at me softly. Next he started nuzzling me. It took me a minute to realize he was calming me down. It was working.

I loosened my death grip on him and nuzzled him back. "I'm supposed to be the one taking care of you, not the other way around," I whispered, then I kissed his head and cuddled him while I pulled myself together. First things first. I needed to get back to my room before someone else came along.

Unlike the racket the steps made with Nor, they were silent

when I crept upstairs. Neither the hallway floor nor the door to my room made a peep either. Once I was safely inside, I put Fuzzy down. He went into the bathroom and slurped up some water while I paced the room.

Okay, everything the house had done so far had been to help me. But the *house* was *helping me.*

Fuzzy came strolling out of the bathroom and looked up at me. He took in the sight of me freaking out, gave me an exasperated sounding, "Meow," and leapt up onto the bed. He sat there looking at me.

Keeping my voice down, I said, "Fuzzy, what the hell just happened? Who were those people, and what were they doing? And holy hell, what's up with the house?" I stopped short. "Oh no, what if it's possessed?"

I looked at the ceiling and the walls, but they looked normal to me. Of course, so had the ones in the mudroom.

For maybe the first time in my life, I felt weird talking to an inanimate object, but I muttered, "Uh, House, you're not possessed, are you?"

There was a sputtering sound from the radiator. To me, it sounded indignant.

I looked at Fuzzy. He didn't seem bothered at all, and if the House were possessed, I was fairly certain he'd be hissing and growling. Instead, he was calmly grooming a paw. "Uh Fuzzy? Since you're a stray, I'm guessing this is your first house, and so I feel I should tell you that this isn't really how houses are supposed to behave. In fact, they don't behave. They're houses. They're supposed to just, you know, sit there."

I contemplated a wall. Feeling ridiculous, I said, "So, uh, House, if you're not possessed, then you're, what, like alive or something?"

There was a short pause, then I heard a single ding sound from the bathroom. I took a few cautious steps into the bathroom. "Uh, was that a yes?"

As I watched, the sink vibrated, and the glass on the edge rocked and clinked against the metal faucet.

Ding.

The house could have chosen to make any number of noises, but it chose to make a "ding" sound that reminded me of the ding you got on a game show when you got something right.

"I see we have a sense of humor," I said to the house.

Ding, ding, ding.

I didn't know how I felt about a house having a sense of humor. I could see where that could go really wrong, so I just said, "Huh, okay. Good to know." I paused. "Um, no offense, but I gotta tell you, this is weirding me out. I've never met a, whatever you are, before. It's gonna take me a little getting used to." The house didn't say anything, so I went back and sat on my bed.

Nope, sitting wasn't going to happen. I decided I needed to get out of the house, take a walk, clear my head. It was still dark, but the sky had already started to lighten.

I got dressed, put Fuzzy on the bed and told him to nap, then headed out. On my way through the mudroom, I realized my laundry was still in the washing machine. I tried the light, and it worked. As I was putting my laundry in the dryer, I realized that the house must've kept the light off to keep me and Fuzzy hidden. For whatever reason, it really was trying to protect us.

I started the dryer, and when I turned off the light, I paused by the wall and whispered, "Thank you. Really." I gave it a nice pat and then went out the back door.

Chapter Fourteen

When I slipped outside, I stepped onto a back porch. I paused for a moment, soaking in the soft hush that precedes dawn. I could feel the forest dreaming around me.

Sunrise was still about a half hour away, but the twilight had lightened enough that I could make out the silhouettes of things. Tugging my sweater closer against the damp chill in the air, I walked down the steps and onto the dew-laden grass. I headed for the outline of a fence across the lawn in front of me.

Parts of the fence were valiantly attempting to remain upright. The rest of the fence had already lain down and called it day. As I approached, I found a gate that was stuck open, hanging from one remaining hinge. I stepped through and the scents of rosemary, basil, and oregano greeted me, making me smile. A garden! Or what was left of one.

To the right of the gate, a variety of herbs had gone wild. The rosemary bush was nearly as tall as I was and was making a run for it over the fence line and into the yard.

I pulled my necklace open, unfolding the pair of scissors tucked inside. I used them to snip a sprig of rosemary. As I waded through the overgrown main path, sniffing the rosemary, I thought of my mom.

The first time she'd shown me the necklace's secret, we'd been in our small, raised-bed garden. I'd been little, only five years old.

"Want to see some magic?" she said.

"Hell yeah!" I said, eyes wide.

"Language, Finn," Mom said, trying to hide a snicker. "You

know the rule."

"'I can talk like a trucker when I can drive a truck,'" I recited. "Sorry, Mom."

"It's great that you're a little sponge. We just want to be choosy about what you're soaking up." She tousled my hair and smiled. Then, with mischief dancing in her eyes, she said, "Okay, now, watch this!"

She'd been wearing the same necklace she always wore, the one that I wore now.

As I watched, she opened the top of the necklace.

I gasped. I didn't know it could do that!

Underneath, there was something metal. With a quick pulling and twisting, the metal unfolded, until a small pair of scissors hung from the chain. "Ta dah!"

I giggled and clapped. "How come there's scissors in your necklace?"

"The necklace is really old. My guess is that these were sewing scissors. Women used to wear folded scissors like these because they were always mending things."

"What's mending?"

"Uh, fixing. Women used to sew all the clothes and things by hand. They were constantly fixing things to make them last, so they kept their scissors with them—kind of the way people keep cell phones in their pockets today because they use them all the time. But women didn't wear pants back then, so they wore the scissors on a chain around their neck or on a belt sometimes. The scissors fold up, so you don't accidentally poke yourself when you're wearing them. And the cover on them makes them pretty to wear."

"Those was there the whole time?" I asked.

"Yup."

"Do you gots other magic stuffs hiding?" I bounced. "A bunny? Do you gots a bunny?"

She laughed. "No bunnies, sorry. But it's a big world, and there's lots more amazing stuff for you to discover."

"Like those?" I asked, pointing to the necklace.

"All sorts of things."

"How come you never shows me before?" I pointed at the scissors.

"You weren't old enough. These scissors are too sharp. But you're old enough now."

Mom had handed me the scissors and showed me how to cut the rosemary. She'd tucked a sprig in my button hole, and then we'd laughed our way around the garden as I began learning how to harvest herbs and vegetables. Later, I'd stood on a chair next to her, and she'd let me add some of the herbs as she cooked. Then, I'd peeped out from the kitchen and watched as a customer ate what we'd made. The trucker had slumped in his chair until Mom brought him his plate. Watching the fresh food smooth the weariness from his face and replace it with a look of comfort had made me want to hug my mother. So I did.

Now, as I wandered, sniffing the rosemary, I could still feel her arms around me.

"Hey Mom, guess what I discovered?" I murmured to the sky. "Oh I wish you could see the house!"

I could almost hear her laugh of delight. She wouldn't be freaked out by the house at all. She'd be banging around in the kitchen while she chatted up a storm, forging ways to communicate with the house, finding out its wants and needs. She'd be making friends.

Me, I was gonna need a minute, so I was fine staying out here for a bit.

I looked at the weed palooza around me. As the sky lightened and revealed more of the garden to me, it became obvious that at one point, the garden must've been magnificent. My heart ached to see the tangled, choked mess it'd become. How Meg could have let this get so fallow was beyond me. I could add it to the list of things I wanted to ask her.

A sound like a door closing broke the quiet. I tensed and snapped my head around toward the house, but relaxed a little when I didn't see anyone. I thought it was probably forest noise I'd heard. But if someone else was awake, I didn't want them to call me back inside, so I decided to get going on my walk.

I left the garden and headed off into the woods. Though the

sun was peeking above the horizon, it was dim in the forest, so I stuck to the first path I found. Looking around me as I walked, I realized that while the garden might be a wreck, the forest was thriving, teeming with life. Decorated with chirping birds and scurrying squirrels, numerous trees nodded in the gentle breeze that rustled their leaves and teased my hair. As I walked, the quiet serenity of the forest sank into me. My shoulders relaxed, my breathing eased, and my mind cleared.

I thought about Meg, Doug, and their visitors. From the way they were skulking about, it was clear they weren't supposed to be doing whatever they were doing. And what about the "no visitors" rule? I was pretty sure Not-Meg and Not-Doug weren't even supposed to be in the house. Given the way the house had hidden me, I was thinking that outright asking about what they'd been up to was a bad idea. There was something going on with that door, that much I knew. I'd have to get a look at the door later. Maybe the house could clue me in to what was going on.

Ah, the house. So the house was alive. But what did that even mean? It seemed to be sentient, but what level of intelligence was I dealing with? It could move stuff around, and it could communicate with me, at least a little. What else could it do? I needed more info.

I mulled it over and decided to take a combination Dad-and-Mom approach. I'd treat the house like a stray: be kind, learn to communicate, but observe carefully for signs that I was about to be scratched or bitten. At the same time, I was going to try to borrow some of my mom's spunk and enjoy the heck out it while I could. When was I going to get the chance to play with a living house again?

Although now that I knew about the house, it made me wonder what else was out there. It wasn't like I was expecting the world to suddenly be full of sentient houses—if there were a whole bunch of talking houses around, the Internet would be going nuts about it. I suspected the house was unique, and that's why the Fosters were so against visitors. They were trying to keep it secret. But knowing that the house existed just confirmed my conviction that there was a lot of exciting stuff out there in the world for me to encounter. It made me itchy to get on my ship and start exploring.

I put the house out of my head and concentrated on enjoying the forest around me. This place was so different from the desert—so many glorious trees!—and I inhaled the scent of leaves and damp earth, committing them to memory.

The path wound so much that I wasn't certain how far I was actually walking, but the woods were much bigger than I'd expected. I'd been walking for nearly an hour when I came across a large pond fed by a stream. I crossed the stream at a narrow point and walked along the far side until I reached the edge of the pond. As I stood wondering if anyone went swimming or fishing here, a ripple broke the surface, a head popped up, and something small and furry swam toward the shore. At first I thought it might be an otter or a beaver, but as it came closer, I realized it was Fuzzy, and he had something in his mouth. He strutted onto the shore, shook himself, and dropped his treasure on the ground, where he started eating it.

"Oh God, no, don't eat that! What is that? Is that a fish? You're supposed to be eating kitten food, not—oh that's so gross."

Fuzzy looked up from the small fish he was devouring, blinked at me, and then went back to eating.

"Fuzzy, what are you even doing out here? You're not supposed to be outside. And what were you doing in the water? Cats hate water!" I realized then that the door-closing sound I heard earlier was the house letting Fuzzy out, to go hunt, apparently. That had been over an hour and a half ago, which meant Fuzzy had been out in the woods all by his tiny self this whole time. The thought that I'd have to have some stern words with the house was immediately followed by the thought that I couldn't believe I'd just thought that.

Fuzzy inhaled the fish. Given the other fish bones nearby, I was guessing it hadn't been his first.

He padded over to me and dropped the fish's head at my feet. "Uh, thanks," I said. I knew it was a sign of affection for him to share his kill with me, and while it was better than mouse guts, I still wasn't going to eat it.

"What am I going to do with you? You're soaked." I picked him up and was relieved to find that he wasn't as wet as I'd thought he'd be. His coat must dry really fast, thank the wet kitten gods for small favors. "Fuzzy the fisherman. Awesome. The vet will never believe me. C'mon fish breath. We're taking you home."

I turned to go and walked a few feet away from the pond, back along the stream. Fuzzy got all stiff in my arms.

"Look, I know you're the wildman of the water and all that, but the woods are no place for you. It's dangerous out here, no matter how pretty it looks."

Fuzzy started vibrating. At first I though he might be cold, but then the vibrating increased to a full growl.

That's when I noticed it had gotten very quiet in the forest. The welcome-to-the-dawn birdsong that had been playing in the background had stopped. I clutched Fuzzy closer and peered into the woods around us. I didn't see or hear anything scary approaching through the brush, but then scary things that eat you don't usually announce themselves, do they?

While I stood there, trying to figure out what to do, it started to rain. On a laugh, I let out the breath I hadn't even noticed I was holding. The birds had hunkered down to avoid the rain, that's why it was quiet. I peered down at Fuzzy. "Oh sure, you'll go swimming, but a little rain makes you freak out? Hah!"

As I spoke, the sound of the rain changed from a gentle pattering to a rapid hammering. From the sound of it, we should have been getting soaked, but where we stood, only a small amount of rain reached us. When I looked up, I could see that the trees were bowing under the force of the rain, creating a natural umbrella that was shielding us from the worst of the downpour.

I had just decided that maybe we should stay where we were until the cloudburst passed, when I caught movement out of the corner of my eye and turned to see that the stream was swelling. Fast. Flash floods were a dangerous fact of life in the desert, and reflex had me scrambling away as the water surged toward me.

The water was rising so fast now that I felt like the water was chasing me as I ran through the trees to escape it. I was going in the wrong direction, running away from the house, but I didn't care, I just wanted to get clear, and then I could circle back. The water kept coming, surging faster now, so I kept going.

Suddenly, I broke through the tree line and onto someone's lawn. The wet grass sent me into a skid, and since I was still clinging to Fuzzy, I couldn't pinwheel my arms for balance. I went down hard on one knee. The wind picked up, and the rain flew sideways, pelting my face so hard that tears formed in my eyes. I ducked my head and folded my body around Fuzzy, trying to protect him the best that I could. I couldn't hear him over the roaring of the rain, but I could feel him growling. I didn't blame him.

I struggled to get back up, but the force of the rain and wind combined with the weight of my sodden clothing made it really hard to stand, and I fell back down again. My teeth started to chatter, and I couldn't tell if the temperature was actually dropping, or if I was just freezing from being so wet. I couldn't stay there huddled on someone's front yard, that was for sure. I picked my head up to peer through the rain and saw a house across the lawn. With a surge, I gained my feet and started struggling across the lawn toward the house.

The wind decided I was its chew toy, tugging and tossing me this way and that across the lawn, as I staggered, looking like a drunk after a bender. I realized it really was getting colder when it started to hail. It hurt like hell when the little bits of ice hit me, and I was pretty sure I was going to be polka-dotted with bruises by the time this was over. I thought that was bad, but then the little hail's older brothers decided to join the party. Huge pieces of ice came thundering down, and the grass around me started looking like a driving range covered in icy golf balls and baseballs. As I neared the porch stairs, a baseball-sized chunk of hail slammed into my head so hard, I nearly went down again. I felt a hot rush where it hit my scalp and got really dizzy.

I stumbled up the stairs onto the covered porch. The door opened, a hand reached out, and I was yanked inside.

Chapter Fifteen

I jerked to a stop. I was standing in a cheery foyer surrounded by white wainscoting and flowered wallpaper. The abrupt shift from "flee the killer hail" to "happy sunny cottage" was too much for my brain, and it locked up. So, I just stood there dripping, gasping for air, and clinging to Fuzzy, while I waited for the lady who'd yanked us inside to say something.

The cheerful surroundings were in direct contrast to the scowl on her face. She had dark, dreadlocked hair that was loosely gathered into a messy bun. She was wearing some kind of drapey sweater thing, and she was standing in front of me, arms crossed.

Her expression changed to alarm, when I started swaying.

She sighed, said, "Come on," stepped forward, and guided me to the left into a kitchen.

"Sit," she said and plunked me down at a table just inside the kitchen door. The table was in a breakfast nook in front of a big window that looked out over the front yard, which was currently covered in so much hail that there was more ice than lawn.

The woman followed my gaze and made a sound that I could only describe as a growl. "If they damaged any of my plants, they're gonna pay." I cringed back into my chair. Her tone of voice made me think that whoever "they" were, they wouldn't be paying with money. But that didn't make any sense. Who did you make pay for the weather? The clouds?

Fuzzy meowed, and I let up on the death grip I had on him. "Are you okay?" I asked. I put him on my lap and ran my hands over him to check for injuries. He had no cuts, and from his purr, he was no worse for the wear. I, on the other hand, started to shake so hard I nearly bounced him off my lap.

"He looks fine," the lady said. "You, on the other hand, are not only soaked, you're bleeding." She went to a cupboard, got a towel, and came back to me. "Don't bleed on my floor. I just cleaned," she said, holding the towel to my head.

"Uh, okay."

"What's your name?"

"Finn…and this is Fuzzy."

She snorted and looked at Fuzzy. "Really? You gonna put up with that name?"

Fuzzy gave her a look and then started to groom a paw. She shrugged and said, "Suit yourself."

"Who are you?" I asked.

"You can call me Zo."

"Zo. Rhymes with No. Which is like Nor—she's next door!" I said in a singsong. "Uh oh, did I just say that aloud?"

"You may have a mild concussion. At the very least, you're sounding like you're a little shocky."

"Shock? Oh not again. Well, at least I didn't start counting your dreadlocks to find out how old you are, so it's probably not that bad." She was looking at me like I was mental, so I said, "Um, I think I might need to stop talking now."

She took one of my hands and put it on the towel so I was holding it in place on my head. Then, she hurried off to the sink, where she put some water in a kettle, which she set on the stove.

It occurred to me that this was the second time in recent weeks that someone had yanked me through a door to safety. This whole being out and about in the world was proving to be kind of treacherous. Or maybe I was just danger prone.

Zo looked irritated. I couldn't blame her. We'd totally just burst in, and now she was stuck taking care of us. I said, "Thanks so much for helping us out. I'm sorry to barge in on you. I know it's early."

She looked over at me, and I must've looked pretty pitiful

because her face softened and she said, "I was up."

She came back to my side and took control of the towel again. "I'll get the bleeding stopped, but I'm pretty sure you're going to need stitches."

Shaking my head to disagree turned out to be a bad idea. The pain that stabbed me made the room swim a bit, and my vision grayed around the edges.

"Easy now. Slow deep breaths. That's it."

She lifted the towel off my head again and gave a "Hmph," which I took to mean I wasn't bleeding anymore, because she put the towel on a counter and left the room. She came back with a blanket, which she wrapped around me. It was warm, like it had just come out of the dryer.

As she returned to the stove and began making tea, I snuggled into the heat of the blanket, still shivering, but less violently. The warmth felt so good that it felt like the water was evaporating off my clothes. I half expected to find a cloud of fog hanging around me, but when I looked down at Fuzzy, he was fog-free and kneading the blanket. I looked up again when Zo placed a steaming cup of tea in front of me.

"Drink." Reaching out to Fuzzy, she asked, "May I?" Before I could answer, he started climbing across the blanket toward her, and she picked him up. She went and grabbed a tea towel, then came back and sat across from me and began toweling Fuzzy off. It couldn't have been an easy job, what with him trying to eat the towel as she wiped him down. When she started drying one of his paws, she stopped, then leaned closer.

"Oh crap. Did he get cut?" I asked, craning my neck to see.

"He's fine. He's just…a little unusual. His toes are webbed."

"Huh. I found him swimming just now. Before the storm. I've never seen a cat swim, nevermind one with webbed toes."

"It happens. Drink." She pointed at my mug and then resumed toweling him.

The mug shook in my hands, sending the hot liquid sloshing around. Fortunately, she hadn't filled it to the tippy top, or I'd have wound up with burns on top of my bruises. Scalded and frozen. What a morning, and the sun hadn't even been up that long.

Thinking of the sun, I looked out the window and nearly dropped the mug when I saw that it was a clear, bright day. Sunlight sparkled off the pools of water left by the melting hail. The poor lawn. It looked like a herd of moose had hosted a kegger on it.

"Yeah, it's a mess," Zo said. "I'll fix it. Stop gawking and drink your tea."

I took a big sip of the tea and choked as it blazed its way down my throat. When I stopped coughing, I glared at her. "Is that whiskey?"

She was grinning. "Drink up."

The first sip was already making me feel warmer. I took another sip. "Whiskey for breakfast. Sure, why not." I couldn't seem to get my brain to work right, so I concentrated on sipping my tea. As I drank, my shivering slowed, then stopped, and the pounding in my head receded to a dull thumping.

I peered into the mug and saw some tea leaves at the bottom, and a bunch of stuff floating in the last of the tea. I looked up at her. "What did you put in here?"

"You mean besides the whiskey? Just some herbs to help with your head. Feeling better now?"

"Actually, yes." I swallowed the last of the tea and reached to set my cup down, but she took it from my hand. She peered into the cup, turning it this way and that, frowning in concentration.

"Uh, are you reading my tea leaves?" I asked.

"And if I am?"

"Cool!" I winced, making a note to keep my enthusiasm turned down to a five or lower. I saw her eyes widen, but before I could tell if it was surprise or alarm, she smoothed her face out. "What? See anything interesting?"

She kept her expression blank. "Mmmm. Hard to say." She put the cup down, then put Fuzzy down on the floor. As he wandered around the kitchen, she came over to me, took a quick look at my head, then said, "You're definitely going to need to see a doctor for that. I'll give it another minute to let the tea do its thing, then we'll take you to get stitched up."

She moved around the kitchen, grabbing a purse and keys, and pulling out a cell phone and sending a text. Fuzzy padded over and stared up at her. Looking down at him, she said, "You can hang out here while we're gone."

"Thank you so much," I said.

"No problem." She set out a dish of water and some cat food for him. She opened a door at the end of the kitchen, and Fuzzy went to investigate. "Litterbox is in here," she said to him.

"Do you have a cat? The way you talk to Fuzzy like he's a person makes me think you have a cat. Well that and all the cat stuff."

"He's outside at the moment," she said. "Don't worry. He won't bother Fuzzy. But to keep Fuzzy out of trouble, I'll shut him in the kitchen while we're gone." She looked down at Fuzzy. "There's lots of good napping spots in here. So you just curl up and behave yourself."

Fuzzy blinked at her.

Her phone beeped. She read the message and said, "My friend the doc said to come right over. Time to go."

I groaned and said, "I can't believe I'm going to need stitches. Meg's gonna kill me for disrupting her schedule...Meg's in the house down the road—"

"I know who Meg is."

"I can tell from your tone that you're another huge fan of the Fosters. Well full disclosure, I'm also a Foster. Distantly. But still a Foster."

She raised an eyebrow and glanced at her lawn. "No kidding."

"Why are you looking at the lawn? It's not like I made it hail."

"Well of course you didn't," she said, looking exasperated. She came over and pulled the blanket from around my shoulders. I was startled to realize I was dry.

"Let's get going," she said.

I stood up, and the thumping in my head increased.

Zo looked me over. "You okay to travel?"

"The room's a bit tilty, but I'm getting on a ship in a couple of weeks, so I'm trying to think of this as good practice for walking around when the sea is pitching."

She gave me a look and shook her head. "Whatever works."

She led me out of the kitchen into a garage and got me tucked into her car. There were a bunch of beads and charms hanging from her rearview mirror. They reminded me of some of the beads my mom had draped inside of Babs. Longing swamped me, so intense that my eyes teared up. I would've given anything in that moment to be able to call my mom or dad and tell them about the crazy morning I'd had, to have them come with me while I got stitches.

Zo climbed into the other side of the car, took one look at my teary eyes, and began digging around in her purse and muttering. She must've thought my head was killing me because she pulled out an enormous pair of sunglasses and said, "Put these on. They'll help keep your headache down to a dull roar."

They were leopard print. And had rhinestones. I put them on anyway. "Thanks," I said. She was right. As soon as I had them in place, they seemed to help my head. The light must've been bothering me more than I thought. I shuddered to think how I would've felt outside in the bright sunlight without them.

She also dug another set of beads out of her bag and added them to the ones hanging around the mirror.

"Those are pretty," I said. "My mom had a whole bunch in her car, too. I still have them hanging in there."

"You don't say," she said and started the car.

We pulled out of the garage into a beautiful sunny morning. Unfortunately, the sunlight just served to highlight the devastation.

I gasped as I took in the wreckage. "Holy shit."

The driveway led away from the side of the house, so we hadn't been able to see this part of the damage from the kitchen. Zo stopped the car. Her hands were white on the steering wheel, her mouth compressed into a flat line.

It looked like someone had bombed her yard. She'd lined

the driveway all the way to the road with a complex series of beds. About an hour ago, it must have been beautiful. Now the plants and shrubs were shredded, bent, torn, and in some places, snapped in half.

She shut off the car, got out, and stomped down a path to the back of the house. I followed her. I caught up to her at the back corner of the house, where she'd stopped and was looking out over an enormous garden. I let out a breath when I realized the garden hadn't been touched. In fact, it looked like the hail had stopped right at the edge of the back of the house. So while the front and sides had been blasted, the back had been spared entirely.

"That's weird," I said.

Zo turned around and strode back to the car.

I scrambled to follow her, chattering as I climbed back into the car. "I mean, good that your garden's okay. But just weird that the hail stopped like that, like it hit a wall," I said, shutting the car door.

Zo looked at the ceiling of the car, shook her head, and started driving down the driveway.

As we passed the ruined beds, I looked at them, winced, and said, "Wow. I am so sorry. What a mess. Look, I'm only here for the weekend, but I can come over tomorrow and help you get started on replanting and repairing some of this, if you want. I'm pretty good with plants." I twisted around in my seat to get a better look. "And I'm pretty sure we can salvage at least some of them."

She glanced over at me, eyebrows raised. "You actually mean that, don't you?"

"Of course."

"Well. That's a kind offer. But what about your Foster family obligations?"

"What obligations? Oh, right, Meg's schedule. Well, she can't have scheduled every minute of the weekend. I mean, it's a reunion not a business conference, and to be honest, you can barely call it a reunion—there's only a few of us."

"A reunion?"

"Well, when I got here, Meg did say it was more of an, uh," I did my best Meg voice, "'intimate soiree,' but yeah." I rambled on for a few minutes, explaining about the invitation and my curiosity about my family.

When I wound down, she was silent a moment. Then she said, "I need to think."

I took that as a "Shut up, Finn." I was glomming onto the fact that Zo wasn't a big talker. Well, at least she was taking good care of me, for which I was really grateful. I decided to give her the space she'd asked for, and spent the rest of the car ride in silence.

Chapter Sixteen

Zo took the same main road I'd been on earlier, but instead of going left toward the Foster house and the strip mall with the pub, she turned right toward the vet.

As we drove, the houses got closer and closer together, and more strip malls and businesses dotted the roadway. I recognized the vet's office as we drove past it.

After about 15 minutes, the houses and businesses were shoulder-to-shoulder, and we reached the downtown area. What I thought of as a town square marked the center of town, but the sign called it a town "common," which seemed adorably New Englandy to me. It had a big grassy lawn, large shade trees with benches under them, and a big white gazebo in the middle. The common was bordered on all four sides by various businesses and restaurants. Some of the buildings looked really old, like the brick might have been there since the town was founded. Despite my current physical state, I was charmed by the old brick buildings and lovely common.

The road we were on was one of four that led into the town's center. Zo wove her way around downtown until she parked in an alleyway a couple of blocks from the town square, behind a building that looked like it might have been a house at one point.

"We're here," she said. She led me up the stairs and in the back door. We stepped into the hallway, and I could tell by the antiseptic smell that we were in the doctor's office.

A woman with caramel skin and long, dark hair approached us. She was wearing a white lab coat.

"Zo," she said. Then she turned her attention to me and gave me a smile and offered her hand, "Hi, I'm Dr. Paige Alexander. Most people just call me Dr. Paige, though."

"Hi, I'm Finn." I shook her hand.

"Let's go in here, and I'll have a look at you." She motioned me into an exam room. "Zo, you can wait in my office, if you like."

Zo nodded, said, "I've got some calls to make," and walked away down the hallway, cell phone in hand.

The doc followed me into the exam room and closed the door behind us. "I see that you're limping a little."

"What? Oh, huh. Yeah, my knee's a bit sore, I guess from when I fell on it." I laughed a little. "Wow, I didn't even notice, I've been so focused on my head."

"It's hurting?"

I nodded. "I'm not as woozy as I was, but the thumping is getting worse again."

"Well, hop on up and let me have a look."

I climbed up on the table, and Dr. Paige donned a pair of latex gloves. The snapping sound made me wince.

She noticed and gave me a reassuring smile as she approached. "I'll be gentle, I promise. Why don't you tell me what happened?"

She was true to her word, and it didn't hurt that much as she poked and prodded my head, as I explained, "I got caught in a sudden storm and got hit in the head with a big chunk of hail."

"Hail? Really." She stopped poking and stepped back to look at me. "Zo's right. You need some stitches." She checked my knee. "Well, the good news is that you don't need stitches in your knee. But, you've got a bad scrape and a big bruise forming, and it's going to be really sore later."

The doc walked over to a counter and pulled out a syringe, a vial, and some other supplies. "So what brings you to our little town?" she asked.

"I'm here for a family reunion." I looked over at her filling the syringe. "I feel like I should confess that I'm a Foster, if Zo didn't already tell you. Given how people seem to react to that name, I'm really hoping it doesn't affect the size of that needle you're looking to jam in my scalp." I cringed as she approached. "Would it help if I said I was distantly related?"

She smiled and stood next to me. "I'm a doctor. I work on everyone. Even the occasional Foster. Like Zo, I tend to be neutral in these matters. Little pinch…"

She leaned toward my head, and I closed my eyes, grabbing onto my necklace for dear life. "Neutral? You make it sound like there's a war—OW!"

"Nearly done. Okay." She patted my shoulder. "That's the worst part. Now everything will be nice and numb. I'm going to clean the cut and put in the stitches. Then I'll bandage your knee."

As she started stitching she said, "In answer to your question, no, there's not a war, per se…well, not a war-war. More of a cold war. Didn't your family tell you? Basically, it's a small town, old families, not everyone gets along…. So, some of us like to be clear we're neutral. Speaking of families, is there anyone you want me to call for you? Did you want me to call your parents to come on over from the reunion?"

A vision of my parents walking through the door, all worried about me, swam before me. It was so visceral, I could feel them in the room. Then it evaporated. I jerked and sucked in a breath.

Dr. Paige stopped stitching. "Did you feel that? Is this hurting?"

"No. Sorry, I'll try to hold still. And, uh, no. No need to call anyone. I'm here alone." I cleared my throat and made a conscious effort to get rid of the raspy, choked up edge to my voice. "Speaking of which, since I'm leaving day after tomorrow for school, will I need to go see a doctor to get these out?"

"Nope. I'm using dissolving stitches that will go away on their own. But I would like to see you on Monday, before you go, to make sure everything is healing properly." Then she added, "So, tell me about school." When I explained where I was going she asked, "Why the sea?"

"You mean other than the fact that it's not the desert?"

I asked.

She smiled. "Lots of places aren't the desert."

"True," I said. Something in her manner made her easy to talk to, so I decided to give her a real answer. "Well, I'm dying to spend some time on the water. But really, I guess what it comes down to is that it's a big adventure. I get to travel and explore and discover new things."

"You mean like discovering other cultures?"

"That's part of it. I've always been fascinated with where people are from and the different ways they do things. My family had a diner—you wouldn't believe the array of characters we had wandering through there."

"I'll bet."

"But it's more than that. In the ocean, there's a real possibility that I'll get to encounter things we didn't even know existed. Did you know that they're constantly discovering new species in the ocean? You'd think by now, we'd know all about the planet we're living on. But the ocean, it's like an undiscovered country. Who knows what else we're going to find."

"Holding out hope for a mermaid or two?"

"I was thinking more along the lines of a funky jellyfish or a giant squid, but I wouldn't mind finding me some nice, chiseled mermen."

We both laughed, and she said, "Okay, all done. Let me just bandage your knee, and you're out of here."

After she'd finished, I hopped down, and she walked me out the door. "I wouldn't play any rugby if I were you, but other than that you should be fine. You can take over-the-counter painkillers for all the aching. In fact, I'd take some as soon as you eat something."

"Thanks, Dr. Paige."

"You're welcome. Follow me. I'll take you to Zo."

As I followed her down the hallway, I said, "Don't you need me to fill out some paperwork? And pay you?"

"The office isn't actually open. We'll deal with all that when you come back on Monday." She opened a door and gestured me to go in, saying, "They're in here."

"Who's they?" I asked. I looked into the office. Zo was there, but so were Lou, Pete, and a really cute red-headed guy I'd never seen before. Dr. Paige went in ahead of me, and I hovered in the open doorway.

Zo looked at the doc. "You're staying?"

Dr. Paige shrugged. "I like her. I'll referee if needed."

Well, that didn't sound good. I said, "Why do I need a referee?"

Dr. Paige said, "Why don't you come in and sit down, Finn."

Instead of sitting, I stayed where I was. My heart rate kicked up, and I was feeling uneasy.

"She looks kind of peaky," said Lou. "Have you had anything to eat?" he asked me.

"No."

"That settles it," said Pete. "Let's go get some breakfast."

"Is that a good idea?" asked Zo.

The cute guy said, "What are they going to do? Make a scene in the middle of town?"

I raised my hand. "Do I get a say in this?" I looked at Lou and Pete. "And why do you want to have breakfast with me? You don't even like me!"

Lou and Pete both looked a little bit embarrassed.

Zo sighed. "Finn, just bear with us. It's important."

"But I already have breakfast plans." I glanced at the clock over the doc's desk. It was 8:30. I was supposed to meet the Foster historical council person this morning, and I had the feeling that Meg would have a fit if I mucked up her plans. Not that I wanted to meet anyone. I was sore all over, and I just wanted to crawl back into bed.

Dr. Paige gave me a solemn look. "I really think you should eat something so we can get some painkillers in you before the numbing agent wears off. And you definitely need to hear what we have to say before you go back to that house."

The way she said "that house" made me wonder if she knew something about the house's special nature. I looked at Zo. "But what about Fuzzy?"

"He'll be fine, I promise."

"I need to call Meg," I hedged.

Lou, Pete, and Cute Guy exchanged looks, but Zo grinned. "Oh, please do. Want to use my phone?"

"No, I've got mine," I said, pulling it out of my back pocket.

"Why don't you step out into the hall for some privacy," Dr. Paige said. When I did, she closed the door, shutting everyone into her office and leaving me alone in the hallway. They started talking the minute the door closed. I just stared at the door for a minute.

Wowee, another odd event. They'd been happening so frequently since I got to this town that it was starting to seem normal. This was the strangest weekend I'd ever had, and it was only Saturday morning.

What on Earth could they possibly want to talk to me about so badly? I looked around the empty hallway. Well, I could make a break for it if I wanted to, which made me feel a little better. I sighed. Thing was, I was curious to know what they wanted. But I did have other obligations.

I walked a little bit down the hallway and called the house. "Hello?"

"Meg? It's Finn."

She laughed. "Is the door stuck, and you need me to let you out?"

"What?"

"I assume if you're calling me from your room, it's because you're stuck and need rescuing."

"I'm not in my room."

There was a pause, and then she said, "What?"

She sounded so shocked that I wondered if she'd gotten up this morning, and first thing, told the house to lock me in.

"I'm not in my room. Look, I went for a walk, I had a little accident, and long story short, I had to get some stitches."

"Stitches! Jesus, Finn." For a moment, the alarm in her voice gave me a nice warm feeling—I felt comforted that she seemed so worried about me. Maybe I was just being needlessly suspicious. Then she said, "Well, how long will it take you to get back here? We're meeting with the councilwoman in half an hour."

The warm feeling evaporated and was replaced by a knot in my stomach. I realized she wasn't worried about me at all. She was worried about her stupid meeting. The complete lack of concern for me made my decision suddenly very clear. I needed food, caffeine, and a ton of aspirin before I could deal with any more Meg.

"I'm fine, thanks for asking, and the doctor thinks I should get something to eat before I do anything else, so I'm going to miss the breakfast meeting thing."

Another pause. "Your car is still here. Do you need me to send Doug to come and get you? How did you get to a doctor's anyway? Where, exactly, are you?"

"Look, I'll explain everything when I get back. I have a ride. I just wanted to let you know I'm going to be late. I'll see you in a bit. Bye." And I hung up. It was rude, I knew it was rude, but I didn't care. Dr. Paige was right. I needed to eat. More, I needed to inhale a pot of coffee to get me thinking clearly.

I walked back up the hall and opened the door. They all stopped talking and turned to stare at me.

"Let's go find some food," I said.

Chapter Seventeen

Lou and Pete led the way, Zo walked with me, and Dr. Paige and Cute Guy took up the rear. We walked out through the lobby of the office, out the front door, and into a bustling, bright morning. I slid Zo's sunglasses back on, and I sighed in relief.

She glanced over at me. "It's only a couple of short blocks. Think you can make it?"

I nodded. I figured walking a little might keep my knee from stiffening up any more than it already was. Lou and Pete headed off in the direction of the town common, and we all followed along.

No one talked. The way they were all rubbernecking, you'd think they were as new to the town as I was. While we walked, I took in my surroundings. The street was lined with a mix of local small businesses and a few small chain stores. As we neared the town common, I could make out a post office, an ice cream shop, and a library among the shops bordering it.

We reached the corner opposite the common, and Lou and Pete went into a building. As soon as they opened the door, a whiff of coffee and fried potatoes swirled outside. The chatter of happy customers reached me. I swallowed hard and stepped inside.

It was a diner. A good one, judging from the nimble and alert staff and the happy faces of the customers.

Okay, I hadn't prepared myself for a diner, but I could do this. I plastered a smile on my face.

Then I looked to my left. Customers were chowing down at a big counter with a kitchen behind it. The man and woman who worked behind the counter telegraphed "owners" in the way they moved and interacted with the customers. As I watched, he turned and smiled at her, put his arm around her waist, and said something that had them both laughing. The customers at the counter joined in.

That burst of happy smashed into me, and it was like it detonated the ball of misery I'd been tamping down. My smile crumpled. Everything I'd been carefully tuning out started yelling for attention all at the same time. My body was complaining that my head pounded, my knee throbbed, and I ached all over. My mind was spinning, trying to grapple with the reunion, the house, the storm, and whatever Zo's people wanted. And my heart was breaking a little more as the happy little scene across the room rammed home the fact that I had no one to talk to about any of it.

The gut punch that I felt slammed me so hard that I stepped back a little.

Dr. Paige looked alarmed and grabbed my arm. "Are you okay?"

I didn't trust myself to speak so I just nodded.

Zo turned and frowned as she looked at me, even though she couldn't see my eyes behind the sunglasses. Then her eyes widened slightly, and she said quietly, "Oh crap. I didn't think."

In front of us, Lou waved to the man behind the counter, who waved back. A waitress came up, Lou murmured to her, and she led us toward the back.

Walking through the diner, I felt like I was drowning.

Zo had a death grip on my arm. "Just breathe," she murmured, while we followed Lou.

As we approached a table in the back corner, Zo said, "We're going to the lady's room," and she marched me past the table, down a short hallway to the bathroom. The bathroom gods were being kind to me because miraculously there was no line.

I went in, shut the door on Zo, and burst into tears. I started sobbing, and I couldn't stop. There was a knock, and then Zo came in and shut the door behind her.

She walked right over and put her arms around me. I was

so surprised that I went rigid. And then I started crying even harder. I cried so hard I was hiccuping, and my head started pounding in earnest. She held onto me and let me cry.

When I quieted down a little, she said, "I know about your parents. I'm so sorry, Finn. I was so focused on…everything else…I just didn't think about it being a diner, run by a happy couple no less. I'm sorry."

It took me another minute to get myself under control. Finally, I sniffled and stepped back, wiping at my eyes. "I don't know what's wrong with me. This is ridiculous. It's not like it happened yesterday."

Zo said, "Well, you've had quite a morning. And grief is like this. You think you've got it under control, and then it sneaks up and sucker punches you."

"Well, the timing certainly sucks." I straightened my shoulders and went over to the sink. My tear-stained face stared back at me in the mirror. I looked pathetic. Splashing cold water on it did nothing to disguise the fact that I'd been crying. "Oh come on. I can't go out there like this." I nearly started crying again.

Zo stepped up beside me, grabbed some paper towels, soaked them in water and turned me to face her. "I can't do anything about your parents, but this, I can help with. Close your eyes."

I did what she said, and she dabbed at my face. The towels felt deliciously cool and tingly.

"How do you know about my parents?"

"I made some calls while you were in with Paige."

"Oh."

"If I were you, I'd have lost my shit long before now. It's a wonder you've held it together this long. Paige said you didn't even cry when she stitched you." Her voice sounded gruff, but her touch was very gentle and soothing.

She stopped dabbing and surveyed me face. "There."

I turned to face the mirror and was shocked to see that I looked totally normal. "How'd you do that?"

She winked. "Trade secret. You ready for this next part? Because trust me, you need to pay attention."

And didn't that sound enticing. I sighed. My head was killing me, but my crying jag had emptied my emotional well, and I felt really calm. Exhausted, but calm. "Depends. How's the coffee here?"

We left the bathroom and joined the others at the table. Nobody seemed to notice that I'd been crying, and I puffed out a small sigh of relief.

I sat on one side of the table, flanked by Zo and Dr. Paige. The boys sat on the other side. It was like being at a seventh-grade dance, boys on one side, girls on the other, complete with awkward silences.

Pete broke the ice by saying, "Breakfast is on us, so please order anything you want."

As I scanned the menu, I squashed the pang I felt forming, and let my professional side take over. It helped me maintain my post-cry calm detachment as I assessed the choices. Good range. All the classics with a few local twists thrown in. A couple of house specialties. Reasonable prices. I nodded. Well done.

In my opinion, the true test of a diner comes down to a few simple things: coffee, eggs, and hash browns. Good diner coffee is worth its weight in gold. And it's surprisingly difficult to find a place that makes good eggs and hash browns.

The waitress appeared with coffee. She introduced herself as Rose, and she served me first. While she served the others and started taking orders, I doctored my coffee, picked up the mug, closed my eyes, and inhaled. No burnt smell, so the coffee was reasonably fresh. I took my first sip and smiled. Real, honest-to-goodness diner coffee. The good stuff.

When I opened my eyes, Rose was grinning at me. "Good, right?"

"Very good. I'm going to need some more, really soon," I said, taking a huge sip.

She laughed. "No problem. I'll be back to top you off in a minute. Can I get you something to eat?"

I ordered the eggs, bacon, and hash browns, and then finished off my coffee as she took Zo's order and left. True to her word, Rose came right back with the pot of coffee, refilled my mug, and retreated again.

As I fixed my coffee, I took a deep breath. Time to get this over with, whatever "this" was. I looked around the table. "Alright, someone spill."

They looked at each other, doing a silent version of "Not it!"

My cranky pants came along and stomped all over my nice sense of detachment. I propped my forehead on my hand and growled at them. "Oh for Pete's sake, no pun intended Pete, unless, that is, it'll get you to man up. Guys, my head is killing me, and this day has already lasted a week. So could we please just get on with it?"

Dr. Paige fiddled in her purse and then slipped me some pills. "Take these. Normally I'd say eat something first, but they serve the food fast here, so go ahead and take them now."

"Thanks." I swallowed the pills and said, "Why don't we start with something easy. You," I pointed to Cute Guy. "You got a name?"

He smiled and waved at me from across the table. "Yeah, hey, hi. I'm Eagan."

"And what possessed you to come on out and gang up on a stranger, first thing on a Saturday morning, Eagan?" I took another sip of my coffee. Food had better appear soon before the filter between my brain and my mouth totally disappeared.

Pete cleared his throat. "Lou?"

Lou nodded, pulled out a cell phone, and set it on the table. It got really quiet around us. I put my coffee down when I realized I couldn't hear any of the diner noises. I looked around behind me, and everything looked normal, I just couldn't hear anything. I sat up straight and looked at Lou and Pete. "What just happened?" I asked.

Pete cleared his throat. "We're just making sure we have some privacy. You ever seen *Get Smart*?"

"What?"

"It's a TV show."

"I know it's a TV show. What's it got to do with anything?"

"Well they had this cone of silence thing," said Pete. "It's like that. We're in a cone of silence."

Lou said, "Well, it's more of a bubble, really. And this one actually works."

I stared at Lou's cell phone. It looked like a normal phone. I'd heard of a cell-phone jammer, but I'd never heard of cell phone as a sound jammer, not that I was up on the latest spy-type gadgets. Well, it wasn't really that much weirder than anything else that'd happened today. "Awesome. Is James Bond going to show up soon? Because I'm really not dressed appropriately to be a Bond girl."

Dr. Paige chuckled.

"How much do you know about the Fosters, Finn?" asked Pete.

I sucked down the rest of my coffee, slumped back in my chair, and crossed my arms. "Again, for the gazillionth time, I'm from a DISTANT branch of the family. Not even a branch. It's like a bump on a leaf on a twig on a branch," *on a frog, on a log, in a hole in the bottom of the sea!* sang my brain, but I didn't say that last part out loud, so the coffee must've been kicking in.

"And that means what?" asked Dr. Paige.

I looked at her and threw up my hands. "It means I don't know anything! Why do people keep asking me that? Meg asked me the same thing. Look, this is my first foray into the Fosterverse, and to be perfectly honest, it's probably my last, the way it's going."

Rose approached our table. As she got closer, the diner sounds reappeared. She walked right up, refilled my cup, topped off everyone else who needed it, and left. The background noise went away again.

"People can just walk in and out of the—what is it, the bubble of bliss?" I asked.

Eagan snickered, and Lou actually smiled and said, "It's just a sound thing."

"Whatever that means," I mumbled. I waved a hand for them to continue.

"So, just to be perfectly clear, are you saying you don't know anything about the Fosters?" asked Pete.

"Yes! What's there to know? What's the big deal?" A thought

occurred to me. Were the Fosters some kind of mafia family? It'd make sense, given the way people acted about them. Oh jeez. What had I gotten myself into?

"Told you," said Dr. Paige.

Pete said, "Okay. Do you want to jump right in, or wait till you get some food in you?"

"Just say what you've got to say."

Pete took a deep breath. "Here's the short version. The house you're staying in is…special."

Understatement of the year, I thought. I leaned back in my chair, sipped my coffee, and avoided making eye contact. "What do you mean by 'special'?"

Pete said, "I don't want to get into a long history lesson—"

"Again, that's almost exactly what Meg said."

Zo grimaced. "I'll just bet she did."

Pete said, "Originally, the Fosters were supposed to share the responsibility for taking care of the house with four other families. But they took the house for themselves."

"So this is some kind of Hatfield/McCoy family feud thing?" I asked.

Lou tipped his head back and forth, saying, "Sort of. Ever since the first Foster took control of the house, all the other families have been trying to get access to it."

"You didn't answer the question. What do you mean by 'special'?" I asked.

Eagan said, "This is taking too long. Look. The house, it's not just a house. It's alive. It's kind of a, well, it's a guardian of sorts, I guess you'd say."

I stirred my coffee and watched the cream swirling in it, like it was the most fascinating thing I'd ever seen.

"You don't look surprised," said Lou.

Eagan sat up straighter. "Wait. Why isn't she surprised? Why aren't you surprised?" He leaned forward in his chair. "Did something happen with the house?"

Rose picked that moment to arrive with all our food. She placed my plate in front of me, and the smell of food chased all other thoughts from my mind for a few minutes. I tasted a little of everything and smiled. Light and fluffy eggs, nice crispy bacon, and hash browns with the right amount of crunch. Yum.

As soon as Rose left, Eagan shifted in his seat and said, "Something happened with the house—I knew it!" He looked at Lou and Pete. "I told you. They wouldn't have attacked her otherwise."

I paused shoveling eggs onto my fork and stared at Eagan. "Attacked me?"

"That wasn't a random storm," said Lou. "That was one of the other families. We're guessing they're trying to take out Meg's primary competition—you."

I shook my head vigorously, then had to wait a moment for the stabbing pain to pass, which just made me crankier. "You're not making any sense. 'That wasn't a storm'—what does that even mean? Oh! Wait! Let me guess. You've got a super high-tech spy jammer thingy, so that must mean there's a supervillain in the mix. And...wait for it...he's got the world domination weather machine!" I did my best villain voice. *"And now, I will smite them with my killer death hail, mwah ha ha!"*

I gave them a level look, changed back to my normal voice and said, "Really? Cuz that doesn't sound crazy at all," then went back to eating my food.

Eagan was snickering, but Lou and Pete looked flabbergasted.

"Also," I said, around a mouthful of eggs, "what competition? I'm not competing with Meg for anything."

They all looked stunned, except for Zo, who said, "She really doesn't know."

"Know what?" I realized I was nearly shouting when they flinched back. But honestly, I was so frustrated I would've banged my head on the table if it didn't already hurt so much.

Instead of answering me, Dr. Paige asked, "Can they do that? Isn't that against the rules?"

"It's looking like Meg's not worrying about the rules," said Lou.

"I don't get it. If you're really this clueless, Finn, why did you show up here, now, at the Fosters?" Eagan asked.

"She thinks it's a family reunion," supplied Zo.

I looked at them. "It isn't a reunion?"

They all shook their heads.

"Well what the hell is it?" If someone said "intimate soiree," I was gonna huck a piece of bacon at their head.

"It's a selection process," said Lou. "To see who will become the next keeper of the house."

"But I don't want to be a housekeeper. I want to be an oceanographer and travel the world's oceans and maybe find me some mermen. I'm boarding a ship for school in like a week."

"Er, I don't think you understand," said Eagan. "It's not a housekeeper as in someone who cleans the house. It's way more than that. The job comes with…perks."

"Which part of 'leaving for school in a week' makes you think I care if there's a dental plan with the housekeeping job?"

"Not those kind of perks," said Lou.

I closed my eyes and prayed for patience. "I. Don't. Care. I'm just passing through here. And Meg knows that, by the way. So there's no reason for your evil villain with the storm machine to bother with me. Which still sounds nuts, by the way. It was just a freak storm."

There was a slight pause, and then Eagan leaned forward. "What happened with the house, Finn?" he asked again. All the teasing was gone, and he looked somber, almost angry.

I pushed the remaining food around my plate with my fork. "I'm not sure what you mean."

They all sat very still, waiting.

I searched for an honest answer that wasn't too specific. "I thought I heard Meg say the house was trying to please me. And Doug said it was just showing some interest."

"Are they right?" asked Lou.

I mumbled, "Maybe."

"Ah." That came from Pete.

"I still don't see why that's a problem."

Pete said, "Meg is the temporary housekeeper and, as such, is the presumptive next choice. But they still have to go through the selection process."

Lou added, "The fact that the house is showing an interest

in you means her job isn't the done deal she thought it was."

Eagan said, "Hang on. How did anyone outside of the house know that Finn's a serious challenge to Meg?"

Pete looked at Lou. "You were right. They must be working with Meg and Doug. It's the only way they'd know what's happening inside the house."

Well, I knew of at least two people who were working with Meg and Doug. But I decided to hang onto that little tidbit for the moment.

Suddenly, all three men sat up straight and looked toward the door. Lou must've stopped the sound thingy because diner noises resumed.

Zo whipped around to look behind us. A glance at her had me craning my head to see what she was trying to incinerate with her gaze.

Two men and a woman made a beeline for our table. The people in the diner went on about their breakfasts, but I looked at the diner owners and tensed. They'd switched into a stance I called "meth heads in the house." Whoever these people were, the owners were worried about trouble.

Rose had great waitress instincts. She trotted up to the trio and said, "Excuse me, coming through, hot coffee," forcing them to separate from their tight knot as she walked between them. She paused in the middle of the group. "Hey guys, you're in luck! The table over here," she pointed to the other side of the diner, "just cleared out. Go on and have a seat, and I'll be right over."

The guy in the lead nodded, and the woman and man went to the table. Lead guy came over to us.

As Rose topped off our coffees, I gave her a smile, and she gave me a wink, before heading off. Then I checked out the guy. He was tall with dark caramel skin and shoulder-length, black wavy hair. He reminded me of a walking storm cloud, all broody and looking like he could let loose at any moment. He even had a charcoal gray button-down shirt to complete the effect.

He surveyed the table, walked over to a nearby empty chair,

snagged it and placed it at the head of the table. He sat down, Lou on one side, Dr. Paige on the other.

Zo said in a voice so cold it gave me chills, "You might want to rethink that."

The moron actually smiled at her. He leaned forward, hands folded on the table in front of him.

Lou, Pete, and Eagan had the tense body posture of men who were about to get into a brawl. On my right, Zo was wearing what I could only describe as a serial killer smile. On my left, Dr. Paige darted glances around the table.

I almost wanted to see what would happen, but I liked Rose and didn't want her to have to clean up a mess. Years of diffusing amped up truckers had given me some practice in this kind of situation. Refuse to take them seriously, keep them off balance, and they couldn't get enough steam going to cause any real trouble.

So I laughed. "Wow. No really, just park yourself anywhere. Manners much? You're lucky someone's nana doesn't come over here and bap you in the head." I sighed and shook my head. Oh thank the aspirin fairies, it barely hurt when I shook it this time. "And you'd be…?"

He stared at me, unblinking. "I'm Gram."

Something about Gram seemed familiar. I smiled, nodded, sipped my coffee. "Let me guess. Based on the whole," I waved a hand up and down, "simmering and pouting thing you've got going here, you're the one with the rainy day death ray?"

They all turned to look at me. The doc was grinning, and I heard Zo snort.

"Death ray?" Gram ratcheted down from simmering to confused.

"Private joke," I said.

"Finn," said Eagan. "This isn't a joke. He *is* the one with the, uh—"

"Weather machine of doom?" I supplied.

"Not exactly, but, yeah."

I took my last bite of eggs and said to Gram, "According to these people, you had something to do with the hail this morning. True?" I took a sip of my coffee.

Gram looked at me a long moment, assessing, then he leaned back in his chair, somehow managing to look both relaxed and arrogant at the same time. "True."

I nearly choked. True? What? I'd been expecting him to deny it. My brain stalled, and a chill ran down my spine. None of this made any sense to me. Were these people all nuts? I mean, no one could actually make it hail. Then I thought of the sophisticated sound jammer sitting on the table, and I suddenly wasn't sure that was the case.

Well, in any event, I could play along. If he insisted on taking credit for it, then he should take responsibility as well.

I tried to keep my tone light and said, "Well Gram, you owe Zo a whole bunch of new plants, and you owe me for some stitches. Hey, Dr. Paige, can you bill Gram, instead of me?"

Whatever he'd expected me to say, apparently that wasn't it because he looked totally nonplussed. He actually blinked. Dr. Paige compressed her lips in a way that told me she was trying not to laugh, and nodded at me.

I said to Gram, "I'm assuming you were just trying to impress me with the size of your—," I waved my hand, "—let's go with influence—because you didn't know that I'm not really part of the whole Foster thing. Because otherwise, that'd mean there was an assault, and you don't look like a total idiot, so I'm sure you know assaulting someone is a felony. So, I'm guessing this is all a big mistake." I paused and took another long sip of my coffee. His eyes were starting to look a little glazed. Good.

"My understanding is that your hail tantrum has to do with the family feud you all have going on. Well you can relax, pal. Repeat after me: Finn is just visiting." I looked at Eagan. "Maybe I should put it on a t-shirt? Would that help?" I shrugged and looked back at Gram, pointed my fork at him. "So, in conclusion, quit playing your reindeer games with me. Oh, and pay up." I chomped my last piece of bacon for emphasis.

He looked at the boys' side of the table. "Is she for real?"

Eagan smiled and said, "Yup. But she's wrong about one thing. You are a complete idiot."

Gram's eyes narrowed. I sighed and jumped in before he could say anything. "You've already established the size of your mighty hail. Was there something you needed Gram?"

"If the other families are getting a chance to make a pitch to you, then I get to have my say, too."

I glanced around the table. Oh. They were representing the other families? I should have figured that out sooner.

I looked at Gram. "And just what did you want to pitch? I mean, besides all that hail at my head."

A crafty look stole across his face and was replaced by a smug smile that told me he was used to getting what he wanted. "A possible alliance. Access to the house."

"I changed my mind. I need a t-shirt that says 'Not a Housekeeper.'" I turned to Zo. "Can we stop at a t-shirt shop on the way home?"

She paused giving Gram the stink eye to glance at me. A small smile tugged at her mouth as she said completely deadpan, "Sure. And you'd better get an extra-large font."

Dr. Paige piped up, "I'd make the lettering day-glo. Maybe add some sparkle. You know, just to make sure they get it."

"Good point." I looked at Gram, gave him a big smile. "Well, I know what I'm doing with the rest of my day. So, back to you. As it turns out, no one else was pitching me anything, but thanks for asking me to be your Foster buddy. Unless you want to be pen pals, I can't help you, but as my mom said, it's always nice to be asked. You can go on and join your friends now. They're looking hungry." Actually, they were looking like they were about to head back over to us.

He hesitated, and Zo said in a mild voice, "The only reason you're still breathing is that you didn't touch my garden. Don't push it, Gram."

Gram met Zo's eyes and froze. I turned to look at Zo, and I froze too. She was smiling again, but it was the kind of smile a dragon would give you right before it barbecued you. In that moment, I totally believed she'd have ended him, given any further provocation. Jeez, and I thought my mom took her plants seriously.

I cleared my throat, turned back to Gram, and gave him a huge, cheery smile. "Okay, then. Have a nice breakfast."

Gram looked at me for a long moment. It was clear he didn't like being dismissed. He stood up, glowered in my direction and said, "We'll talk again later, when you're alone," and he walked off to join his friends. Because that didn't sound like a threat at all. When I looked over at their table, I saw that they'd angled themselves so that they were blatantly watching our every move.

I turned back to Lou. "Can you turn the sound squisher back on?"

"Don't," said Zo. When I looked at her, she said, "They'll be able to tell. He'll come right back over."

"Time to go," said Dr. Paige. She waved for Rose, who brought the check over. She also gave me a last top off of my coffee, bless her.

When she left, I asked, "Were you guys planning on pitching me to be allies, like he said?"

As he paid the bill, Pete said, "Oddly enough, making an alliance wasn't our main purpose today."

Eagan gave me a big smile and said, "Though we wouldn't be against it."

"But you are representatives from the other families?"

Pete said, "We're not here in any official capacity. But yes, Lou, Eagan, and I are each a member of the other families. Dr. Paige isn't, though. She just has to deal with the lot of us."

I looked at Zo. "And you?"

"Technically, I'm a neutral party," she said.

"Technically?" I asked.

"They destroyed my yard."

I looked around the table. "So what is it you want from me?"

Lou said, "For now, just information. We're trying to figure out what's going on. We've suspected that Gram's family might be working with Meg. If she officially becomes the housekeeper, and Gram forms an alliance with her, then the balance of power among the families is going to shift."

"And that's a bad thing?"

"You've met Gram. Would you want to give him more

power than anyone else?" asked Eagan.

"I see your point."

"Look, Zo is going to give you all our numbers," Lou said. "Just consider giving us a ring if there's something you think we need to know."

"You want me to be a mole? This really is a James Bond novel."

"Just think about it, okay?" said Eagan.

Dr. Paige glanced over at Gram. "We'd better get going. Gram's looking antsy."

While I finished my coffee, Lou leaned forward, "Finn, I know this all seems bizarre, and we haven't even scratched the surface, really. But when you go back to the house, keep in mind that the Fosters have a whole agenda that for some reason they haven't seen fit to read you in on."

It was becoming clear to me that everyone at the table had an agenda, but I just nodded. I was finished with my coffee, so I stood up.

We walked to the front of the diner, and on my way by, I waved at Gram and sent him a big smile. He didn't smile back, but he didn't glare. I was hoping that was a good thing.

Chapter Eighteen

We made it back to Zo's car with no further ado. To my surprise, no one tried to convince me of anything or hound me for more information. Instead, they chatted about the weather, about the annual fall influx of tourists, and about how good the food always was at the diner. But they did the rubbernecking thing again. Now I realized that they weren't sightseeing. They were keeping a lookout for Gram and his family, worried they were going to try something while we were out in the open.

When we got to Zo's car, I thanked them for breakfast, and Lou, Pete, and Eagan kept on walking. Dr. Paige stood with me and Zo for a moment, reminded me to come back on Monday, then retreated into her office.

Zo and I climbed into her car.

Zo pulled out her cell phone and said, "What's your number? I'm going to text you all their contact info."

I gave it to her. While she typed her text, I sank back into the seat. I rubbed my eyes. So much to process. I ran back over the conversation, turning the bits of information around in my mind. I felt like I'd been given a few of the edge pieces of a really complicated puzzle. Just enough to see the outlines, but not enough to know what the overall picture would be.

Zo was absorbed in texting with someone, so I let my mind continue to wander. With all the weird gadgets and the tense rivalries, it seemed like maybe there was some kind of high-tech, Tony-Stark-level thing going on. But on the other hand, there was the house, which felt more like something in the Harry Potter zone.

As soon as the Harry Potter thought slipped through my head, I heard my parents' voices, saying, "Now, Finn. Use your science!"

My mouth twisted in a wry smile. "Use your science" had been a favorite refrain of theirs while I was growing up.

My mind flashed back to the day they'd come across me in the living room, waving a stick and yelling, "Lumos!"

I'd looked at them, frustration wrinkling my forehead, and said, "It won't work!"

After they put the stick high up on a bookshelf "to rest," they sat me down for a chat.

My mom said, "Finn, it's just a story. It's all pretend."

I frowned and said, "Nuh uh. There's magic out there. I know there is."

They exchanged concerned looks over my head, then dad said, "Actually, you're right. There is magic," I felt a smug smile forming, but it flopped back into a scowl when he added, "It's science magic."

That sounded a lot like something he'd say when he wanted me to enjoy something gross, like cooked carrots.

Dad wasn't deterred. "Did you know that there are all sorts of cool, mysterious creatures in the ocean that light up like they have their own magic wands?"

I shook my head.

Mom picked up what Dad was throwing down. "Remember the fish in *Finding Nemo* with the light bulb hanging off him?"

I nodded. That guy had almost eaten Dory. Of course I remembered him.

Mom said, "Well that's a real kind of fish."

I said, "Nuh uh!"

Dad said, "Yup. The ocean is full of real-life creatures that are amazing. Get this, there are these itty bitty guys called ostracods that glow like one of Harry Potter's patronus charms."

"Really?"

Dad nodded. "Yup. If a fish eats the ostracod, the ostracod will turn on its glow, and it makes the fish barf up the ostracod."

Mom and I said, "Ewwwww," but we both giggled.

Dad said, "Then the ostracod just swims away in a glow-ing blue cloud. It actually looks like a much cooler version of a patronus charm, if you ask me. Here, I can show you some pictures."

We'd spent the rest of the afternoon looking through old *National Geographics,* and my obsession with the ocean was born.

From then on, my parents made a game of using science. Any time I was tempted to think something was magical, we'd find a way to science it.

And sciencing it was what I needed to do now. Between Lou's sound dampener and Gram's weather machine, it would seem that there was a lot of advanced tech in play. This wasn't even remotely my field—it was a miracle we had a computer in the house, given what a pair of Luddites my parents were. It oc-curred to me that if they had this much gadgetry, they probably had weapons that were just as advanced. So far, this had been a cold war, according to Dr. Paige, so I assumed no one was blowing anything up. I found myself fervently hoping they kept it that way. I wouldn't want any of them causing any damage to the house.

Oh, the house! Now that my scientific mind had woken up, it started running around having a field day. The house was fas-cinating. I had so many questions that I didn't even know where to begin. Obviously, there was a lot more to learn there.

I noodled about the situation a little more until Zo inter-rupted my pondering with a "Done." She put her phone in her purse and started the car.

My phone didn't chime, so I checked that I'd gotten her text. It was there. And so were a bunch of missed calls from Meg. I must've accidentally put my phone on mute when I hung up on her earlier. I sighed. She was not going to be a happy camper when I got back.

I put my phone, and thoughts of Meg, away. I wanted to take advantage of the chance to talk with Zo, short as the ride home was.

As she pulled onto the street, I said, "Well breakfast was…

interesting."

Zo glanced at me, then back at the road. "Interesting?"

"Under the circumstances, my other option was something along the lines of 'this is all kind of whacked' so, yeah, I think 'interesting' is the safe way to go."

"Hmph."

After a moment I said, "You guys say the house is alive, right? Which brings up a whole bunch of other questions. Do you guys know why the house is alive or where it came from? And, besides it being alive, which is cool and all, why is everyone so hot and bothered to have access to it? You guys said it's a, what, a guardian? What's it guarding?"

Zo nodded. "Those are all excellent questions."

Which, apparently, she wasn't going to answer. I pushed on. "Well, I don't know about the house, but I have a theory about the rest of it. These families are all in a cold war, right? You've got competing interests, in this case families instead of countries, looking to gain control of a valuable asset. To do that, they've wound up engaged in an arms race. Each of them is constantly inventing these crazy advanced gadgets to try and one-up each other and gain access to the house. Given the level of tech they've got access to, I'm betting they're all heavily involved in shady government agencies. Ooh, is this is a thing where each family is loyal to a different government agency? Like, a battle of the alphabet soup agencies—sort of like *Batman vs. Superman*, but instead it's FBI vs. CIA vs. NSA?"

"I see your caffeine has kicked in."

"You bet. So am I right?"

Zo was quiet for a minute. "You say you want to leave here. If you really are planning to go, then the less you know the better."

"Is this a *Godfather* thing where they'll just keep pulling me back in?"

She rolled her eyes. "It makes you a target. You've already seen how much fun that is. Besides, it's not my place."

I harrumphed.

"Look, Finn, we're trying to strike a balance here. Something is really wrong with this round of the selections. That hasn't happened before. Since changing the status quo could have… we'll call them impressive negative consequences—"

"Like Gram?"

"Among other things. It's in everyone's best interests to make sure you at least know the basics. But, there's this little dance of telling you enough to be helpful, but not telling you so much that you get sucked into all this permanently."

"Well, thanks. I appreciate it."

"Don't thank me yet. You've still got to get through the rest of this weekend."

"It's only a day and a half. How bad can it be?"

Zo said, "You had to say that, didn't you."

I stopped asking questions and sat mulling things over for the rest of the drive. We arrived back at Zo's house, and I found Fuzzy curled up with a black-and-white cat twice his size, both of them snoozing in a sunbeam.

"I see you made a friend," I said.

Fuzzy stretched, yawned, and I picked him up. The black-and-white cat blinked at me. "And who are you?"

"That's Moonpie. Thanks for keeping an eye on Fuzzy, pal." Moonpie blinked at us and went back to sleep.

It seemed to me that people who named their cat Moonpie shouldn't balk at the name Fuzzy, but I said nothing. Besides, Moonpie fit him.

"C'mon, I'll give you a ride to the house."

"Uh, Fuzzy really doesn't like the car."

"Well, he's just going to have to buck up. You're in no shape to hike for an hour through woods."

Fuzzy and I got into Zo's car, and she drove us back toward the Foster house. I don't know if it was because he was feeling more settled overall, or if it was because I had both hands on him instead of on the steering wheel, but Fuzzy sat quietly looking out the window and didn't make a peep the entire drive.

"The turn is kind of hard to find," I said.

"I know where it is," Zo said.

We drove past the woods I'd walked through earlier that

morning. I spent a few minutes studying the sun-dappled trees. "Does all of this belong to the Fosters?" I asked.

"Yes."

"Wow, it's huge. And it's really beautiful. House aside, I could totally see people fighting over the property."

And speaking of fighting people, from the gazillion missed calls on my phone, I had the feeling that Meg was a tad bit irritated at my absence. I clutched Fuzzy and tried to psych myself up to prepare for the forthcoming drama. I wasn't sure if we'd be talking full-on *Real Housewives*, but I knew there'd be drama.

As she approached the driveway, Zo said, "I take it I have your permission to drive you up to the house?"

"What? Oh sure!"

She turned into the driveway and I said, "I know the Fosters have some strict rules about who can visit, but at this point I think they can just stuff it. You're my guest, and you're welcome to come on in to the house with me. I'm really grateful to you for all you've done for me—and Fuzzy—and I'd be happy to make you a cup of coffee or tea, if you'd like one."

Zo smirked. "I'd love to see the look on Meg's face. Thank you for the offer, but no. I've got some things to do."

"Well my offer stands for tomorrow. I'm totally happy to drive on over and help you start righting your yard. Just let me know if you need me."

Zo looked touched. "Thank you for that. Ah, we're here."

The giant trees loomed before us, marking the entrance to the clearing where the house stood. I did a little wave at them, then blushed when Zo shot me a look.

"I, uh, really like the trees."

"I can see that."

Zo drove around the circular driveway and stopped in front of the house. A black luxury car that hadn't been there before was parked near Babs in the little side lot.

"Oops, looks like the council lady is here," I said.

Zo frowned. "Be careful, Finn."

I shrugged. "What are they going to do? Give me a firm

talking to? Please, it wouldn't be my first, and probably won't be the last. And if they kick me out, well that just means I get to finally visit the ocean all that much sooner."

Zo just shook her head and gave me a reluctant smile. I climbed out of the car with Fuzzy. As I started to walk away, Zo powered down the passenger side window. "Call if you need us."

"Okay."

I walked up the steps, which made happy-sounding little squeaks as I climbed, like I was walking over a pile of squeaky toys. When I reached the porch, I put my hand on the porch column, gave it a little pat, and the whole house sighed. I turned around to find Zo watching, eyes narrowed, gaze darting between me and the house.

The front door burst open, and Meg charged out onto the porch. "Finn!" She stopped short and looked over my shoulder at Zo.

Zo sent her a serene smile, gave me a little wave, and drove off.

I turned around, and Meg's face looked pinched.

"You've got really nice neighbors," I said, and I walked past her into the house.

Chapter Nineteen

Once I'd entered the house, I headed straight up the stairs.

"I'm just going to put Fuzzy in my room. I'll meet you in the kitchen," I called to Meg, who'd followed me inside. I sprinted up the stairs before she had a chance to respond.

When Fuzzy and I got to my room, I shut the door behind us quickly. Then, I stopped short. The room was bigger. It'd been cozy in there yesterday—comfortable for sure, but there was barely enough space for me and Fuzzy to play without tripping over my suitcase.

Now there was at least twice as much space between the bed and the bathroom. And where had those two chairs come from?

I supposed the house had its reasons for rearranging. I shrugged and decided to go with it.

I deposited Fuzzy on the bed and put some fresh water in his bowl. "How do you think I should handle this?" I asked him. He yawned.

I yawned, too, and looked longingly at my pillow. I'd have loved to take a nap with him, but I knew if I didn't appear in the kitchen promptly, Meg would be banging on my door.

I wondered how much I should tell Meg about my morning. I thought over the dinner last night, and from the way Nor and Wil were behaving, I was pretty sure they knew all about the house and the different families involved in the feud. That meant I was the only one left in the dark.

It put a sick little knot in my stomach, thinking that they all felt they could just lie to me. Maybe it was what Zo said, they were just trying to keep me from getting sucked into the family feud. But I had a sinking feeling that, at least in Meg and Doug's case, their motives weren't that noble.

I decided to be as withholding as they were being. I wouldn't lie, but I wouldn't tell them everything either. I was curious to see just what bits of information they decided to dole out to me. Not to mention that I really wanted to figure out what they were up to.

I walked to the closest wall and gave it a gentle pat. "Thanks for the room upgrade. How you doing buddy?" I asked.

The floor board under me grunted.

"Well, I hope your morning has gone smoother than mine." The floor moaned.

"That doesn't sound good. That sounds like I feel, and I had to get stitches. What have they been doing to you, you poor thing?"

The house didn't say anything, so I gave the wall another pat, and then went over to give Fuzzy an extra pat so he didn't get jealous.

"I'll be back soon," I told Fuzzy. Then I grabbed his bottle and went down the back stairs to the kitchen.

Meg was standing next to the sink, arms crossed. I could hear voices from the dining room, next to the kitchen.

I smiled at her, crossed to the kettle, and took it to the sink to fill it with water. "Well, I had quite the adventure this morning." I slid a glance her way. "Seems like you've been having adventures of your own…" I saw a shadow of unease cross her face, "you know, with the council person arriving."

Any unease Meg felt got smushed under the weight of the frown she sent me. "What the hell happened to you, Finn? I've been calling you all morning."

"Yeah, sorry. I just saw that. I had my phone on mute and didn't realize it."

"What happened? Are you all right? You said you needed stitches?" She eyeballed the bandage peeping through my hair.

"Yeah, I'm fine, thanks," I turned the stove on and settled in next to it. That put some space between us, with Meg holding position near the sink on the other side of the room. "I went for a walk in the woods this morning—"

"Did you trip or something?"

"No. Well, yes, actually, but that's not why I needed stitches." I watched her closely as I said, "It was so weird. There was a freak storm."

She went very still.

"And you won't believe this, but I got hit in the head with a chunk of hail big enough to cut me," I pointed to my scalp.

Meg pasted a sympathetic smile on and said, "I'm so sorry Finn. That must've been scary. And painful."

I sighed. "Yeah, not my most fun morning."

"How'd you wind up with Zo?"

"I was lucky enough to stumble onto her lawn, and she took me to get stitches."

"Really? Huh. She's usually not particularly fond of the Fosters." Meg picked a piece of lint off her sweater. "I bet she gave you an earful about us."

I laughed. "Have you met Zo? She's not very talkative."

Meg gave me a stingy smile. "Where'd she take you to get stitches?"

"This doctor downtown. Super nice lady. She did a great job. Wanna see?" I took a step forward, and Meg took a step back.

"No thanks."

The water was getting hot, so I started moving around the kitchen, preparing Fuzzy's bottle.

Meg asked, "So what doctor?"

"Dr. Paige? She's great. She's right downtown."

"Uh huh. And she said you needed some breakfast? Did Zo take you somewhere?"

I thought Meg might do some fishing for information about my morning, but this was about as subtle as throwing sticks of dynamite into the water to blast the fish out. Too bad for her that I wasn't about to be bullied into giving out info until she ponied up some of her own.

I smiled and batted my eyes. "Yeah, downtown. You've got all sorts of great food, and your downtown area is so cute. I'm dying to go back there and go shopping. I'm thinking I'll scoot out for some sightseeing later today."

Meg's lips thinned. "Should you be out running around with your injury?"

"Hmm. You're right. And there could be another storm. Do you get a lot of freak storms around here?"

"Freak storms?" Nor was standing in the doorway. She came in and planted herself by the kitchen island.

"Hey, Nor. I was just telling Meg about my exciting morning." I shifted back to my position near the stove and finished making Fuzzy's bottle, repeating just the bare bones information that I'd given to Meg. Somewhere in the middle of my tale, Wil drifted into the doorway, leaning on the doorframe as he listened to me.

When I got to the part about the hail, Nor and Wil looked at Meg, who avoided looking at either of them. It was enough to confirm my suspicions that I was the only one here that was out of the loop. Great.

When I'd finished, Nor strode over to Meg. "I'm done with this little charade you've got going on here. To say you've been stretching the rules is generous." She pointed at me. "And now, she got hurt. That's so far outside the rules, that I'm pretty sure it's actionable."

Wil said, "Nor—"

"Wil, I'm not worried about being politically correct. It's clear after my interview with Sarah that I've got no chance of being the housekeeper, and even if I did, I wouldn't stand by for this." Nor whirled to me. "Are you really alright?"

"Yeah. Besides the stitches, I've got some spectacular bruises, but basically I'm okay." I wondered if Nor realized yet that she'd said "housekeeper" in front of me, and if it was an accident, or if she'd done it on purpose. But Meg sure had noticed. She'd winced.

Nor said, "You were lucky. I know it probably doesn't seem like it, but it could've been a lot worse." She turned back to Meg, who was glowering.

Meg said, "Fine. You don't like the way I've handled things, that's your problem. As you said, you've got no shot at being—"

she flicked a glance at me, and I gritted my teeth as I watched her struggle to come up with a way not to say "housekeeper." She plowed through with, "—uh, you've got no shot at being in charge here. So you don't get a say. And you'd better not be implying that I had anything to do with this—"

"With what?" a female voice came from the hallway.

Meg shot Nor a venomous look, then smoothed her face into a respectful smile, as she turned to the voice. The rest of us also turned to the doorway, and Wil stepped aside to let a woman into the room. She had that well-preserved thing going that meant I couldn't tell her age. I'd put her somewhere north of 40, but beyond that, I couldn't be sure.

She and Meg might have shared the same stylist. Her suit was tailored to perfection, her skirt the exact length to be proper but fashionable. Her shiny hair was swept into a chic French twist, and, of course, she didn't have a hair out of place. Her jewelry was tasteful but looked old and original in a way that made me think of fancy auction houses and private estate sales. All of it was done with an exacting sense of taste and refinement. The woman dripped money.

She walked into the kitchen. Her presence filled all the extra space in the kitchen so that the big room suddenly felt crowded. She zeroed in on me, and came forward smiling, hand extended. "Hi, I'm Sarah. You must be Finn," she said, heels click-clacking as she walked over to me and took my hand.

She had a firm handshake, and she made eye contact the entire time, not being the least bit subtle about assessing me as we shook. She let go of my hand and turned to Meg and Nor. "Now, Meg has nothing to do with what?" Her voice was pleasant, but it had that kind of iron schoolteacher edge to it that let you know she expected an answer, and she expected it now.

I could've weighed in, but I folded my arms and watched.

Nor switched into what I imagined must be her lawyer-meeting-a-client mode. She became polite, detached, and businesslike. "Finn here was telling us about the storm she encountered this morning. She was hit by hail so large she required stitches. Is that correct, Finn?" she asked, turning to me.

"Yup," I said.

"I'm sorry to hear that, Finn," Sarah said. She looked at Nor. "But I'm not sure what this has to do with Meg?"

Meg shrugged and looked confused.

Nor nodded, "Me either. But I'm wondering, since Meg's in charge and all, how this could have happened under her watch? I mean, given the objective of this weekend, I could see where it might raise some concerns for you and the council. Because either she was fully cognizant of the events, which is one set of problems, or she didn't notice this was happening on the property, which is, perhaps, a bigger issue."

Meg was doubling down on her look of confusion. Wil had pursed his lips and crossed his arms, and was leaning against the wall, observing.

Sarah looked thoughtful. "Well, I can see where this bears further discussion. And Finn, this must all sound a bit confusing to you," Sarah said. When she looked at me, I did my best to look wide-eyed and totally lost. "We should have a little chat."

I held up the bottle. "I have to feed Fuzzy…uh, he's the kitten I'm fostering this weekend."

Sarah smiled. "Of course. Why don't you see to your kitten, and I'll have a quick word with Meg. I'll send someone to fetch you when I've finished with her. Okay?"

"Sure."

"Meg?" Sarah said and walked out of the room. Meg followed along behind her.

I heard them walk down the hall and into the dining room. Deciding to escape while I could, I tossed a "See you in a bit," at Nor and Wil.

I began to head out of the kitchen, only to pause and do a double-take. A longer look down the dark hallway confirmed I was correct. Blending into the shadows, there were two men, dressed in black, bracketing the door to the dining room.

I gave them a little wave and a "Hi guys."

One of them nodded at me, but something about the way they were standing did not invite further conversation.

I turned back around into the kitchen and raised a

questioning eyebrow at Nor. I lowered my voice to ask, "What's with Shaggy and Scooby there in the hallway?"

Nor barked out a laugh and said, "Sarah's assistants."

"Assistants?" What were they assisting Sarah with, fending off a swarm of ninjas? I was thinking that "assistants" had to be a euphemism because they sure looked like bodyguards to me. Then again, maybe I was being small-minded. I supposed assistants could be into wearing all black. And could be so fit that their shirts pulled across their shoulders. And that they could have spent time in the military, which would account for them standing at parade rest in a hallway. They could. But I didn't think so.

My skepticism must've shown because Wil added, "It's standard. Council members always travel with them."

"Oh." What did members of a historical council need with big, muscled assistants? Although, given my morning, I could see where having secretaries with fringe benefits might come in handy.

I shrugged and headed out of the kitchen again. I didn't try to talk to the assistants. But, as I crossed the hallway, I had the creepy-crawly feeling on my skin that made think that Shaggy and Scooby were watching me closely.

Chapter Twenty

As I walked through the mudroom, I realized my clothes were still in the dryer, so I snagged them and carried the armful of laundry up the stairs with me.

When I reached my room, Fuzzy was sitting on the bed, staring at the door, waiting for me.

I dropped the laundry in a heap by my suitcase, then scooped Fuzzy up and assumed my feeding position against the headboard. As soon as I offered him the bottle, he started slurping away. I'd thought maybe he wouldn't want it, given his demonstrated appetite for solid food, but apparently Fuzzy wasn't ready to give up his liquid diet yet. I made a mental note to put out some kitten crunchies for him to nibble on, too.

I smiled as I watched Fuzzy guzzle. The whole crazy morning fell away from me for a minute, my mind emptied, and I just enjoyed watching him.

A quiet knock on the door snapped me back to the present. "It's Nor. Can I come in?"

I couldn't ignore her. She knew I was in there feeding Fuzzy. And besides, she'd stood up for me in the kitchen.

"Sure." I stifled a sigh as I watched my moment of peace and quiet exit as she entered.

Nor slipped into the room, softly closing the door behind her.

"Well, that's ridiculously cute," she said, taking in the sight of Fuzzy with his bottle.

"I know, right?"

"Can you talk while you're feeding him?"

"Uh, sure."

She snagged a chair, dragged it over closer to the bed, but didn't sit down. "Do you have a dollar?"

"Uh, yeah, I think so."

"Great. I want you to hire me."

"What?"

"You know I'm a lawyer, right?"

"Yeah."

Nor looked around the room, spotted my purse, and brought it over to me. "I want you to hire me," she said, "before we talk. That way, everything we say is covered under attorney-client privilege." She sat on the edge of her chair, leaning forward, hand out, palm up, waiting for the dollar.

I blinked at her.

"Did you know you furrow your brow when you're feeling skeptical? One of the things we'll need to work on is your game face—you're too easy to read. Which is one of many reasons why you can use my help."

"Er...I can't afford any more lawyers," I said. I'd been grateful for their help, but just the thought of a lawyer brought me back to the mounds of paperwork involved in dealing with my dad's death and the diner. As if grief wasn't bad enough, it turned out it came with a ton of paper cuts.

"I'm waiving my usual fee so it's not a problem," said Nor. "A dollar will suffice as a retainer." She hesitated, then added, "The dollar isn't even strictly necessary. It's a symbolic gesture. But an important one."

I didn't know what to say to that. To stall for time while I tried to think it through, I asked, "What do you get out of this arrangement?"

"Good question." Nor leaned back in her chair and crossed her legs, hands wrapped around one knee. "While you were gone this morning, did someone tell you this isn't a reunion?"

I thought about pussyfooting around the truth. But my instincts said I might want to trust Nor, and Fuzzy didn't seem to mind her, so I said, "Yes."

"Good." My surprise must've shown because she said, "Hey, I've been lobbying to read you in since you got here. Meg overruled me. No offense, but you getting hurt is actually going to work in your favor because," a predatory grin appeared, "now I have grounds to circumvent her authority."

I didn't know what to say so I sort of nodded at her to go on.

Nor continued, "I figured someone had said something to you because you didn't look surprised when I mentioned being housekeeper. At some point, I'd like to know the details of who you talked with and what they said. But we're short on time, so for now, in broad strokes, what did you learn this morning?"

"Not much. All I know is this is like some kind of competition to be the housekeeper."

"Technically, it's a 'selection process.' But you're right—in essence it's a competition. So, to answer your earlier question, what I get out of working for you is two-fold. If you've officially hired me to work for you, whether you win or not, any interactions we have will remain confidential," she said.

I nodded. "You're covering your ass. When I lose, no one will know for sure how much you helped me or how. Clever."

A cunning gleam lit her eyes, and she smiled as she said, "*If* you lose. And if you win, you give me first shot at pitching myself to be your general counsel while you are the housekeeper."

I couldn't imagine why someone would want to be the lawyer for a housekeeper, or why a housekeeper would need something as fancy as general counsel. I supposed I could find that out later. For now, I needed to know, "What's in it for me?"

Nor uncrossed her legs, leaned forward on her chair, resting her arms on her thighs. I nearly leaned back from the intense, focused look she was giving me. It was like being probed by a laser.

She gestured toward the stitches on my head. "This weekend isn't going the way it's supposed to. You've already gotten hurt, and we still have another day to go. And, you haven't even gotten to the hard part yet."

"There's a hard part?"

Nor shook her head. "You want info, you need to hire me." When I hesitated, Nor added, "I think by now it should be clear to you that you need to find out what's going on. And to really answer your questions, you need to talk to a Foster. Right now, I'm your best option for a number of reasons."

She started ticking them off on her fingers. "First, I'm here. Second, it's in my best interests to help you. Not only am I fully incentivized from a career standpoint, but I'll also be legally bound to work for your best interests once you hire me. And third, though you have no way of knowing this, I'm really good at my job." She relaxed the intensity of her gaze, sat back, and grinned at me. "Plus admit it. You kind of like me."

She was right. I did like her. "Fine, you're hired." Fuzzy had finished his bottle, so I wiped his chin, put the bottle down, and fished a dollar out of my wallet. I guess I'd picked up some static from Fuzzy's fur, because when I put the dollar in Nor's palm, I got a little zap feeling, and my hand tingled.

Nor didn't seem to mind because she smiled and said, "Outstanding. Now, what do you know about the house?"

I glanced down at Fuzzy who had begun grooming himself. "Not much." Though I wasn't making eye contact, I could feel Nor's gaze boring into me.

"But you know something."

I shrugged. "I know it's...special. Alive, somehow." I reached behind me, above the headboard, so I was touching the wall. "It's kind of amazing, actually."

The house shifted around us, letting out a soft murmur that sounded a bit like a purr.

Nor's eyes widened and that gleam reappeared. "It's fairly evident that the house has been trying to communicate with you. But it hasn't been clear if you've understood that or been communicating back with it, at least on purpose. This is excellent, but try not to hold a conversation with it in front of Meg or Sarah, okay? At least for now."

"Okay." I'd already decided to keep my chats with the house private, but it was interesting to me that Nor thought it was a necessity.

"What else did you learn this morning?"

"I didn't get a lot of details. I do know that there are some other families feuding with the Fosters over the house. They did

say that one of the other families caused the hail storm. I think
they have some kind of gadget. Hey, do you know about the
other families?"

"I do."

"Maybe you can answer this for me then. What's up with
all the weird gadgets they have? Don't laugh at me…but…are
they with some top secret government agencies or something? I
mean, how else would they have access to the kind of tech that
allows them to control the weather and sound and stuff?"

"Control sound? Wait, who did you meet with?"

"You said we don't have time to go into that. And if we're
short on time, I want my questions answered before we get
to yours."

"Okay, fair enough. One thing though. Why do you think
they're using gadgets?"

I blinked at her. "Well, L—er, one of them had a cell phone
that had some kind of sound dampening function. And then
the other guy was bragging about his weather prowess, so I just
assumed he also had some kind of high-tech gizmo…how else
would they do it?"

"This is why you need me."

Another knock sounded on the door. "Can I come in?"
called Wil.

I looked at Nor, who said, "I would."

"But we're not done talking. I've got a lot more questions."

"As your lawyer, my first piece of advice is to let him in.
Trust me."

In for a penny, in for a pound. "Yeah, come in," I called to
Wil. It wasn't my fault if I sounded less than enthusiastic.

Wil stepped into the room, quickly and quietly shutting
the door behind him. He paused, sizing us up, scoping out
the room.

"Nice view," he said, strolling past Nor, over to the window.

I thought he was being sarcastic about the tree blocking the
view. I was about to tell him I liked the feeling of living in a treehouse, when I turned my head to find that there was, indeed,
a nice view out the window. The tree that had been blocking

the window had moved to the right. Or the house had moved the window to the left. I was pretty sure it was the latter, given that I hadn't seen any Ents on my walk through the woods this morning. Although, on second thought, the way things were going, I really wouldn't be that surprised if the tree had scooted over on its own.

"Yup, nice view," I said. "So, what's up?"

Fuzzy had stopped grooming to watch Wil. After a moment, he must've decided Wil wasn't worth growling at because Fuzzy climbed into my lap and settled down. But he kept his eyes open, watching Wil and Nor.

Wil leaned against the wall, arms crossed, looking out the window and said, "I want in."

"I'm sorry?" I asked.

"On whatever you're planning. I want in."

I rubbed my eyes. This was like Gram all over again. What the hell was happening this morning? I was Miss Freaking Popularity all of a sudden.

I was about to tell him we weren't planning anything, when Nor crossed her arms, mirroring his posture, looked him over, and said, "What do you have to bring to the table?"

I thought, *Would ya look at that. My dollar's already hard a work.*

Wil kept looking out the window. "Knowledge."

"I thought that was what Nor was for," I said. Neither of them smiled at my rhyme, but I did. Hanging out with Nor was gonna have another advantage. With all the things that "Nor" rhymed with, at the very least she was gonna be good for hours of mental rhyming games.

Wil said, "I know more about Foster history than anyone outside of the council. At this point, I probably know more than most of the council members themselves." He rubbed either side of the bridge of his nose, under his glasses, as though they were digging into him.

"How does that help us?" asked Nor.

Us. She'd said "us." I was part of a team now. For someone who'd been alone for months, that one little word was a big deal.

Wil said, "You're joking, right?" He stared at me. "I'm not sure what your end game is, Finn, but you want to get through the rest of this weekend, you're going to need all the help you can get."

He pointed to Nor. "She's going to be great with the rules, and she's a shark at the negotiating table."

He turned to Nor. "Of course, I looked you up when I found out you were in my round of selections."

He looked at me. "Nor isn't just any regular old lawyer. She's the youngest person to make partner at her firm, ever, and has negotiated two of the biggest international deals in the Foster clan's history."

He pushed off from the wall and walked over to stand next to us. "I would have looked you up ahead of time, too, Finn— that's pretty standard for the selections. But no one knew you were going to be here. Including Meg, by the way, who only found out last minute."

"Is that unusual?" I asked.

Nor shrugged, but Wil said, "There have been occasional wild-card candidates in the past, but they're rare. And certainly none in the last hundred years or so."

Nor raised an eyebrow at Wil and said, "You're not the only one who can do research. I looked into you as well."

She turned back to me. "Wil here blew through high school in two years, is a Rhodes scholar, holds two doctorates, and is rumored to be working on a third—and he's not even thirty yet. He parlayed his Rhodes connections into a series of traveling professorships and, as a result, has an extensive network of academic contacts around the globe."

Nor smiled at him. If she'd smiled at me like that, I'd be backing away and looking for exits. I gave him points for not flinching. "What is it that you want from Finn, Wil?"

"I want a guaranteed position as the liaison between Finn and the council, should you become housekeeper, Finn."

Nor said, "That would not only secure you a position as a council member, but it would also put you on the fast track to becoming head of the council."

Wil smiled at her.

Nor nodded and said, "Smart. And you're already covered if Meg wins, since yesterday she all but promised you a position with the council. Of course, you realize that at least part of the reason she did that was that she anticipated that you'd be so consumed with the idea of being elevated to a council member that you'd fail to bond with the house." At the look Wil gave her, she held up her hands and said, "Hey, I'm as ambitious as they come. I'm not judging you. But I hope you're cognizant of the fact she's trying to play you."

Wil shrugged. "I can handle Meg."

I stared at them for a moment then said, "This is all very… interesting. But what I don't get is why you aren't making deals with each other? From what I understand, either of you has just as much chance to become the housekeeper as I do."

Nor said, "Unlikely. My test with Sarah this morning pretty much confirmed it for me." She shot a look at Wil. "And I'm inferring from the fact that you're here that you don't expect to be advancing, either."

Wil gave Nor a level look. "I think it's safe to say that I'm no longer near the top of the scoreboard."

He started to pace. "Now that I'm basically out of the running, am I looking out for my own self interests? Of course I am. It's no secret that I've been aiming for the council my entire career. And it's because of my ambitions, because I've made this family my career, that I need to step in here.

"Look, I've read most, if not all, of the transcripts of the previous selections." Nor started to interrupt him and he cut her off with, "Don't ask me how I got ahold of them. I wasn't screwing around when I told you my Foster knowledge is—"

"Scary?" Nor said, but she said it with a small grin.

"I would've gone with 'thorough' but yes, scary works. During the selection, the type of maneuvering Meg's doing—offering me a plum position, trying to distract me—that's not unusual. Selection candidates building alliances among themselves," he paused in his pacing to gesture back and forth between me and Nor, "is not unusual, either. But a completely clueless—sorry, Finn, but it's true—a totally uneducated candidate, someone with absolutely no knowledge of our family or the real world? That's unheard of." He starting pacing again.

Okay, I knew I'd grown up in the west end of nowhere, but to say I didn't know anything about the real world was uncalled for. I was about to growl an objection, but before I could, Wil started up again.

"And then there's that!" He pointed at my head. "She's got stitches, for Christ's sake. Candidates are supposed to be safe from outside interference during the selection. It's one of the basic rules. It shouldn't have happened. It shouldn't be *possible* for it to have happened."

Wil came to a stop by the bed, between Nor and me. "Ladies, to put it bluntly, something is very, very wrong. And Finn, this isn't just about you. It's not just about Nor or me either. This won't make sense to you right now, but the selection process, it's important for the whole family."

I glanced at Nor. Her face was dead serious, and she was nodding in agreement.

How could this one job be so important? It was a housekeeper position for crying out loud. Oh man, these people took themselves way too seriously.

Wil said, "In summary, my position is this: I want to help you because my whole career is tied up in this family. I did not work my ass off to get this far and have things fall apart now, when I'm so damn close to a council position. And you, you need help. You've needed it since you got here. And now, with things going off the rails so spectacularly, you really need it. I'm offering my considerable expertise. You should take it."

Nor looked at me and said, "He knows more about the history here than I do. And, for what it's worth," she eyed him up and down, "I think he's a decent guy. I vote yes, let him help you. But it's up to you, Finn."

I looked at Fuzzy. He hadn't flinched when Wil came closer, so I guessed that was a good sign. Plus, the house hadn't tried to prevent Wil, or Nor for that matter, from entering my room, so that was something. A smile tugged at my lips as I wondered if it was a good or bad sign that I was basing decisions on the dispositions of a kitten and a house. I said, "Why don't you pull up a chair, Wil?"

He snagged a chair and dragged it toward the bed.

Two chairs, two people. It was like the house had known they would be coming.

"Did you guys plan this? Plan on coming to see me together?"

Nor and Wil traded a look.

Wil said, "Not exactly. Nor talked to me this morning, while you were gone—"

"I was trying to convince him that we needed to read you in," said Nor.

So that's how the house had known to place the chairs and to make space for them. I was both impressed and a little creeped out.

Nor must've noticed my discomfort and thought it was about working with her and Wil because she said, "You need allies, Finn."

And, there it was again. Allies. I sure felt like I'd been dragged into some weird war. Maybe I should be wearing army fatigues. Certainly a helmet seemed a good idea.

Fuzzy must've felt my frustration because he rubbed his head against me. I petted him while I took a moment to organize my thoughts. I weighed my words as I went, saying, "While having friends is always nice, I'm afraid you guys are missing a crucial point. Had anyone bothered to tell me that this was a competition—a selection process, whatever—the point is, I never would have come here. I've been very clear about the fact that I've already got plans—I'm enrolled, tuition paid, boat literally leaving the dock soon."

Nor looked grim. "This is one of the reasons I wanted to talk to you. I've never heard of anyone going through this process who didn't know what they were in for. I'd like to think that they'd fill you in before you accepted the job, but let's just say that what I've seen so far doesn't fill me with confidence. I'm afraid there's every chance you're going to enter into a binding contract without realizing it until it's too late."

"I'm not stupid. I know how to read a contract," I said. "And besides, that's what fancy schmancy lawyers like you are for—to get people out of supposedly ironclad contracts."

"Not this kind of contract," said Wil. "It gives a whole new meaning to binding."

"Look, even if they offered it to me, which I still think is unlikely, I'm not taking this job." I patted the wall behind me again. "No offense, sweetie."

The house didn't respond.

Nor and Wil both looked like they didn't believe me.

"I should have gotten the t-shirt," I mumbled.

"What?" asked Wil.

"Nevermind," I said. I rubbed Fuzzy's chin for a moment and then asked the question that I'd been pondering pretty much since I'd gotten there. "What if I just leave?"

The house groaned around us. It did not sound happy.

"You can't," said Wil.

"What do you mean I can't? I'll just grab my bag, grab Fuzzy, and boogie on out of here," I said.

"The house is under orders not to let any of us leave the property until the final round of the selection process is over," said Wil. "We were there when Sarah ordered Meg to do it, and we all watched Meg give the instructions to the house."

"It's not the house's fault," said Nor. "It can't refuse a direct order from the housekeeper."

"The house can do that? It controls the property?"

Nor and Wil nodded.

"Well then, how come I got hurt? I thought the house likes me."

Wil said, "You had your, er, incident, right near the edge of the property. Protection has been weakening at the borders for a long time, but it's gotten particularly bad in the last few years."

Nor said, "How many people know that? I didn't. Most Fosters, in fact, wouldn't have access to that kind of information, and certainly someone who isn't a Foster shouldn't know that there are weak spots, never mind where, exactly, the weak spots are. Finn, my guess is that someone has been surveiling the edges of the property, waiting for an opportunity, and when you happened to stumble into an area that's weakening, someone took advantage of it."

I thought back to the part where I was in the forest, when it had started raining. At first, I hadn't gotten wet because the trees had bent to form an umbrella over me and Fuzzy, protecting us. At the time, I'd thought it had just been the rain weighing them down. Now, I wondered if that hadn't been the house reaching out, trying to help.

Nor said, "The house should alert the housekeeper if anything is amiss. So either Meg didn't know or she allowed it to happen."

Wil was starting to look a little panicked. "You can't assume Meg was involved with what happened. It might have something to do with her being a temporary housekeeper—maybe she just didn't know."

"What if she did?" countered Nor.

I waved my hands, "Regardless, this is a whole other level of crazy. They can't hold me here against my will. That's…that's… kidnapping. Or hostage taking. Or some other kind of messed up -ing."

"You can try taking it up with Sarah when you meet with her," said Nor.

"You might fail your test," said Wil, "in which case, I don't see why you'd have to stay for the official contract tomorrow."

"Speaking of which," Nor said. "We need to prep you for your test this afternoon."

A knock on the door interrupted whatever she was going to say next.

Chapter Twenty-One

"Who is it?"

"It's Doug."

Nor hopped out of her chair and sprawled herself across the foot of the bed. She waved at Wil's feet until he put them up on the chair where she'd just been sitting.

I raised an eyebrow and called, "Come on in."

The door opened and Doug stood in the doorway, his gaze sweeping the room. I saw something cold and calculating flit across his face before he smiled. Even with a grin in place, the smile didn't quite reach his eyes.

"Having a little party? How come I wasn't invited?" His words had his usual teasing tone, but there was a stiffness in his posture that put me on edge. The fact that Fuzzy had sat up in my lap and was giving Doug the evil eye didn't help.

"Just hanging out, shooting the breeze," said Nor. I had to applaud her. It sure didn't look like we were in here plotting, what with her sprawled across my bed, casual as could be, no lawyerness in sight.

"We're just passing time, waiting for Sarah," I said. "Want to join us?"

"While I'd normally love the opportunity to climb into bed with two beautiful women, I'm afraid I'll have to take a raincheck."

Nor and I both rolled our eyes, which turned his half-smile into a genuine grin. It faded, though, as he added, "Sarah wants to see you." When we all started to shift to get up, he said, "Just you, Finn."

Well this sucked. Nor and Wil were just about to get to the good part and give me some answers. Hopefully, meeting Sarah would be quick so they'd still have plenty of time to prep me for whatever was going to happen later this afternoon. If I knew what was coming, maybe I could purposefully tank the test. Then I could leave. That made me smile.

Doug thought I was smiling at him and sent me a grin that made my toes tingle. Too bad he was such a twit. That boy could melt steel with those grins of his.

I stood up and put Fuzzy on the bed. "Just give me one sec," I said to Doug.

While he, Nor, and Wil made small talk, I grabbed the kitten kibble from the vet bag and put out some crunchies for Fuzzy in the bathroom. I retrieved him from the bed, brought him into the bathroom, and showed him the kibbles.

"These are for you. I know they're not fish, but you might want to give them a try," I kissed the top of his head and put him down. I added, "And please, stay in my room while I'm gone" as much for his benefit as for the house's. Hopefully, the house would make sure Fuzzy stayed put until I returned.

I emerged into my bedroom to find Doug, Nor, and Wil had migrated to the hallway, where they were clustered, waiting for me.

"Have fun," said Nor. "Come find us later, and we'll hang out some more."

"Okay," I said, closing my door behind us. I gave her and Wil a small wave and followed Doug down the front stairs.

"Where's Meg?" I asked.

"She's doing some stuff for Sarah. You can catch up with her later, though."

I wasn't in any big hurry to get into it with Meg again, so I hoped she'd stay busy for a while and maybe I could get a nap before I had to deal with her again.

Back downstairs, Shaggy and Scooby were still hulking about in the hallway. They both scanned me thoroughly, but they didn't make any move toward me, so I must've passed muster.

I paused outside the doorway to the dining room. Now that I was close to them, I could see them more clearly. I blinked. They were even bigger than I thought. They looked like they were chiseled from stone. Assistants my pink panties. These guys had to be bodyguards.

Shaggy and Scooby didn't seem like the right names for them anymore, so I said, "Hey Thor," with a nod to the one with the shoulder-length blond hair on my right. "Heimdahl," I nodded to the man with the coffee-colored skin on my left. They both glanced at me and nodded back, but neither cracked a smile.

Doug coughed and I turned to see him trying not to laugh, so at least someone was amused.

"Sarah," he called out. "Finn's here."

"Come in," Sarah called.

Doug waved me into the room, then headed off down the hallway toward the kitchen.

I stepped into the dining room. Sarah had commandeered the room and set up camp at the head of the table. The heavy furniture and sheer size of the table should have dwarfed her. Instead, she dominated the room.

The laptop, briefcase, and tower of paper next to her all fit with the Commander-in-Chief vibe she projected. The dainty formal tea service laid out near her, not so much. It was kind of like seeing a tank with a circlet of daisies hanging from its gun.

Sarah stood with a smile and gestured me toward her. "Finn, come in, come in. I hear you've had quite the morning. Please, sit down." She motioned me into a chair.

"Hi, uh thanks," I said as I sat down. Her smile was welcoming, but she radiated authority in a way that made me feel like a kid in the principal's office. I found myself sitting up really straight in my chair.

"Would you like some tea?"

Sarah started pouring before I could respond so I said, "Sure, thanks."

She was still smiling. There was nothing hostile in her

movements. But there was such a sharp intelligence in her eyes, and the assessing look she gave me was so penetrating, that I got nervous. I blurted out, "Is this the test?"

She smiled wider, eyes twinkling. "Well, I thought first, we could have a little chat. Get to know one another. We can get to the test later, if that's all right with you."

"Okay."

She placed a cup of tea in front of me, then sat down.

"There's nothing like a good cup of tea. Between you and me, I drink way too much of the stuff. But I can't seem to help myself." She sipped her tea, closing her eyes and sighing with pleasure.

I added milk and sugar to my cup and took a sip to be polite. "I feel that way about coffee. But this is really good."

Sarah took another sip of her tea, peering at me over the brim of her cup. I tried not wiggle and fidget under her gaze.

She said, "Relax, Finn. You're a Foster. All Fosters are welcome here. But I must admit—and don't tell the others I said this—I take a particular delight in getting to know some of the more distant branches of the family." She took a sip of tea. "You've really never met any of your relatives before?"

I shook my head.

"How unfortunate. And here you thought this weekend was a reunion, and you'd finally get to meet some Fosters. If I were you, I couldn't help but be a bit disappointed. By the way, who sent you the invitation?"

"Didn't you?"

"No. I did not."

"Oh. Well, I have no idea. There was no name on the invitation or the envelope. It was just a fancy invitation, like you get for a wedding."

"How interesting."

I hadn't thought so before, but she seemed perplexed. I filed it away for later consideration.

"Well, in any event, this weekend is so much more than a simple family party. Though it's not what you expected, it's actually much better than a reunion. It's the opportunity of a lifetime, really."

"Oh?"

"I'm certain by now you've realized that our house here is quite special. And I'm sure that by now someone—perhaps your breakfast companions this morning—filled you in on at least the basic purpose of the weekend. I'm here to give you a fuller understanding of the situation."

"Okay." She'd said "breakfast companions" in a way that made me think she knew all about the diner this morning. Whether she actually knew anything or was just trying to get me to spill details, I decided it'd be wise to tread very carefully with what I said.

Still, I couldn't help but ask, "How come you guys didn't just tell me what's going on yesterday? Why all the secrecy?"

Sarah nodded, looking as though she'd expected that question. "I apologize for the confusion. No one was prepared for you to turn up to a selection with absolutely no knowledge of the Fosters. Meg didn't know exactly how to proceed and was waiting for me to get here to clear things up. She was trying to follow the rules, and in the process, made things seem more… complicated than they are."

"Oh." I didn't know if I was buying it, but it seemed like a good idea to hear her out.

"I don't think it's a good use of our time to fill you in on the whole Foster history right now. Let's start with the more immediate issue, the house. You do know it's special?"

"I do."

"Excellent. Well, something so special requires special care. Makes sense, right?"

"Sure."

"So we in the council go to extra effort to ensure that the housekeeper is someone extremely well-suited to the job. That's where the selection process comes in."

"Uh huh." I considered interrupting her to explain that there was no way I was going to be the housekeeper. But I realized I really wanted to hear what she was going to say. I wanted answers. I had the feeling that Sarah had them.

"Part of my duties is to give an orientation of sorts to potential housekeepers. Actually, it's required that I fully brief each candidate about being housekeeper. I'd appreciate it if you'd be patient enough to hear me out."

"Okay."

"I know that, compared to the other candidates, you're a bit behind the curve—"

"If by 'behind the curve' you mean, 'have no idea what's going on,' then yup, you're right." Oops. That sounded more bitter than I'd intended.

"Well we can't have that," she said and gave my arm a little pat. "And, again, I apologize. Had I known, I would have come yesterday and given you a proper orientation as soon as you arrived. But I'm here now. And we've got a lot to cover."

I sighed. That did not sound fun.

Sarah looked me over for a moment. "You know what? Why don't we go for a tour of the house while we talk? Kind of a show and tell, if you will."

"That'd be great." I didn't have to fake my eagerness. I was dying to look around the house. And anything would be better than sitting here getting a lecture.

She topped off her cup of tea, then stood, cup in hand. I rose and stepped back, letting her take the lead as we left the dining room.

I let out a slow breath, and some of my tension left me as I followed behind her. Sitting at that big table with the formal tea set, I'd felt like she was going to grill me or test me.

But now she was strolling along with a teacup in her hand. It made her seem a lot less scary. Which, I had to admit, was probably why she was doing it. Well, it was nice of her to make an effort to put me at ease. I felt the nervous knot in my stomach relax a little.

In the hallway, Sarah spoke to her assistants. "Please make sure we have some privacy," she said as she strode past them. They nodded.

I followed after her to the front door. The assistants had closed ranks and moved off down the hall, lurking at a discreet distance.

"What's with Hall and Oates?" I asked.

"Hall and Oates? I thought they were Thor and Heimdahl?"

I blushed a little. "You heard that, huh? I haven't landed on the right combo yet, but give me time, I'll get it."

She gave me an amused grin. "I'm looking forward to it. In the meantime, don't worry about them. A certain lack of privacy comes with being on the council—we've always got various people trailing after us. But good assistants do have their uses." She lowered her voice and winked at me, "Watch this."

She turned and called, "In about ten minutes, I'll need some more tea."

Both Hall and Oates nodded.

Sarah turned back to me, grinning. "Every job has its perks! Speaking of which, let's talk about the house and being its housekeeper."

We were standing at the front door. She turned around and faced into the house, like we'd just stepped inside. The doors to the rooms on either side of the hallway were still closed, as they'd been every time I'd seen them so far.

Sarah gestured to the door on the left side of the hallway. "Let's start over here. After you."

I walked to the door and turned the knob. The door opened easily—no comments from the house.

"Oh cool!" I strode into a parlor/sitting room. Of course, the ceiling, floor, and walls were made of wood. It was a little dark, so I asked, "Is it okay if I open the curtains?"

"Of course," said Sarah. She stood just inside the doorway, sipping her tea.

I walked to the window, whisked open the curtains, and turned around to survey the room. Under the window was a small table and two chairs. There was a fireplace opposite the door, and arranged in front of it was a horseshoe-shaped seating area consisting of two couches and an armchair, with a low coffee table in the middle and end tables by the ends of the couches. A few other random chairs were placed around the room, including a rocking chair that sat near the fireplace.

There were built-in shelves and cabinets lining the walls. My fingers itched to open the cabinets and explore them, but I didn't think this was the time for it. Maybe later.

I wondered why we didn't have dinner in here last night. The dark wood everywhere gave it a cozy feeling that certainly would've made last night less awkward. Out loud I said, "It's the kind of place that makes you want to have a bunch of friends over for a board-game night."

"You're not far off the mark. At one time, it was a formal sitting room for entertaining visitors," said Sarah. "There's all sorts of interesting oddities in here that have collected over the years. You should take a peek in the cabinets."

It was so close to what I'd been thinking a few minutes ago that I wondered if my curiosity was obvious. Maybe Nor was right, and I needed to find a game face. I smiled at Sarah and said, "Sure."

I walked over to the nearest wall. The built-in shelves went from the ceiling to a bit more than halfway down the wall, then the cabinets took up the rest of the space to the floor. I reached for the knob and twisted it.

"I think it's stuck," I said.

"Ah well, the house is old, and sometimes things stick. I can have Meg take a look at it later. Maybe we should continue on," said Sarah.

I wasn't about to give up my chance to get a peek that easily. "Hang on a sec," I said. I gently worked the knob back and forth, muttering under my breath, "Come on sweetie. You can do it." With a tiny snick, the latch gave and the door swung open, giving us a view of the crammed contents.

Behind me, I heard Sarah take a breath. I turned and smiled, "I know! Pretty cool, right? Just look at all this stuff!" The cabinet had a series of cubbyholes at the top and a few widely spaced shelves underneath. Every inch was crammed with a variety of bric-a-brac. Some of it looked really, really old.

I said, "Well, this is an antique dealer's dream. You could spend a whole afternoon in here just searching through the cubbies."

"Speaking of searching, you don't happen to see a pair of eyeglasses anywhere do you?" Sarah was pacing around the room, peering under chairs and tables. "I had them earlier today, and I can't find them. I must've put them down somewhere when I was walking around the house earlier."

I gave a last longing glance at the contents of the cabinet, then shut the door with a sigh. I gave it a little pat of thanks before I walked over to join Sarah.

As we searched around, Sarah said, "Let me tell you a little more about the position. While the title is that of housekeeper, you wouldn't be responsible for cleaning, if you don't want to be. The housekeeper is expected to work with the house to help it stay functional. The house will communicate its needs to you, and you will see that those needs are met. But how you do that is your decision. You can hire any staff you need. In the past, some housekeepers have preferred to do everything themselves, right down to actual housekeeping tasks like cleaning, while others have preferred to act as an overseer."

"As long as the staff are Fosters?"

"Correct. From time to time, different Fosters will visit the house. I, for example, and other members of the council are likely to visit. In those instances, you would make sure that everything is ready for our visit, that food has been ordered, that kind of thing."

"Kind of like an innkeeper?"

"A bit, yes. Again, you can be as hands-on as you like, or you can staff it out. The most important thing is that things here run smoothly. And that the house is happy. How you accomplish that is entirely up to you."

I had a lot of experience from the diner that would easily transfer to running the house. But I had a million questions I wanted to ask, not the least of which was how did one keep a living house happy? What kinds of things did it need? Did it eat? Did it have special care instructions? I couldn't imagine what they'd be. I mean, maybe it preferred lemon-scented furniture polish. Oh god, maybe it had allergies, like to certain kinds of cleaning products. Who knew.

I shook my head and reined in my thoughts. I wasn't actually interested in the job, and I wouldn't let her suck me into considering it.

We'd been looking for several minutes, and we still hadn't found any glasses. Sarah said, "I don't think they're in here. I'll find them later. Let's continue the tour, shall we?"

Chapter Twenty-Two

"Okay, where next?" I said, following her out into the hall.

Sarah nodded at the closed door on the other side of the hallway, near the stairs.

"Let's go in there next," Sarah said. Teacup in hand, she moved past me and over to the door. Hall appeared, topped off her tea, and retreated. Oates was still skulking about at the far end of the hallway.

She tried to turn the doorknob one-handed, but it was huge, and she had trouble getting a grip on it.

"Let me," I said.

She shot me a grateful look and stepped back.

I used two hands and tried to open the door. Though the knob felt incredibly heavy, it turned when I applied some effort. But when I pushed, the door stuck shut.

"Oh dear. This door is always so finicky. I swear, you'd think a living house wouldn't have the same problems that regular houses do. But wood is wood, I suppose. Well, if we can't get in this way, we can go through the other door off the mudroom. That's what we did earlier."

"It might be alright. Sometimes you have to kind of pull and lift up a bit with these older doors. The wood swells, and you just have to give it a little help." I tried wiggling the door a bit, but it didn't move much. Whispering "C'mon big fella," I turned the knob, bent both knees, gave a tug up and a swift shove of my shoulder. The door groaned at me, but it scraped forward, and swung open.

When I walked into the room, I wooshed out a "Whoa."

The room was huge. It ran the length of the house, and like every other room, was all wood. But unlike the other rooms I'd seen so far, this room was empty.

The windows were different in here, too. They ran in long verticals, nearly floor to ceiling. For some reason, the curtains were open on all the windows, and I wondered if the house had opened them for me, since I'd opened the curtains in the other room.

Though the windows let in plenty of light, the sunlight didn't have much to do, other than illuminate the drifting dust motes and the dark wood of the floor and walls. A few forlorn ceiling-to-floor bookcases lined the walls, but they just looked lonely, devoid of all but a few books as they were.

The click-click of Sarah's heels changed to a more hollow, echoing clomp-clomp sound as she entered the room behind me.

"What is this place?" I asked, my voice bouncing around the room.

"It's had various uses over the years. At one time or another it's been a library, a study, a music room, even a dance room. Recently, it's fallen into disuse."

Looking at the polished floor, all I wanted to do was to whip off my shoes and see if I could slide from one end of the room to another. Instead, I walked to a window in the far wall and sighed at the view of the forest. "I can see why someone would look out these windows and be inspired to make music."

Sarah smiled. "You could easily make this a music room again. One of the benefits of being the housekeeper is that the position comes with a substantial decorating budget, which is renewed annually. The housekeeper has absolute autonomy in redecorating the house, so you could turn any room into anything you want, really."

"Huh," I said. "I'd have thought you historical council people would be more hands-on than that, given that this is a historic place and all."

"We are deeply grateful to our housekeepers for their service and consider it a great honor to make their stay here as comfortable as possible. That, of course, includes encouraging them to make this place as much their personal dream home as they can. A happy housekeeper makes for a happy house."

From the little I knew about historical preservation, that didn't sound at all right to me. But this wasn't an ordinary house, so it sort of made sense that the usual rules wouldn't apply.

"That's nice of you." I gave her my most bland smile and tried not to let her see how much the idea of a huge redecorating budget made the wannabe designer part of me bounce with glee.

Sarah took a sip of her tea. "If Meg stays on as housekeeper, I understand that Doug has been lobbying for her to turn this into a sort of rec room. Something about a big screen TV, video game consoles, a pool table, a foosball table, and so on."

I smiled, "That sounds like Doug." I was sort of surprised that he planned on staying here with Meg, though.

"In addition to the redecorating budget, the position comes with a generous salary—think more along the lines of top-level management."

"For a housekeeper job?"

"Next to being a member of the council, the housekeeper position is the most prestigious job in the family. So of course the pay is commensurate with the level of prestige."

Well, now it was making sense to me why Meg wanted the position so bad. Being a regular housekeeper didn't seem like her thing. Wads of cash and a whopping ton of clout, now that sounded right up her alley.

Sarah watched me as I drifted around the room. I trailed my fingers along one of the shelves. Was it my imagination or did Sarah just seem to flinch a bit?

I decided to try an experiment. I reached for a book, watching Sarah out of the corner of my eye. Yup, she tensed. It was subtle, but it was there.

Huh. I turned my attention to the shelves in the room. There wasn't a lot to see. I reached to put the book back and nearly dropped it. An arrow had appeared in the grain of the wood on the shelf in front of me. It was pointing to the left.

I pulled down the other book on the shelf and flipped through it while I thought.

Okay, the house was trying to tell me something. And it was being stealthy about it. The house wasn't talking to me. Instead, it was making sure that only I saw what it was communicating. My guess was that it didn't want Sarah to know what it was doing. Interesting.

"Old books are neat," I said. I cringed inwardly at how lame I sounded. Sarah seemed to buy it, though.

She said, "Well feel free to look around as much as you like." She was smiling, but there was an alertness to her that hadn't been there before.

She'd said that she was required to give me a speech about being housekeeper. I wondered if she was also required to let me look around as much as I wanted. If so, maybe she was just tense because she wanted to move things along.

I returned the book and walked to my left. When I got to the next bookshelf, another arrow was waiting for me, pointing to the left. I didn't want to look obvious, so I paused where I was. This bookshelf only had one book on it. Again, I took it down, and again Sarah flinched. What was she worried about?

I meandered from bookcase to bookcase, seemingly fascinated by the books I was finding, but really just following the arrows. The house led me to the far end of the room. With no windows along the back wall, the shadows pooled in this part of the room. When I turned to look at her, Sarah was standing at the other end in a beam of sunlight, sipping her tea. The brightness at her end just reinforced how dim the area was where I was standing.

I turned to look at the next bookcase. There was no arrow on the shelf that was at my eye level. There wasn't anything else on the shelf either. In fact, the last two bookcases back here appeared to be empty.

The floor under my right foot jiggled a little. I looked down. The wooden floorboards had rearranged themselves to form an arrow pointing toward the bottom shelf of the bookcase.

It was too dark to see what was down there from where I was standing. How was I going to get down there without looking obvious?

"Looks like I've run out of books," I called to Sarah.

"Ready to move on with the tour?" she asked.

"Sure. Let me just tie my shoelace," I said.

I knelt on my unbruised knee and fiddled with my shoelace. I kept my head angled toward my shoe, but slid my gaze around me, trying to figure out what the house wanted me to know.

A small glint caught my attention. To my right, deep in the shadows, on the bottom shelf of the bookcase, was a pair of eyeglasses.

When I looked up, Sarah was still sipping her tea, trying to cover the fact that she was keeping an eye on me. Good thing it was so dim at my end and so bright at hers because she couldn't see me that well.

"Might as well do the other one while I'm down here," I mumbled loud enough that she could hear me. I switched feet and started retying my other shoe while my thoughts scurried around my head.

Okay, I had to figure out what was going on, fast.

I sent a glance Sarah's way. She strolled over to the window next to the door and looked outside, while she waited for me to get it together.

She was definitely checking out what I was doing. But she didn't seem particularly alarmed at where I was kneeling.

I realized two things.

One, Sarah didn't know exactly where the glasses were, but she knew they were somewhere in the room. That's why she'd been tensing when I pulled things off the shelves. It also explained why she didn't look any more tense than usual at my current location.

And two, the glasses hadn't wound up where they were by accident. No way could Sarah have dropped and kicked her glasses all the way into the shelf without hearing or noticing.

So someone had put the glasses there, likely on Sarah's orders.

Sarah had probably given the glasses to her assistants and told them to hide them somewhere in this room. You know, because the room was obviously empty. Nothing to see here. Best to just whip through and keep on going.

It was especially smart, handing the glasses off to someone else. If she didn't know exactly where they were, she couldn't accidentally give away their location.

But why go to all the trouble to hide the glasses in the first place? It made no sense. Unless, of course, she was trying to see if the house would help me find them.

Which was exactly what was happening.

And that meant that despite what she said earlier, this was it.

I was taking the test.

Chapter Twenty-Three

Son of a bitch. She flat out lied to me.

Okay, fine. She wanted to play games? Well, game on, lady. I could play, too. I wasn't sure how yet, but I was going to figure it out, fast.

Whatever I decided to do, I was pretty sure that I shouldn't leave the glasses behind. At the very least, the house wanted me to have them, and since it had gone to so much effort, I wanted to make it happy. Plus, having the glasses would give me some options. And I really needed some options because I still wasn't sure exactly what game these people were playing.

"Distract her, please," I whispered to the house.

Sarah was still standing in front of the window. She turned to look at me, and the curtain nearest to her swayed as though she'd bumped it. A shower of dust sprinkled down on her.

"Oh dear," she said, hastily stepping out of the way. She set her teacup on the windowsill and began brushing at her suit.

While she was momentarily occupied, I made my move. The shadows worked to my advantage, obscuring my movement. Lightning quick, I reached over, snagged the glasses, and tucked them in the side of my shoe under my pant leg. I was already standing up by the time Sarah finished swiping away the dust on her skirt.

"You okay?" I asked. My voice sounded strained to me, but she didn't notice.

"Just a little dust. It's no problem." She retrieved her teacup and turned to me. "Well, I think you've got an idea of the potential of this room, and of the overall decorating potential you get to wield as the housekeeper. Shall we continue on?"

"Sure."

I had to physically restrain myself from stomping across the room.

I was so angry that all I could do was smile and plot. I knew if I opened my mouth, yelling would commence, and any subtlety was going to go right out the window. So I plastered my "dealing with a customer-from-hell" smile on my face. And I used my anger to set the more devious section of my brain into motion.

As we went back out into the hallway, Sarah was saying something about how the local Fosters could build or obtain any furnishings I wanted. I nodded occasionally, but mostly tuned her out.

Okay, so first I had to figure out what kind of test this was. Pass/fail—find the glasses/don't find the glasses? Or, were there different sections to the test? If I could figure it out, maybe I could mess with her test results. Hell, I could even flunk the test on purpose if I wanted to. My brain cells started rubbing their hands together in evil glee.

Sarah said, "Ready to go upstairs?"

"Absolutely," I smiled. Sarah looked a little alarmed so I toned the smile down from hungry tiger to curious house cat. "I can't wait to see what's next."

We paused in the hallway when Sarah waved to Hall and Oates, who strode forward.

Who was she kidding? These guys moved like they were extras in an '80s Sylvester Stallone movie. I redubbed them in my head: the dark one was Tango, and the one with the hair was Cash. Sarah handed Cash her teacup. "Are the others in the kitchen?"

"Yes."

Sarah nodded and turned to me. "Upstairs?"

I headed up the stairs, Sarah behind me. There was a pause, and then I heard a heavy tread. A glance confirmed that Tango was following behind us, again at a distance.

What did he think I was going to do? Toss her down the

staircase? I smiled at the thought before I caught myself and suppressed the section of my brain that thought we should give that some consideration.

At the top of the stairs, Sarah turned around and faced a closed door at the front of the house. "This is the master suite. The room is Meg's right now, so I don't feel comfortable intruding on her private space, but let me just say that it's light and airy, lots of windows and lots of space." Sarah turned to face down the hallway toward the back of the house. "As you can see there's plenty of room for the housekeeper to spread out. You can turn any of these rooms into anything you like. For example, you could have an exercise room and a sewing room and a craft room and an office—you can have them all. You don't have to pick and choose."

"And there's plenty of room for guests," I added.

"Yes, of course," said Sarah, striding down the hallway. I followed her, but to my surprise, she didn't stop at any of the rooms. Maybe now that she thought I'd flunked at least part of the test, she'd just breeze through the rest of her tour.

I glanced at my door on the way by, longing to check in on Fuzzy, but Sarah was already near the end of the hall.

Oh the hell with it. "Hang on." I poked my head into my room. Fuzzy was asleep on my pillow. For a second, I debated sliding into the room, locking the door, and curling up with him. But I could only imagine the chaos that'd cause, so I backed out and closed the door.

Sarah stood at the head of the back stairs, waiting. "All good?"

"Yup, my kitten's asleep," I said, as I approached her.

"Great. Then we have time to go see the outside," she said, and started down the stairs ahead of me.

I glanced behind me before following her, and sure enough, Tango was still following us. So weird. I faced forward again and noticed that the door to the right of the stairs had popped open a bit.

"Hey Sarah?" I called. "What's in here?"

As she clacked back up the stairs to reach me, I pulled open the door. A set of stairs led upward. A dry, musty smell wafted down the stairs, making my nose itch.

Sarah appeared next to me and said, "Oh, that's just the attic. You're welcome to explore it on your own time, but it's not part of my tour. It's a dusty mess, full of junk and spiders." She shut the door with a shudder, turned to the staircase and said, "After you."

I shrugged and trudged down the stairs. Spiders didn't particularly bother me, but I knew that some people freaked out over them. I could always check the attic out later.

We reached the bottom of the stairs, trekked through the mudroom, and over to the back door. Cash was standing by the kitchen doorway. Nor, Wil, Meg, and Doug were inside, milling about. They all turned to look at me as I followed Sarah outside, but no one said anything or made a move to follow us. Uh huh. I bet it was because they weren't allowed to. Because, you know, I WAS TAKING A TEST. I swallowed my scowl and went out onto the porch with Sarah. Of course, Tango followed us.

With the sun out in full, I could see that the garden was much bigger than I'd realized. It stretched back to the far tree line.

"As you can see, the yard needs some work," said Sarah. "As housekeeper, you can landscape the property any way you want, and you have a whole army of Foster family gardening staff at your disposal to help you."

My fingers twitched at the thought of salvaging that lovely wreck of a garden. I asked, "How did the garden get so fallow?"

"Gardening isn't everyone's thing. Each housekeeper gets to make their own choices about such things. In fact, it's not even necessary to have a garden at all. I think Meg's plan is to plow it under, and plant some grass. You could too, if you like."

Get rid of the garden? I was really starting to dislike these people. I didn't trust myself to say anything, so I nodded at Sarah and tried to hide my dismay.

"Let's stroll," she said.

I glanced at Sarah's shoes. If she wanted to teeter along on the lawn in heels, well, that was her prerogative. As for my own shoe, the glasses tucked in it still felt secure, so I shrugged and said, "Sure."

We stepped off the porch, and Sarah led me to the left. I was disappointed to see that she moved as gracefully as if she was inside—no teetering in sight. The ground was soft, but somehow, even with her pointy heels, she didn't sink in at all. Of course she didn't. Heaven forbid she get mud on her shoes.

"The house sits on a few hundred acres, which, as you've seen, are quite beautiful. It's another advantage to being housekeeper. You have access to all this pristine land."

We reached the edge of the woods and Sarah turned, walking around the side of the house. When we walked under my bedroom window, I looked up to see Fuzzy looking out the window at me. I must've woken him up when I checked on him. I gave him a little finger wave and mentally begged him to stay put in my room.

We reached the front edge of the house, but we didn't head for the front door like I expected. Sarah continued on, heading along the driveway and away from the house. After a glance and a wave from Sarah, Tango, who'd been trailing us, stepped up onto the porch, where he took a position watching us as we followed the driveway.

Sarah used her serious voice to say, "Now that you've heard about some of the advantages of being the housekeeper, we can circle around to one of its major disadvantages."

"Oh?"

"I'm sorry to say that being housekeeper makes you the focus of a lot of…jealous energy. Given the special nature of the house, there are other people who want access to it. Of course, part of the housekeeper's duties is to protect the house from outsiders. And that, unfortunately, angers the people who don't have access. I'm so sorry I didn't have a chance to warn you about any of this before you went on your walk this morning. How are you feeling, by the way? How's your head?"

Nice of her to ask this far into the tour. I said, "I'm fine. A little sore, a little tired. No big deal."

"Well, I want you to know I had a chat with Meg, and I feel

confident she had nothing to do with your…incident this morning. The whole thing was just bad timing."

"How so?"

"You just happened to be at the wrong place at the wrong time. The house is old, you know, and I daresay it's feeling its age. Aren't we all, though? Ah well." She sighed and gave me a wistful smile. "Anyway, while age is certainly a factor, the truth is that whenever we're searching for a new housekeeper, the house is especially vulnerable. With only an interim housekeeper in place, the house isn't up to full strength. To take advantage of that fact, our enemies watch the borders of the property and look for ways to cause trouble. That's why it's in your best interest to stick close to the house until the weekend is over. For your own safety."

That explanation had holes so big you could drive a truck through them. But I didn't point them out. Instead, I said, "Well, I don't really have a choice, do I? You've given orders that we have to stay here."

"As I said, it's for your own safety. And it's not like you hadn't already planned to be here."

When she put it that way, it almost sounded reasonable. But I still felt like a prisoner. "What if I relinquish my spot? Then can I leave?"

"I'm sorry, but for the safety of all you candidates, it's best if we all stay put till we're done. If it's any consolation, I'll be sequestered here as well."

Actually, that made things worse, but I didn't think I should say that. I glanced at Tango. I wondered if the real reason he and Cash were here was to enforce Sarah's orders. I could totally see them tying me to a chair if I tried to make a break for it.

We reached the two enormous trees that formed the entrance to the grove where the house lived. I wandered over to the trunk of the closest one and ran my hand along the bark. Looking up into the canopy made me wonder if climbing up and changing my physical perspective would somehow give me a better mental perspective on this whole test thing. My best bet now was to go talk to Nor and Wil and see what I could do about getting out of here.

Sarah had moved several feet away from the trunk and appeared to be deep in thought.

I wandered over next to her. Time for me to end this and get away from her. I said, "So, in broad strokes, that's it then? That's the pitch you're required to give me?"

"Well, really, this is just an outline. There's a lot more to it."

"That's okay. I'm good. Let me save you some time and effort. I don't want the job. Had anyone bothered to ask me, or told me what this whole weekend was really about, I would have told you that from the start." Some of my anger was creeping into my voice.

A little voice in the back of my mind reminded me that if I'd never come here, I'd never have seen these glorious trees, never met the amazing house, never met Fuzzy.

I pointed out to that little voice that that just made things worse. Now I was going to be sad about all the new things I'd be leaving behind. I got even angrier as I realized that I was going to be forced to lose more stuff. Because, you know, I hadn't lost enough already.

The little voice shut up.

While this little debate was going on in my head, Sarah was giving me another one of her assessing looks. She raised an eyebrow and said, "Don't you want to know about the extra benefits that come with working with the house?"

"Not really, no. " And if she started in about a 401k I was gonna start yelling. Sarah sighed, so I added, "But hey, you've done your duty. Said your thing. So, thanks for that." I couldn't help it. The "thanks" dripped with sarcasm. Maybe she wouldn't notice, but if she did, I didn't really care.

I started to walk away, back to the house.

Sarah said, "And where do you think you're going?"

"The tour seems to be winding down, so I'm going back to the house."

"No."

Chapter Twenty-Four

Sarah stepped in front of me. Then she made a show of nudging the ground with the pointy toe on her fancy shoe.

At first, I thought she was drawing a literal line in the dirt, daring me to cross it. I started to laugh, but gasped instead. The patch of ground I was standing on turned to liquid. It sucked me in, up to mid-calf, then solidified around my legs.

I yelped and tried to pull myself free.

"What the hell! Did you do this?"

She smiled.

Oh for pity's sake.

Gram could make it hail.

Lou did the sound dampening trick.

Of course Sarah would have her own wacko gadget.

I kept pulling at my legs, panting as I tried to break free. Sarah stepped out of range of my flailing arms. Far enough away that I couldn't grab her. Or slug her. Which was sounding better and better as I struggled.

"What did you...how did you—let me out!" Fists balled at my side, I stopped struggling and glared at Sarah.

She said, "We're not quite done yet. And I require your full attention while we complete this next part of our talk."

Despite her skirt, Sarah squatted down. She put one hand on the ground and closed her eyes.

What was she doing?

Her eyes snapped open, she looked startled, and then a cold, hard light entered her eyes. She flicked a glance at me, then stared at my right leg where it met the ground.

I could feel the dirt around my legs liquefy again. I tried yanking my legs out, but it was like standing in quicksand. The harder I pulled, the harder the mud sucked at my legs.

The mud felt like a living thing as it oozed up my pant legs and down my socks and shoes. I felt the mud slide between the glasses and my skin, and then the glasses slipped out of my sock and were sucked away. A moment later, they sprouted from the ground next to Sarah's hand. The ground around my leg became solid again.

How did she do that? My mind boggled trying to figure out what kind of gadget could make dirt behave that way. Maybe it was hidden in one of her rings or her bracelets? It occurred to me that I was so far out of my league that it would have been funny if I wasn't so freaked out.

Sarah looked at the glasses, then looked up at me. It was not a happy look. Keeping her eyes on my face, slowly she stood up, leaving the glasses on the ground between us like a gauntlet.

Crossing her arms, Sarah stared hard at me. Then, she paced a slow circle around me. She didn't say anything, but she looked me over from every angle. By the time she started a second circle around me, my skin was crawling.

From behind me, she said, "Cheating, Finn?"

I knew she was trying to spook me, but I didn't know why. Not sure how to play this, I tamped down on my anger and went for clueless, which wasn't that big of a stretch. I had no idea what she was up to now. "How can I be cheating when you said I'm not being tested?"

A pause. "Indeed."

Sarah reached my front again and faced me. She gave me a small smile. "Well, I dare say you've figured out by now that our little tour did include round two of the test, or else, why hide the glasses from me?"

She leaned in a little, and I had to work really hard not to lean back. "I really do not approve of you trying to throw the results of the test. It just isn't done."

She straightened away from me, and I felt like I could

breathe again. I said, "I wasn't throwing anything." Well, at least I hadn't decided yet exactly what I was going to do, but she didn't need to know that. "I was gonna give you the glasses when we were done."

She arched an eyebrow at me, and some of my irritation broke through. "Hey, it's not my fault! I wasn't sure what the rules were since you a) didn't explain them to me, and b) you totally lied to me in the first place about not doing the test yet." I glared at her. "So can I go now?"

I tugged on my legs again. I was still stuck. I couldn't help but ask, "What did you do anyway?"

The smile she gave me sent a shiver up my spine. "This little demonstration? This is nothing. Just something to get your attention. To show you, Finn, that the Fosters have so much to offer."

I nodded. "This is majorly advanced tech, I'll give you that. But you've made your point. I'm impressed. Now let me out."

"Tech?" The creepy smile she was wearing bloomed. "What makes you think this—" she swept a hand toward my imprisoned legs "—was done by some kind of tech?"

That sounded like what Nor had said. "What else would it be?" I asked. An uneasy feeling swept through me. It had to be tech, didn't it? That was the only thing that made logical, scientific sense.

Sarah clasped her hands behind her back, a smug smile playing on her lips, as she strode back and forth like a commander in front of her ranks. Or a warden in front of her prisoner. She said, "How is it that you think I was able to trap you in the ground just now? For that matter, how is it that you think someone was able to target you with hail this morning?"

I frowned. "I don't know. Some kind of high tech gadget."

She laughed. "Really? You jumped straight to technology? How interesting. Your parents really didn't tell you anything, did they."

I'd already answered that question like a zillion times so I just gave her a look.

"Didn't it occur to you, Finn, that maybe the things

happening here could have a different explanation?"

"Like what?"

"Like something more…supernatural."

"You mean like magic or something?"

"Exactly."

It was my turn to smile. "No."

"And why not?"

With a snicker, I said, "Because I'm not an idiot. And because I live in the real world, that's why." I sounded sure of what I was saying, but a niggling doubt joined my sense of unease. No way was I giving her the satisfaction of seeing it, though.

"Ah, how apropos that you should bring that up. You have been living in the world, but the real world, so to speak, is a much broader place than the sorry hobbled version your parents confined you to. Lucky for you, that's all about to change."

"You want to start trading 'Yo mama' insults, let's go. Otherwise, leave my parents out of this."

Sarah raised an eyebrow. "Really? That's what you got out of what I'm saying?"

I gave her my best look of pure disbelief. "Oh I heard you. You're trying to sell me on the idea that all the weirdness I've been seeing is magic. Okay, lemme guess…the next thing you're going to tell me is that the house is magic, too. And then I'll be so excited that I'll be all—" I clasped my hands together like I was begging, "'Oh please can I be the housekeeper?'" I put my hands on my hips. "Man, you must be really desperate to resort to this line of bull—er, baloney."

I shook my head. "Just out of curiosity, are you going to whip out a wand and a pointy hat for effect? Ooh, and a broom. You should definitely have a broom."

Sarah gave me a long look. I glared right back at her.

Sarah said, "This isn't Harry Potter, and I'm not Dumbledore."

"I'll say."

"And as you've seen, I don't need a wand."

She had me there.

Sarah resumed pacing back and forth in front of me and assumed a lecturing tone. "You like science, Finn, so let's think about this scientifically. What you think of as magic is really just a way to manipulate energy. Some people have a natural gift for working with the energies given off by different types of materials. People in the Foster bloodline, for example, have a talent for working with earth-related elements, like plants and minerals.

"Other families have other strengths. You encountered the family who can manipulate water this morning. Your father's family is adept at working with animals. Actually, he was a hybrid, like your mother—and you, for that matter—but you get the idea."

"You make it sound like there's all these magical people running around."

"We're a small percentage of the population, but there are more than a few of us."

"If there was really that much magic in the world, then people would know."

"Would they? People see what they want to see. And generally speaking, people are so absorbed in their own little lives that they don't really focus on anything outside what they know."

The little voice in the back of my brain was wondering if maybe what she was saying could be true. But she'd done nothing but mess with me since I'd met her, and I wasn't inclined to believe something so outrageous without some serious proof.

My gaze roamed as I thought, and it landed on the house. That made me pause. The house was alive, there was no denying that. I'd been thinking of the house like a rare animal, sort of like finding a bird you'd thought was extinct. But maybe it was more like finding a dragon. If the house was not just a one-of-a-kind animal, but more of a magical being, well, that would go a long way toward explaining why so many people were all hot and bothered to gain access to it.

And if the house were magical, then it was possible other magic existed as well.

Holy crap.

I needed to get out of there so I could think all this through. Alone. Arguing with Sarah seemed to be a good way to remain stuck, so I figured my best bet was to go along with her enough that she'd set me free.

"Say I believe you," I said. "So what?"

"So being housekeeper gives you access to a kind of magic that only exists one place in the entire world. Think of the research you could do. Think of the skills you could develop."

"I need to think a minute."

My head was spinning. Magic. Actual magic in the world. I couldn't decide if it was really possible, or this was yet another game.

For a moment, I let myself entertain the idea that Sarah was finally telling the truth. My inner scientist poked her head up and suddenly I was brimming with questions. If it was true, it'd be so exciting! So much to discover. So many new things to learn about.

If it was true.

I shook my head. No way was I going to give Sarah what she wanted and get all excited right here in front of her. On the other hand, I needed to play along a little until I got out of this. So I said, "Well, I have to say, that all sounds nice."

"Nice?"

I tried to sound more positive. "No really, it does. But I don't have any special skills. There's nothing to develop. So you know, thanks, but still no thanks."

She pursed her lips. After a long moment she said, "It was my understanding that you want to be an explorer. Go off and investigate and discover new things."

I wasn't sure where she was going with this, so I gave her a tentative, "That's why I'm going to school."

She nodded. "But your curiosity is limited to the ocean? You're not interested in pushing the boundaries of scientific knowledge unless you're on the water?"

When she put it that way, it sounded ridiculous. I shrugged.

"As housekeeper, you have the opportunity to interact with

a truly unique entity. You also have the opportunity to learn to harness and manipulate energies you didn't even know existed five minutes ago. But you're going to turn that down without even giving it serious consideration?"

Well hell. She had a point. I hated it, but she had a point. "Fine, I'll think about it."

"Excellent. Then we can proceed."

I didn't like the sound of that. Not one bit. "Do I have a choice?"

"Finn, I didn't make the rules of selection, but I'm bound by them. And so are you. Once you've started testing, you must continue until you either fail or get to the final round. Then, you have a choice."

"I'd like to state for the record that I object. I was never given the choice about being involved in any of this in the first place. I shouldn't be forced to continue now. This isn't fair!" I yanked at my feet but I was still stuck. I let out a growl and tugged a bit more until I finally gave up.

Sarah waited a minute. "Are you finished?"

"Yes." My fists were clenched and if she'd stepped closer, I would've shoved her just to have the satisfaction of seeing her sprawled in the dirt.

"Good. While I have your undivided attention, we might as well move on to the next section of the test."

I huffed out a sigh and shrugged, crossing my arms. "Lemme guess. I have to find another pair of glasses."

Sarah looked down at the glasses, still lying on the ground between us. "Ah, yes, I'd forgotten about those. I'm done with them now."

She stepped on them. She took her time, crushing them under her foot. When she was done, the ground gulped down the broken remains.

I swallowed hard.

She asked, "What's your favorite flower?"

"What?" I was still staring at the empty spot on the ground.

"Your favorite flower?"

"Uh…."

I tried to think how this could backfire on me, but I didn't know enough even to be able to hazard a guess.

"It's the bloom from the saguaro cactus," I said, just to be difficult. I mean, I loved the saguaro blooms, but mostly I chose it to be a pain in the ass. The tall cactus only grew in the desert, so I wasn't sure if she even knew what I was talking about.

Sarah's smile just widened. "And are you still fond of mazes?"

I went cold, and my arms dropped to my sides in shock. I'd loved mazes as a kid. I used to sit on a stool in the diner and do them while Mom and Dad worked. That way, I was entertained, and they could keep an eye on me, but I wasn't underfoot.

The only way she'd have known that was…"You were in the diner," I said. "You, or your minions. You guys were keeping tabs on me? On us?" Meg had said they kept track of the family, but this felt way more invasive than that, like being spied on.

Sarah's smile widened so much that I was starting to wonder if she could unhinge her jaw.

My stomach churned, and my hands curled into tense little fists.

She winked at me and said, "Watch this."

Sarah crouched down and touched the ground again.

The ground under us trembled, and I pinwheeled my arms for balance. I broke out in a sweat. The quiet vibrations sounded and felt a lot like what had happened the night of the sinkhole. And just like then, the noise and vibrations increased. But instead of a hole opening up, the section of ground we stood on flowed upward. When it stopped, we were on a hill, overlooking the lawn.

Sarah looked up at me. "So you can really enjoy the view," she said. Then she turned her back on me. As she turned, I thought I saw her lips moving, but if she was saying anything, I couldn't hear it. She placed both hands on the ground this time. The low rumbling started again.

In front of me, saguaro cacti began springing from the ground, fully grown. It can take 10 years for a saguaro to grow an inch and about 100 years for it to grow its first arm.

These guys were taller than I was and were sporting multiple arms each.

When the rumbling stopped, the lawn between me and the house was filled with cacti.

Sarah surveyed her work.

"Oh yes," she said and stomped her foot.

In unison, all the cacti flowered.

I hugged myself with my arms while I gaped at the field.

Sarah sauntered over closer to me. "Notice anything special?"

Besides a zillion flowering cacti in the middle of a New England forest? Er…I looked closer. I started to speak, cleared my throat, tried again. "It's…it's a hedge maze. Made of cacti."

Sarah smiled. "Not my personal choice, but I give you points for originality."

I could see the porch of the house. Tango was still standing there, keeping watch. Unlike me, he didn't look surprised at all. In fact, he look bored.

Sarah turned her back on the maze, and then studied me closely. "Now," she said. She raised her hand, did a little wave, and our hill sank back to its original level. A ring of saguaros popped up around us, the ones behind me so close that I yelped and cringed away when they flowed out of the ground. When they stopped growing, the sharp-needled cacti formed an impenetrable horseshoe around us. The only way out was the entrance to the maze.

I wanted to back away, but I was still stuck in the ground, and there was nowhere to go anyway. It occurred to me that I was basically a human saguaro, feet rooted, arms in the air. All I needed was a flower, and I'd be all matchy-matchy with my cohorts around me.

Sarah turned from me and faced the maze. My jaw dropped again. They were moving! The saguaros shuffled themselves around, opening a straight lane between us and the house.

"Your job," said Sarah as she began strolling down the lane, "is to use your innate earth magic to safely navigate the maze and make it back to the house."

I gaped at her. Then I started struggling again and sputtered, "But I don't have any magic!"

She reached the edge of the house at the other end of the lawn. She didn't turn around. Instead, she gave me a little finger wave over her shoulder.

My feet came loose. I was tugging so hard that when they suddenly popped free, I stumbled backwards, stabbing my flailing arm on a cactus. I yowled and jerked forward so fast that I fell over on my face. As I toppled over, the maze closed up, and the straight, wide path across the lawn disappeared.

Chapter Twenty-Five

When I scrambled to my feet, I spent a few moments stomping around my small enclosure, rubbing my arm, and swearing. Finally, I calmed down enough to really look around me.

It didn't look good. I was surrounded by cacti. Beautiful flowering cacti, sure. But Sarah had grown them extra big—really tall, lots of long arms, and so many wicked-looking thorns that it looked like the cacti had fur. Evil, stabby fur.

She'd packed the cacti close enough that their arms intertwined. Any remaining space between them was filled in with abnormally long thorns that looked more like small spears. If I tried to squeeze between the cacti, I'd wind up as saguaro shish-kebab.

The only opening past the cacti was the opening to the maze.

I flopped down on the ground, pulled my knees up to my chest, and put my forehead on my knees.

Okay, so Sarah was a dick. I'd been raised to be respectful of my elders, but a girl has limits. I peered around me for a second and put my head back down with a groan. I needed some stronger words to describe Sarah.

I spent a few minutes coming up with colorful names for Sarah, then forced myself to concentrate and review my situation.

Well, with one day still left to go, I felt fairly comfortable in saying that this reunion sucked, my extended family sucked, and I should've just gone straight to the ocean.

But then I wouldn't have met Fuzzy. Or the house.

I sighed.

Well, on the plus side: magic. Looking around me, I felt pretty sure that magic existed.

Actual magic.

I smiled, despite myself, as a little spark of sheer delight tickled its way through me. It made me want to stand up and do a little dance around the clearing.

I didn't think I, personally, had any kind of magic skills. And I'd never seen my parents do anything I'd consider magical, but then, it was looking like they'd taken great pains to shelter me from all this. Given the amount of crazy that seemed to be going along with all the magic stuff, I couldn't say as I blamed them.

And speaking of crazy, I sat up a little straighter and examined the hedge maze in front of me.

If I understood Sarah correctly, the idea was to force me to use some kind of earth magic to make my way through the maze. I wasn't entirely clear on why I'd need magic to do that.

I climbed to my feet and stepped cautiously forward into the entrance of the maze. I barely had enough room to walk without touching the thorns. The entrance path was only a few feet long. Then the path reached a T intersection that branched left and right.

I reached the T and glanced left to see that the path in that direction branched again almost immediately. I looked right, and while I was looking, the cacti shifted and changed the configuration of the path. My mouth dropped open. Some of them just moved their arms around. But two actually tottered across the path to new spots. What had been another T intersection was now a right angle bending to the left.

Wow.

I stood there staring for a moment before I realized I should get out of there before my exit closed up behind me.

I backed out of the maze and returned to my little holding area.

Well, now I knew why I'd need magic to navigate the maze. It wasn't just a matter of solving a regular maze. I'd need the magic to find a way through the shifting paths or to force a path through like Sarah had done. Otherwise, the maze would keep moving around me. At best, I'd be stuck in there until they decided to let me out. At worst, I'd get really hurt by those thorns. And I'd already found out that these people didn't really care about inflicting damage on the way to getting what they wanted, so I found it likely that I wouldn't come out of this unscathed.

The thought of being hurt made me realize that my stitches were starting to twinge again. I needed to get to the house, get something to eat, and have some more painkiller soon, before my headache came rip-roaring back, and I couldn't think at all.

This was…argh! So. Not. Fair.

I stomped around the clearing some more. Sarah knew I was injured. How dare she leave me out here! And how dare she make the challenge so potentially harmful! Sure, I'd picked the saguaros, but I was betting it wouldn't have mattered what flower I'd picked. Sarah would've found a way to make the challenge suck hard.

I wondered if Meg had done this test yet, and if so, what flower she'd picked. Maybe her test had been different, but I was really hoping it was the same as mine and that she'd picked roses. The thought of the thorns snagging on Meg made me stop stomping. I got a visual of Meg yelling at a rose bush. I knew it wasn't nice of me, but the mental image of Meg, her silk blouse half-untucked, dirty, and wrinkled, her perfect hair sticking up in 80 directions in a snarled mess, well that image made me smile.

Bringing out my mean side helped me to stop feeling sorry for myself and to turn my attention to fixing the mess I was in.

So. Magic. I had to do some magic.

Okay, fine. I just had to experiment a bit till I found something that worked. Kind of like trying different ingredients until I came up with a great new recipe.

I knelt down and touched the ground the way I'd seen Sarah do. I focused on the way the ground felt under my fingers and searched for any kind of weird feeling—some kind of tingling or zinging or something.

I didn't feel anything. Neither did the saguaros, apparently, because they kept on doing their thing.

I tried to concentrate on what I wanted. I visualized a path opening up across the lawn, like the one Sarah had made. Then I tried visualizing the cacti freezing in place. I even tried imagining a glowing line showing me the path through the maze.

Nothing happened.

For the next hour, I ran through every magical word I could remember from *Harry Potter*, every bit of elvish from *Lord of the Rings*, and any kind of spell I could remember Giles or Willow saying on *Buffy the Vampire Slayer*. I even said "Abracadabra."

Still nothing.

By then, my headache had moved from twinging to low-level throbbing. I flopped down on my back on the grass. I felt like Gandalf giving up in disgust in front of the Mines of Moria. But I didn't have Frodo to figure this out for me. I was on my own.

As I lay on the grass, I wondered how long Sarah would leave me out in cactus jail before she'd decided I'd failed. I wouldn't put it past her and Meg to leave me trapped until the whole selection thing was over tomorrow. They'd finally send the saguaros back wherever they came from, revealing my blue corpse, curled into a ball right where I was now, dead of hypothermia. Awesome.

I stared up at the sky. Well, if I had to be stuck in a weirdo magic cactus cell, at least it was a beautiful day for it. My saguaro prison was right at the entrance to the house's clearing, so I was under the canopy of one of the two giant oaks. One of the tree's gnarled roots was poking through the grass near me, and I rested my hand on it. The combination of the strength in the root under my hand and the way the sunlight played with the swaying leaves overhead soothed me.

I sighed. "You're lovely, you know," I told the tree. "Both you and your husband over there. We don't have trees like you back where I grew up." I shot a nervous glance at the saguaros. "Er, not that there's anything wrong with having a bunch of cactus around."

I contemplated the tree overhead. "You guys need names. You may already have names, but these people are kind of idiots, so I'm betting that you don't." I ran my fingers along the root while I thought for a moment. The way the trees were kind of holding hands over the road reminded me of an elderly couple who used to frequent the diner. "I'm gonna call you Libby. And your husband over there? I'm gonna call him Todd."

A branch overhead bobbed in the wind.

I laughed. "If I didn't know better, I'd swear you like your name."

Given the way the branch was waving around, I thought the wind must be starting to blow. Surprisingly, the saguaros were doing something helpful and sheltering me from the brunt of whatever wind was kicking up. But if it got windy enough, I'd start feeling it.

I groaned. Wind would mean the temperature would start dropping soon. Break time over. I needed to think of something else to try.

As I stood up, another gust of wind must've hit the branch, because it bobbed low enough that the very tips of a few leaves tickled my hair.

I laughed and reached up to run my hand through the leaves. "Too bad I'm not a squirrel. I could just run up your branch and be out of here pronto."

There was a tug at the branch, and I let go of the leaves, watching as the branch bobbed back up toward the tree. I returned my gaze to the saguaros, chewing on my lip as I tried to think of a solution.

A rustling sound made me look up again. I gasped and jumped back as Libby bent forward and extended the branch I'd just been touching until it rested in the center of my little clearing.

"Uh," I said, as I stared at the branch. My eyes traveled up to stare at the tree.

Libby had given me a way to climb out. Like a squirrel. Like I'd just said.

Um, was I communicating with a tree?

I didn't think this was what Sarah meant about using magic—I was pretty sure she meant for me to do something with the saguaros.

But I seemed to be talking to a tree, and it was talking back, sort of, which sure wasn't normal—did it count as using magic?

I didn't care. If it got me out of there, I was all for it.

I inched my way forward, careful not to step on any of the leaves or smaller branches while also avoiding the stabby cacti. I found the thickest part of the branch that I could reach, boosted myself up, and threw a leg over the tree limb, preparing to sort of scooch my way upward.

Libby had other plans.

As soon as I was fully astride, she hoisted her branch up and me with it. I squeaked and lunged forward, so I was lying on my stomach along the branch, arms and legs wrapped around it in a desperate hug. When the branch stopped moving, I was hanging far above the saguaros, safely out of their reach.

Chapter Twenty-Six

Adrenaline roared through me. It fixed my headache. But I had to take a few minutes to convince my heart to stop gallivanting around my chest.

Once I felt relatively calm, I pushed myself up to a sitting position and worked on getting my balance. Libby had lent me a thick, sturdy branch so I didn't feel too worried about it breaking. Me falling off of it, well that was another matter. I told myself I just had to be careful and go slow.

I swung a leg over so I was sitting side-saddle and started wriggling and scooting my way down the branch toward the trunk. When I reached the trunk, I wobbled my way to my feet, threw my arms around the trunk, and hugged Libby with all my might.

"Oh thank you!" I said.

When I stopped hugging Libby, I turned around so my back was to her trunk and took a look around. Well, I'd wanted to climb these trees. Looks like I'd gotten what I wished for.

I wasn't at the top of the tree, but I was quite a ways up from the ground. I realized there was no wind. All that branch waving I'd seen must've been Libby, trying to talk with me. How cool was that?

My gaze snagged on the saguaro maze. I frowned. It was even worse than I'd thought. No way I'd ever have made it through there without getting shredded. The saguaros were moving around so much that it looked like they were dancing. Square-dancing saguaros. I shook my head and said to Libby, "Are you seeing this?"

I looked beyond the saguaros to the porch of the house, which was empty. Well, at least they weren't all out there having margaritas, laughing and placing bets on how long it'd take me. So, small mercies.

A flicker of movement caught my eye. I saw Fuzzy hop up on the porch railing. Before I could call out to him, he dug his claws into one of the porch's posts and started shimmying his way upward. I guess the house didn't like Fuzzy's claws, because by the time Fuzzy got to the porch's roof, the house had shoved out a series of little steps for Fuzzy, leading up to the roof.

Once Fuzzy reached the house's roof, he found a flat section and stalked back and forth, eyes trained on the maze.

I was pretty sure he was looking for me. It was bad enough he was on the roof. The last thing I needed was for him to go wandering around the maze looking for me.

I waved and called out, "Fuzzy!" Hopefully, he'd see me, see that I was alright, and go back inside.

He stopped pacing and looked right at me.

I waved again. "It's okay," I called.

He let out a plaintive, pitiful-sounding "Meooooow" to let me know just how much I'd worried him.

Guilt trip achieved. I waved and smiled and used my calm voice when I said, "See, I'm fine, no problems here. Everything's fine. I'll be there soon. Good boy. Stay. Stay, Fuzzy."

I leaned back against Libby and rubbed the frowny spot between my eyebrows. I didn't even want to think about how I was going to get him off the roof. Maybe the house could help me. Of course, the house had let him up there in the first place. I had no idea what the hell the house was thinking. The house and I were gonna have a chat when I got out of this.

Okay, one thing at a time. I had to get over there first.

I figured all I had to do was climb down Libby, circle around the saguaros by walking through the forest, and then go in the back door of the house. No problem, right?

I turned to Libby and looked for a place to step down. Of course, there was a small, dead tree branch that had gotten stuck in the crook of the tree, right where I needed to step, so I tossed it to the ground.

I heard the thud when it hit the dirt. Then I heard something else.

I stopped short and looked down. The damn saguaros were moving over and forming a ring around the bottom of the tree.

Seriously?

I gritted my teeth. Wow, Sarah really didn't want me to pass this test. She'd done something to the saguaros so that they were going to actively mess with me until I figured some way to command them to stop or to make them disappear altogether.

Sarah knew I'd never used magic before, and certainly not on the advanced level she'd displayed. She'd made this test impossibly hard.

I did not have time for this crap. I had a kitten to save.

I looked over at Fuzzy, and my anger turned to horror. He was standing on the lowest edge of the roof, across from the closest cactus, and was glancing between the roof, the saguaros, and the tree limb where I was standing.

I saw him crouch and do a little butt wiggle.

"No! Fuzzy, no. Don't you dare!" I used my stern voice.

He heard me. I saw him pause and twitch his tail at me.

"Stay! Stay! Fuzzy...No!"

The "no" came out as yell as he launched himself off the roof. I could feel my heart lodge in my throat as I watched him. He turned his leap into a sort of glide and landed on the top of the nearest cactus. On one of the enormous flowers, no less.

He looked elegant and unruffled.

I was so scared I wanted to throw up.

What if he'd landed on the thorns?

I didn't have time to contemplate that gruesome image because he launched off his current cactus and landed on a big flower on the next one. He continued to sort of sail from one cactus to the next all the way across the maze.

At some point, I realized I should breathe.

As Fuzzy approached, Libby stretched out a branch for him. On his last jump, he landed on her branch, then climbed his way over to me.

He seated himself in front of me, looking up. "Meow," he yipped at me. He looked extremely proud of himself.

"Fuzzy!" I snatched him up.

"Are you crazy? Argh! Oh my god, are you okay?" I kept on yammering while I checked him over. I checked through his fur. I checked every pad on each paw. Twice. I didn't find a single thorn or scratch. I shook my head in disbelief. He was totally fine.

In fact, I think he was enjoying all my fussing because he was purring like a maniac.

I had tears in my eyes as I clutched him to my chest. It was one thing if I got hurt in all this insanity. But it was in no way okay if Fuzzy was harmed, even a little. He purred while I quivered against Libby's trunk and said a thank you to whomever was acting as Fuzzy's guardian angel.

While I tried to stop shaking, I attempted to process what I'd just seen. My family had taken in a lot of strays. I'd seen cats do some incredible things—jump impressive distances, open and close doors, and climb up super high.

But I was pretty sure that what Fuzzy just did was not typical, even for a cat.

I held him up so I was looking into his eyes. He *looked* like an ordinary kitten. But there was no way I could delude myself into thinking that body gliding across the cacti was normal. Hell, the whole fishing expedition this morning wasn't normal, either.

I tucked him back against my chest. It was becoming obvious to me that, at the very least, the house and Fuzzy seemed to have some kind of communication going because the house seemed to like pleasing Fuzzy. But was the house having some kind of weird effect on him? Could you get dosed with magical energy the way you could get dosed with radiation? If so, maybe it wouldn't be permanent. And at least he wouldn't be here very long. We were leaving on Monday.

My heart clunked at the thought of giving him over to the vet. I nuzzled Fuzzy's fur, letting his purr soothe me. Between leaving Fuzzy and having Dr. Paige poke at my scalp to make sure it was healing, Monday was shaping up to be a suckfest. Not that today had been a picnic. And, of course to get to Monday, I had to get out of this mess first.

I said into Fuzzy's fur, "While I love your company, Fuzzy, that was not a bright move. Now you're stuck up here with me, and I'm fairly confident that no firemen are gonna come and rescue us. You got any ideas on how we're gonna get out of this?"

If he did, he wasn't saying. Instead, Fuzzy got tired of me holding him and started to squirm. I realized I couldn't climb down the tree and hold onto him, so I put him down next to me on the tree limb. He sat and groomed the fur I'd mussed while I tried to plan our escape.

I mentally replayed the way Libby had bent down to scoop me up, trying to figure out how I got her to move and how she might be able to help us now.

"Too bad Libby's branches don't reach all the way to the house. I could just walk above the stupid cacti. Any other thoughts on how we might avoid the saguaros?"

Libby swayed. I gulped, closed my eyes, and clung to her trunk until she was still again.

Fuzzy chirruped at me. I opened my eyes to see him jump to the next tree branch down and to the left.

My heart skipped a beat, and I yelled, "Fuzzy! No! Come on, give me break!" I started clambering after him.

"Stop."

He did not stop.

"First thing when we get out of this, I'm teaching you what that word means. That and 'no.' Just…hold still. I swear I'm stuffing you down the front of my shirt the second I get my hands on you. Stop, dammit."

He waited for me until I got to his branch. The he jumped down and to the left again. He went to the next branch, waited for me to catch up, and then moved on before I could grab him.

If the house was at twelve o'clock, Fuzzy stopped jumping around when he'd positioned himself at nine o'clock. He sat there waiting for me again. This time, when I got to his branch, he walked out along the branch another few feet. This was not good news. I'd been sticking near the trunk and using it for balance.

I didn't want to go out along the branch.

But of course, I would for Fuzzy. And he knew it.

I begged. "Fuzzy, please come back. Please."

He sat on his haunches and stared at me.

"Really? Argh." I inched away from the trunk a little. "How am I supposed to go out there and get you? I need something to hold onto—I don't have claws you know."

A leaf tickled the side of my neck, and I looked to see a branch waving at me from my right. Libby leaned the branch toward me. I reached out, clutched the branch, and used it to help me balance as I walked along the limb I was standing on.

"Thank you, Libby. You're the best tree ever."

Keeping my eyes glued to the branch beneath me so I could keep my footing, I inched my way toward Fuzzy. As soon as I got close, he strutted another foot down the branch, then sat again.

I stopped moving. "Would you quit it? Where do you think you're going? You're going to fall off the end of the—oh."

I'd been so busy looking at my feet that I hadn't looked ahead.

Libby had arranged her limb so that it lined up with a big tree branch from the tree next to us. A nice, thick climbing branch.

My thoughts churned. I played back the last few minutes. I'd said out loud that I wanted a way to walk above the saguaros all the way to the house. Then Libby had swayed. I'd closed my eyes, so I hadn't seen her move.

But Fuzzy had. He'd seen what she'd done and somehow understood.

Score another point for Libby.

I swept my gaze down the edge of the forest. If I could get the other trees to work with me like Libby was doing, I could make my way clockwise around the left side of the house and totally avoid the maze. The trees were really close to the house there and maybe I could get dropped off close enough to the house to make a dash for it.

I looked down at Fuzzy. He had that expression that cats get when they are waiting for you to come to your senses and follow their superior cat logic.

Tail in the air, Fuzzy sauntered the rest of the way down Libby's limb, hopped onto the next tree's waiting branch, and walked all the way across the branch toward the trunk. He turned around so he was facing me, sat down, and meowed at me to hurry up.

"Okay, I get it. I'm coming."

Looking over at Libby's branch that I was clinging to with my hand, I said, "Thank you, Libby. I bet this can't be comfortable for you, holding this position, so I'll get a move on, but, really, thank you." I scurried as quickly as I dared down Libby's branch.

When I got to the part that overlapped with the next tree, I looked at the tree ahead and said, "Er, hey. Wanna help me out?"

Nothing happened.

Something clicked in my brain. Maybe I needed to be touching the tree.

I put one foot on the new tree's branch. "Uh, hi tree. Permission to come aboard?"

The tree swayed a little and scooted its branch closer to Libby. I took that as I yes.

I decided to press my luck. I asked, "May I, uh, have a little help please?" and reached toward the nearest branch overhead. To my delight, the branch bent down. I let go of Libby and, grasping the new branch, I stepped onto the new tree and walked toward Fuzzy.

Fuzzy leapt to another branch before I reached him. I didn't follow him right away. First, I hugged my new tree. "Thank you, tree, for helping me. I'm very grateful for your help. Could you please help me get to the next tree?" While I was talking, I thought about where I wanted to go next.

The new tree shivered a little in response. I gave it a gentle pat, then turned around to look at Libby.

She had resumed standing in her usual pose, limbs arranged

gracefully around her. I waved at her, then I turned back to my new tree.

This time, I looked to see what was happening around me.

I was still separated from the house by the saguaros, who were still waving their arms in the air like they just didn't care. My current tree was bending a branch to line up with the next tree to our left that was big enough to climb. Fuzzy hopped and climbed his way to this new branch bridge, showing me the way to get there without falling and impaling myself on an overeager cactus.

He turned around and yowled at me, trying to get me to follow him.

So that's what I did. I let Fuzzy lead, and I tree-walked my way above and around the saguaros.

Occasionally, I'd knock some debris loose from the tree I was in. Within moments, a few saguaros would surround the trunk of the tree. After the third time it happened, I gave up on the idea of climbing down at some point and decided to try and enjoy the experience. Because there was so much to enjoy.

Since I had to be really careful not to fall, I paid extra attention to the details around me. I was surprised to discover how individual each tree was, as different from one another as people are.

The bark had a wide range of colors. The texture varied, too, from smooth to sandy to bumpy, and everything in between. The bark even had fingerprints of a sort, forming patterns unique to each tree.

The trees dressed in their own particular styles, too. They were garbed in leaves of varying numbers, shapes, and sizes. Some trees had just a small number of strategically placed leaves and showed a lot of limb while others were covered from neck to toe. The leaves had just started to change color so, in addition to the variations in shades of green, a whole host of other colors gave each tree its own fashion palette. It reminded me of kids playing dress up, layering whatever clothes and colors made them happy.

Oh, and when the trees moved! It was like watching tree

yoga. Each tree would gracefully bend and flex, then hold the position until I'd moved on.

I got a sort of rhythm going. I'd ask for permission, then I'd cross into a tree and make my way toward the trunk, where I'd hug each tree, thank it, and ask for its help in moving on. To my surprise and delight, none of them even hesitated. I didn't even get a sense that it was any trouble for them. On the contrary, they seemed like a bunch of kids playing.

Next, I'd follow Fuzzy as he showed me the easiest way to get to the next crossing point. Once I crossed over, the tree I was leaving would resume its original position.

As I crossed from tree to tree, I grew more confident of my balance. Pretty soon, I was startled to find I was grinning from ear to ear. I still wasn't sold on my having any innate talents—this could all be part of the house's influence somehow. But the evidence indicated that I was communicating with trees. With trees! Not to mention that I was following a very unusual kitten.

I giggled. I couldn't help it. I felt like I should be carrying a glittery magic wand and wearing a gauzy fairy princess dress that billowed in the breeze along with the leaves. Despite my inner skeptic, I admitted that the experience truly was magical.

By the time we'd circled around the side of the house, it was late afternoon. Fuzzy stopped as we reached a tree that sort of lined up with my bedroom window.

I looked across to the tree that was next to the house, the one that used to block my window. It was really young. Too young to support my weight.

Hm. The tree I was currently in was the closest forest tree to the house. So continuing to climb around the treetops wasn't going to help me.

Maybe it was safe to climb down?

I looked below me. So far, the saguaros hadn't spread past the front edge of the house. I could try making a dash for it.

Fuzzy had other ideas. He walked out on a branch that grew in the direction of the house.

"Fuzzy, the tree can't bend that far. There's no way the tree can stretch from here to the house. Come back here. We've got to climb down now."

Fuzzy looked at me and then continued another foot down the branch.

"Meow," he called.

I looked from the branch to the house. Despite Fuzzy's optimism, I didn't see any way that the tree could reach the house, no matter how much it bent. And I didn't want it to overextend and hurt itself, or worse, topple over completely.

I stared at the house for a minute.

The tree couldn't reach the house, but…

Hmm.

I had an idea. I hesitated, but then I figured, why not try.

"Uh, House? Hi? Can you hear me?" I cleared my throat and tried again. "Hey uh, House? Any chance you could extend me a, uh, I don't know, something like a balcony…from under my window…you know, so we can hop off this branch onto it?"

The house was silent. It didn't creak. It didn't groan. It didn't even sigh in exasperation. It just sat there. Still. Like a normal house.

I looked at Fuzzy. "Maybe I have to be inside the house for it to hear me?"

A sudden cracking sound startled me so much that I nearly fell off the branch. I had a small heart attack until I realized the crack wasn't the branch breaking. It came from the house.

I flailed about for a few moments struggling to regain my balance. When I had myself under control, I looked at the house.

I stood riveted.

Parallel to the ground, the floor of a balcony flowed out of the house's side. When the balcony approached our branch, the rate of growth slowed, and then stopped altogether when our branch dangled over it. Beautiful posts in the shape of small trees popped up along each side of the balcony floor. The branches at the tops of the tree-shaped posts wove together to form a railing that lined either side of the balcony.

"Wow." The way things were going, I was going to have to come up with some better words to express my awe, but really, "Wow" pretty much covered it.

Fuzzy hurried down the tree branch and leapt gracefully onto the balcony. He ran across it and in through the window, which opened for him as he approached.

I scrambled after him, albeit much less gracefully. I went as far as I could down the branch, then sort of jumped/fell onto the balcony below, landing with a thump that reverberated through the floor. Fortunately it held.

I looked back to see the tree resuming its natural position. I waved a thanks, then hurried after Fuzzy into my room.

When I climbed in the window, I was greeted by the sound of crunching. I popped my head into the bathroom to see Fuzzy chowing down on his kitty kibble.

A wave of exhaustion washed over me. The room blurred, and I got really dizzy. I stumbled over to the bed and the last thing I remembered was pitching forward before I blacked out.

Chapter Twenty-Seven

I dreamed that I was surrounded by sagauros, and they were taking turns pummeling me in the head with their thorny arms. Each time they hit me, I'd get a sharp spike of pain in my head, followed by a deep aching.

I forced myself awake from the dream. When I opened my eyes, the saguaros were gone. The headache wasn't. My head hurt so bad I thought I was gonna barf.

"She's awake." I turned my head to see Wil and Nor. That small movement made my vision blur and my stomach lurch.

I swallowed hard.

"Is your head killing you?" Nor looked concerned.

"Mmrf."

"Don't try to move too much, Finn." She moved closer to the bed. She was holding a cup with a straw sticking out of it. "Drink this. It'll taste really sweet, but try to drink as much as you can."

I got my head about a half inch off the pillow, drank what I could, and lay back.

"Give it a few minutes. The sugar will help with the energy drain. There's pain killer in there, too, to help with the headache."

I knew that I had questions, but before I could concentrate enough to ask them, I fell asleep again.

Something cold and wet on my lips woke me up again.

I opened my eyes to find Fuzzy's nose nudging my mouth.

"Ugh. Blech. Thppt," I said, spitting and sputtering as I turned my head. "Okay, okay. I'm awake." I did a quick systems check. My headache had toned its assault down from murder to mere breaking and entering—it was still there, but it wasn't trying to kill me anymore. When I'd turned my head, my vision didn't blur. I wasn't nauseous. I decided to try sitting up.

Fuzzy and I were alone in my room. It was full dark outside. A look at my watch told me that it was 9 o'clock, so I'd been out at least three hours.

My door opened, and Nor came in carrying Fuzzy's bottle.

She closed the door behind her and came right over to me, a look of relief on her face. "Oh hey, you're up again. How are you feeling?"

"Better."

She scooped up Fuzzy and sat with him in the chair. She said, "I'll take care of him. You drink the rest of that shake."

I sat up, and leaned back against the headboard and sipped at the shake. "Where's Wil?"

"He's keeping the rest of them at bay until you have a chance to recover."

"Recover? Nor, what happened? I remember getting back here to my room and then I just—"

"Passed out?" Nor ran a hand through her hair. "The short version is that you used too much magic too quickly and suffered a severe backlash."

Wil came into the room, shut the door behind him, and stopped short. The same look of relief I'd seen on Nor's face washed over his. "Oh thank God, it worked."

Nor said, "Wil came up with that concoction."

Wil said, "Do you even remember waking up and drinking it?"

I nodded.

He huffed out a breath. "Okay good. That's really good." He rubbed his nose under his glasses.

"Why are you guys so worried?" I asked, finishing the shake and putting the cup on the table next to me.

Nor's lips compressed into a thin line. "What Sarah just pulled? It's—"

Wil said, "Irresponsible? Dangerous? How about we go

with inexcusable." He started pacing.

"I was going to say unconscionable, but all of those are also true."

Wil wrung his hands as he paced. He said, "Finn, there's so much you need to learn…magic, it comes with a lot of rules and procedures. You don't know *any* of them. Hell, you didn't even know magic existed till Sarah told you."

"I was trying to ease into telling you when Doug interrupted us earlier," Nor said.

Wil nodded. "So what the fuck Sarah thought she was doing, giving you a test that would require the level of magic it did…" He threw up his hands in the air.

I looked at Nor. "The professor just said 'fuck.' This is really bad, isn't it?"

Nor nodded.

"How bad?"

Wil said, "Well, let's see. If you use magic, and you don't know what you're doing, all sorts of delightful things can happen. There's the minor stuff," he started ticking them off on his fingers, "exhaustion, headaches, nose bleeds, passing out. Then there's the really fun stuff like, say, nerve and brain damage. It goes downhill from there." Wil stopped pacing and sat, pinching his nose again. "It's going to be chaos when the council hears about this."

Nor raised an eyebrow, "Good thing you've positioned yourself to charge in and help them settle things down."

Wil smiled. It reminded me of Nor's shark smile. "Hey, it's not my fault I have firsthand knowledge of this weekend's events. And that I'm a walking encyclopedia about the history of the house. And that I could be invaluable in helping them sort through this. I just happened to be in the right place at the right time."

I couldn't give a flying fig newton about the council or Wil's political maneuvering right now. I was too busy being terrified.

Nor noticed. She leaned forward and took my hand. "As your lawyer, I took the liberty of acting on your behalf while you were unconscious. I informed Sarah—in front of Meg and

Doug—that her actions were dangerous enough to skirt the line of committing an assault. Sarah knows that I can't prove intent, so an assault charge wouldn't stick, but just bringing a case against her would seriously damage her standing with the council—it could even be a cause for having her removed. I informed all of them that they were to leave you alone until you gave me instructions to allow them access. So, for the moment, you're safe here. There's no need to worry."

Wil's evil grin reappeared as he looked at Nor. "Speaking of positioning, you just stood up to the head of the council. I give it a week, tops, before that makes the rounds. If you weren't already partner, I'd say you just earned yourself a ticket to the top. But I'm sure you have something in mind that you can parlay all this into."

Nor gave him a knowing smirk but didn't say anything.

I stifled a sigh. The more I learned about Foster politics, the more I wished my mom had taken my dad's last name when they married. Okay, Nor and Wil were acting in their own interests. They'd been upfront about that, and I really couldn't expect any less, given that we'd known each other for like five minutes. But, their personal strategizing aside, they'd still both helped save my bacon in their own ways.

"Thanks," I said. "Thank you both, for looking out for me."

Wil gave me a half-smile. "See I told you I'd come in handy. That concoction I gave you for your magic hangover? That's only written down in one place that I know of."

"How'd you even remember it?" I asked.

Wil tapped his temple and smiled. "Photographic memory."

Fuzzy hopped up next to me, and began kneading me and purring. He seemed happy, too, that Wil's hangover cure had worked.

I asked, "Speaking of hangovers, how's the house? It must've taken a lot of magic for the house to do what it did. Are you okay house?"

The house was silent.

Nor said, "We think it's sleeping."

Wil said, "According to the records, any time the house

gets too low on energy, it needs to, well, basically to take a nap to recharge. It's kind of like a milder version of what happened to you. Given the house hasn't been at full strength for a while, and it doesn't have a full housekeeper at the moment, my best guess is that it just overdid it a bit." Wil scrubbed his hand across his face. "Another reason the council is going to have a fit—the house overtaxed itself because of what Sarah did. I don't *think* there'll be any permanent damage. Hopefully, it'll wake up soon."

My eyes teared up. I didn't mean to hurt the house when I asked for help. Wil didn't know that the house was actually even more drained than he thought because it'd helped me last night and throughout the test.

Nor saw my eyes welling and patted my leg, "Hey, it's okay. The house is a creature of magic and, unlike you, knows what it's doing. I'm sure it's fine. It just needed a break."

"Are you sure?"

"Pretty sure. We were watching that whole balcony thing at the end there. That trick with the gorgeous banisters weaving together like that? Yeah, the house could've put up plain posts. Or none at all. Instead, it did those intricate woven-branch posts. The house knew we were watching, so I'm fairly certain that, in addition to paying homage to what you had just accomplished, the house was also giving Sarah the finger. If the house was able to exude that much attitude, then I'm sure it's fine. It's just tired, is all."

"Ok." I hoped when it woke up that it didn't feel as crappy as I was feeling. Physically, the nausea had passed, but I was achy and disoriented. Emotionally…I was a jumble. Confused and terrified on one side, while on the other I was a wiggling puppy of delight because holy cow, magic!

But mostly, listening to how silent the house was, I felt like I'd done something bad and had screwed everything up. I really, really wanted out before something even worse happened. "If the house is asleep, does that mean it's not working?"

Nor shook her head. "The house's protection magic remains in place, whether it's awake or not. It just can't communicate while it's sleeping. So, no, you can't leave."

I blushed. That's exactly what I'd been thinking. My urge to get the hell out of there was nearly overwhelming. Sarah had said I couldn't opt out of tests until the final one. Since this latest one could've turned my brain to mush, I really didn't want to do any more.

I looked at Nor and Wil. They'd been super helpful and were doing the best they could. But bottom line was that they'd both acted in ways that would bring them the most benefit. I suddenly felt desperate for some outside perspective.

I asked, "We can't go out. But people can come in, right? I was able to come back to the property after Sarah put the 'you shall not pass' ban in place, right?"

Wil looked confused. "Right. Why?"

"I need another favor," I said. My stomach rumbled. "But first I need to eat."

Chapter Twenty-Eight

Wil volunteered to go to the kitchen. While he was gone, I told Nor what else I needed. She looked thoughtful but nodded and didn't argue with me.

I'd no sooner put my phone back in my purse than Wil returned with a tray set for two.

"I didn't want them to know you were awake yet, so I told them I was getting sustenance for me and Nor while we maintained our vigil." He handed me the tray. "Try to eat as much as you can."

No problem there. I went from hungry to ravenous with my first bite of food. Halfway through my second sandwich, I looked up to find them smiling. "Ish thish normal?" I said around a mouthful of food.

Nor said, "Being that hungry after such a big magic drain? Yup."

Wil added, "It's a good sign, actually."

I ate everything in sight in under 10 minutes. I woofed it down so fast that even Fuzzy was looking impressed.

Wiping my mouth, I asked, "Do we need to feed the house?"

Wil said, "You can't. Only the housekeeper knows the house's precise needs, including what, if anything, it needs to eat. And only the housekeeper can attend to them."

Well that was a stupid system. I said, "Meg had better be doing that part of her job better than she's been doing everything else."

I set the tray aside and tried standing up. I had the kind of pulling exhaustion you feel when you climb out of a pool. Not only are all your muscles tired from swimming, but you also go from the water buoying you to having to fight gravity all by yourself.

"How do you feel?" asked Nor.

"Tired, but I'm not dizzy." I took a couple of experimental steps. "Yeah, I think I'm fine." I looked at Wil. "Thanks again for the miracle shake."

"No problem. Just glad it worked."

I walked around the room, making sure I had my sea legs. I had a ghost of a headache, and I felt like I could sleep for a year, but I could function. "Wil, are they all in the kitchen?"

"Meg and Sarah and her assistants were in the dining room, but they converged on the kitchen as soon as I set foot in there. I assume they went back to the dining room when I left. I don't know where Doug is. Why?"

"I need to go outside."

Wil asked, "Why?"

I said, "The less you know the better. Look, you're still playing both sides of the fence right now, which is fine since you've been up front about it, but it means things could get sticky for you. If Sarah asks you where I am, you'll have to tell her. Then you'll feel bad about ratting me out. It's not fair to put you in that position. Don't worry, I'm not going far."

I looked at Nor. "I'm thinking the back door is out. That leaves the front door, which actually works better for me, anyway. Do you think you guys can provide me enough cover to slip out?"

Wil looked confused but he said, "The bodyguards, er, assistants are going to be the biggest problem."

"They go where Sarah goes. I bet if both you and I go to the kitchen, they'll all cram in there with us," said Nor. Her smile had an edge to it when she said, "I'll tell them that it's taking so long for you to wake up that I want to talk compensation and possible medical care options. I can't wait to see what Sarah has to say, particularly now that she's had time to stew since I dropped that assault threat."

Nor stood up and grabbed the tray with the empty dishes.

"If anyone tries to duck out and come check on you, I'll head them off—tell them you're still sleeping and not to be disturbed. Maybe throw around a few more threats. I'm sure I can come up with something."

Wil followed, a rueful smile in place as he said, "This ought to be interesting."

I looked over at Fuzzy, who was sitting on the bed watching us intently. "I'm just going to duck outside. Are you going to stay put if I leave you?" I took a couple of steps toward the door. Fuzzy ran across the bed, leapt down to the floor, and was snaking around my ankles before I could put my hand on the doorknob. I looked down at him. "I take it you're coming with me." I picked him up, and he started purring. "Okay, pal. I'm just stepping out for a minute, so you can come too. But I'm carrying you."

"What's outside?" asked Wil.

"You're just going to have to trust me," I said, as I snagged my purse and slung the strap diagonally across my chest.

I could see the wheels spinning in Wil's head, but he said, "No problem."

Nor said, "Don't worry, we've got this. Take whatever time you need." She turned to Wil. "I'm ready for some fun, how about you?" and headed for the door.

Wearing a wry smile and shaking his head, Wil followed her.

Nor and Wil went down the back stairs, making a lot of noise as they went. While they telegraphed their positions, I scurried quietly toward the front stairs, Fuzzy clutched in my arms.

I tuned into the house as I went. I was startled to realize I could actually tell it was asleep. I could *feel* it. That stopped me, a bolt of alarm running through me. Was that a good thing or a bad thing, being able to tell the house was sleeping?

I sighed and kept going. Even if I hadn't been able to feel it, I'd have been able to hear it. The floorboards were behaving like normal floorboards for once: neither oddly loud nor suddenly silent. They just creaked like old wood always creaks.

I crept down the front stairs, hugging the wall, hoping

the shadows would hide me. I could hear Nor and Wil in the kitchen. I scooted down a few more stairs. If Tango and Cash were still by the dining room, they'd see me when I reached the next step. If they were by the kitchen, I'd be out of sight until I reached the door.

I tiptoed down another step and looked. The dining room doorway was empty. I ghosted down the remaining stairs. Yup, they were all by the kitchen. Nor and Wil must really be working it because both Tango and Cash were blocking the doorway, facing inside.

Heart thumping, I darted across the foyer, opened the front door, and slipped outside. I closed the door behind me as quickly and softly as I could. I didn't hear any footsteps following, but I wasn't going to wait around to make sure.

I dashed across the front porch, down the steps, and to the left. Babs was waiting for me where I'd left her. I unlocked the front door and collapsed into the driver seat, shutting and locking the door behind me.

I put Fuzzy on my lap and leaned my forehead against the steering wheel. "Oh Babs." All the confusion and misery of the past two days poured out of me with those two words.

I sat like that for a few minutes. Just the short jaunt to the car had eaten all my energy. I considered climbing into the backseat and taking nap, but a knock on the passenger side window jerked me upright and sent my heart racing again.

I leaned over and unlocked the door.

The door swung open, and Zo peered in at me.

I waved her inside with a, "Thanks for coming."

She climbed in and shut the door.

Fuzzy stood up, yawned, and climbed out of my lap and into the backseat, where he curled up and zonked out. Guess he thought I'd be fine on my own with Zo.

Zo surveyed the interior of the car. Her gaze caught on the assortment of beads and doodads hanging from the rearview mirror. She gave it a little nod and said, "Your mother's work?"

I looked at the beads. "Yeah."

Zo studied them with a look of approval. Then she turned

to me. She looked me over, frowned, then said, "Tell me."

So I did. Maybe I should have played coy like I did in the diner, but I was past playing games. Zo had helped me this morning, and of the people I'd met today, I felt oddly safe with her. Plus, she seemed to know what was going on. Once I finished filling her in, maybe she'd be willing to share more.

I told her everything. I got to the part where I learned that there's magic, and she just nodded.

"You knew? About magic?" I asked.

"Of course."

"And Lou's sound thingy, that wasn't his phone was it—it was some kind of magic?"

"He uses his phone as a sort of…quick activation trigger, but yes, it was magic."

"And Gram's weather machine is not a machine? It's also magic?"

She nodded.

"Thanks for the heads up," I muttered.

At Zo's impassive look, I just sighed and continued with my story.

When I got to the part about Fuzzy hopscotching across the cacti, she gave him a long look. He lifted his head, blinked at her, and then went back to sleep.

When I told her about blacking out, her eyes snapped back to me. She nodded when I told her about the drink Wil had given me and sat quietly while I told her what Nor and Wil had said.

When I wound down, we sat for a moment in the dark.

Zo broke the silence. "Why did you call me here?"

In a small, hesitant voice I said, "Wil. He dropped the F-bomb. And Nor, she was physically guarding me…I…"

"Say it."

I swallowed. "Could I have, you know, died?"

She didn't hesitate. "Yes."

Somehow knowing that for sure helped steady me. I blew out a breath. "Okay. This is so not what I signed up for."

Zo shrugged. "Life is like that."

I barked out a laugh. I wasn't going to get a bunch of warm feelies from Zo, but I could sure count on her to cut the crap and give it to me straight. Which was what I'd been betting on when I texted her.

I gave her a lopsided grin. "You guys said this selection had gone pear-shaped. And to send up a flare if things got interesting. Trying to whack the candidates...does that qualify as 'interesting' enough?"

"It's certainly unusual. Unheard of, actually. A certain amount of competitive gamesmanship is expected. But this is... different."

That just confirmed what Wil had told me. Wil, who prided himself on knowing more about the Fosters than even the council. Yet here was Zo, a non-council member—hell, a non-Foster—with the same knowledge. Curiouser and curiouser. I looked at her, considering. This was not the time for it, but I really wanted to ponder the mystery of Zo at some point.

She said, "So what is it you think I can do for you?"

"Well, I'd prefer not to die. Or have my brain ooze out my ears. Or be horribly maimed—you get the picture. If you could help me avoid that, then that'd be good."

"I thought you had Nor and Wil for that."

"I think..." I searched for the right words, "...I think that they're doing the best they know how. Obviously they have their own agendas, but they are trying to help me, and I think they'll continue to do so as long as it's in their best interests." I thought for a moment and then added, "They're both cutthroat, but not in an actually-going-to-murder-someone way. I don't think either of them would be party to a murder or even be able to keep quiet about it. But that said, they seem to be very limited in what they can do. I need to think outside the box here. You are, literally, outside. I'm hoping you can give me some options. And fast."

"Hmm. And what makes you think I'm willing to help you?"

"I don't know. I just do."

Zo stared out the window. She seemed to be having some kind of an internal debate so, for once, I kept my mouth shut.

After a while, she shook her head, sighed, and turned to face me, "Do you still want to leave?"

It was my turn to look out the window. After a long moment I said, "I don't know." Zo waited while I sorted through my thoughts. "I've barely had time to process this," I said, "so if this doesn't make any sense, just bear with me." I shook my head and said, "As much as it pains me, and it does seriously pain me to say this, but Sarah was," I made a gagging noise, "right. In one respect. This is too much of an amazing opportunity to just blithely dismiss it out of hand. I at least need to consider taking the position."

"So things have changed."

"Not necessarily. I need time to think! And yeah, yeah, yeah, I know—there's no time. But I mean, come on. Give me a minute here. I just found out there's magic in the world. Freaking magic! And then there's the house...I really *like* the house. Not just what it can do. But it's, well, it's...nice. And funny. And creative—you should have seen that crazy balcony. And it's got some snark, which is a whole other level of awesome. Forget Sarah and the Fosters, I at the very least owe it to the house to consider this seriously."

"Ah. Then there's something you should know."

A cold pit lodged in my stomach at her tone. "What do you mean?"

"Didn't you wonder if there was a catch to all this?"

"Well, actually, yes. The position sounds too good to be true. The amount of money they're throwing at it alone is enough to make me wonder what they're hiding. Why?"

She didn't say anything.

"Zo...?"

"I'm thinking."

Zo sighed and stared out the window. I could see the wheels turning. The longer she was quiet, the tighter the knot in my stomach got.

"You said Sarah took you on a tour of the house and property?"

"Yes."

"I take it she left out the graveyard."

I twisted to face her. "I'm sorry, the what?"

"I'll take that as a yes."

"Do I want to know why there's a graveyard on the property?"

Zo gave me a smile. It wasn't a nice smile. "Probably not. But I'm going to tell you anyway."

When she spoke next, it was in a soft, emotionless voice that nonetheless seemed to take up all the space in the car. "The job with the house is a lifetime appointment."

"A lifetime appointment...that's a big commitment."

"Once you are housekeeper, you can never leave."

"What do you mean? People leave lifetime appointments all the time—things come up—family issues, health issues, etc. I mean, look at the Supreme Court...or the Pope, even."

Zo caught my gaze and held it. The way she was look-ing at me made me go very still. "It's not just that you can't leave the job. If only it were that easy. No, you can't leave the property. Ever."

Chapter Twenty-Nine

"I don't understand."

Zo turned away from me to look out the window again. She had the look people get when they're peering into the past. "It's the bargain your ancestor made to keep the house away from the others. One Foster housekeeper, blood-bonded to the house, keeps the house in Foster possession. For the spell to remain intact, the housekeeper must always be on the property."

"That's…that's…" I didn't know what to say. My brain had locked up again. Every time I thought I'd gotten over the last hurdle in this wacky weekend, something else came up.

"So you see, you have a much bigger decision to make than you thought."

"Were they going to tell me?" I shrieked it loud enough that I made myself flinch.

Zo just gave me another look. "I feel fairly certain that Nor and Wil were going to tell you, but they got waylaid by your test—"

"—and then I was unconscious, so they haven't had the chance."

Zo nodded. "Whether they told you or not, the Fosters are required to disclose the terms of the bargain before the final bond. It's part of the process."

My brain kicked back into gear. "But I wouldn't have had time to process and make an informed decision if they sprung it on me in the last minute. It might have been enough to make me back down. Who am I kidding, I'd totally have said no. In fact, now that I'm thinking about it, 'no' seems like the obvious answer."

I fidgeted, touching things inside Babs, jingling the rear-view mirror doodads for comfort.

"Perhaps. But if the answer were obvious, I doubt you'd be this uncomfortable."

Mostly my brain was hollering, "Oh hell no!" and was ready to put Babs in gear and drive to the edge of the driveway and stay there until they let us out.

But a very quiet voice underneath was wondering what a life here, as the housekeeper, might be like.

I'd have to give up everything. School, travel, the ocean. And I'd be trapped. Isolated in the middle of nowhere with no way out. It was like the desert all over again. Just with rain and more trees.

I felt sick. Then I felt sicker when with a dawning horror, my brain circled back to earlier in the conversation. "And the graveyard?" I asked.

Zo said, "The housekeeper lives here until they die. Then they are buried here."

"Ewwwwwww! Even when you're married, it's only supposed to be till death do you part. Not 'and then we keep your corpse here for all eternity so we can keep taking advantage of you and sucking any last nutrients out of your carcass.'"

Zo shrugged. "It's good for the soil. Possibly good for the house, too."

"Wow. I mean, wow. That's really special. I mean, they should put that on a brochure. The Fosters: We take giving it your all to a whole new level." I leaned forward and thumped my head against the steering wheel a few times before resting my face on the wheel. "Hi, welcome to your new job. Here's where you'll live. Oh and here's where we'll bury you. Have fun!"

"Are you done?"

"I doubt it." I sat up again. "This is god awful. I mean this whole thing. I keep saying it can't get worse—"

"That's part of your problem. You need to stop saying that."

"—and then it does." I twisted in my seat to look at her again. "Speaking of which, okay what else?"

"What do you mean?"

"What else is going to come along and catch me off guard? Are there zombies rattling around here? I've got a graveyard to contend with now, so are we talking undead, too?"

"Don't be ridiculous, Finn."

"Ridiculous? Seriously? I'm the one who's ridiculous? This whole situation is ridiculous! Magic houses, magic people, magic trees…oh for Pete's sake." I was shrieking again so I clamped my mouth shut and thunked my head back down on the steering wheel.

"*Now* are you done?"

"I think so."

"Good because I need you to listen."

I sat back in my seat and leaned my head against the window, looking out at the dark forest as she talked. Looming over us, the trees could've felt creepy or threatening, but after today, I thought of them as my friends and was comforted by their presences.

Except now I was wondering where the damn graveyard was.

Zo said, "You have some big decisions to make."

"No duh."

She raised an eyebrow at me.

"Sorry. I don't mean to be disrespectful. I'm really very grateful for any help you can give me. Please continue."

"Decisions."

I sighed. "Can't you just get me out of here?"

"Let's say I could. Is that what you want?"

I leaned my head against the window. After a moment I said, "I don't know."

"As I see it, that's your biggest problem."

"Really."

"Yes."

"Not Sarah and Meg and whoever else is possibly trying to kill me?"

"No."

"Huh." I slumped into my seat and closed my eyes. The weariness in my voice surprised me when I said, "I just don't know. I used to know. Up until this afternoon I was absolutely sure of what I was doing. Then that whole thing happened with the cacti and the trees, not to mention Fuzzy and the house. And now I have doubts. Stupid saguaros.

"And now, I can add that whole 'you can't leave' bombshell. To stay here, commit my whole life to this place...that's...well, it's asking a lot. Maybe too much. I need time to really think this through. And I can't think straight here!"

"Well, you're going to have to."

There wasn't anything I could say to that. She was right.

We sat in silence a moment, then she asked, "Why did you ask to meet me here?"

I wrinkled my forehead. "I told you, I can't leave the property, and I'm hoping you can give me some help getting through the last day."

"Yes, yes. But why did you ask me to meet you *here*?" She gestured at the car around us.

"You mean in Babs?" I thought about it for a moment then decided to tell her the truth. Blushing a little, I said, "I know it sounds stupid, but I feel safe here."

Zo gave me a gentle smile. "Not stupid at all. You see these?" She pointed to the plethora of thingamabobs dangling from the rearview mirror. "They're charms. Your mother charmed Babs."

She pulled a vial out of her purse, dumped some powder in her hand, whispered something, and then blew the powder into the air. It sparkled as it flew around the car. The powder seemed to dissolve. A moment later, the inside of the car started lighting up. Symbols appeared, glowing like they were under a black light. They were everywhere. On the dashboard, the ceiling, the steering wheel. On the windshield and every window. It was like having my own little starry night sky twinkling at me inside of Babs.

I was whipping my head around, mouth gaping open, trying to take them all in. But they faded from sight almost instantly.

"Don't look so dismayed. They're still there. You just can't see them."

I closed my mouth and stared at Zo. "What are they?"

"Your mother warded this car six ways from Sunday. It was originally hers?"

I nodded. "Until she died. When I was old enough to drive, I inherited it."

"Ah. Well, she made it as safe as extra-humanly possible."

"Too bad she wasn't driving it when she was killed."

Zo frowned and looked thoughtful, but didn't comment.

"How come the spells still work?"

Zo said, "Some spells expire quickly, others last longer. Do you have any kind of yearly maintenance you do for the car?"

I nodded. "Once a year, I use a special wax to keep the paint from peeling. We used to sing this silly little song while we waxed, so I keep up the tradition, and holy crap, that's not just a song, it's some kind of spell." I groaned. "And let me guess: the wax is 'special' alright, just not in the way I thought."

Zo nodded. "It's likely a way to charge the magic in the car."

I looked her over. "So I see you do magic, too."

Zo gave me a look that said "well duh." She leaned forward and scrutinized the dangling charms, staring hard but not touching any of them. After few minutes, she pointed and said, "That one. Grab that one."

I untangled the string of beads she pointed to and pulled it off the mirror. This string had black, purple, and turquoise beads.

Zo said, "You can take the string with you without weakening the overall protection on the car. Keep it on you at all times for the rest of the weekend."

I asked, "What does the charm do?"

"For all intents and purposes, it's a protection charm. But it's a powerful one, specifically keyed to your immediate family. It will limit any damage you might incur."

"And keep me from dying."

"One hopes."

I looked at her, my uncertainty showing.

Zo said, "You asked me for options. I'm giving you one."

"Okay…is this all you can do?"

Zo rolled her eyes. "Of course not. But in this particular

situation, it's the best option for you. Given your lack of experience, if you attempt to do any magic, you're likely to do more harm than good at this point. Your mother, on the other hand," she swept a hand around the car, "knew what she was doing. You trust your mother?"

"Of course!"

"Then let her help you."

Invoking my dead mother was a sure way to get me to comply, and I had a feeling Zo knew it. I said, "Okay." I tucked the string of beads in my pocket.

"No, put them in your bra. Next to your heart."

"Why?"

"Because I said so."

Well, I'd asked for her help. I did as she said. I yanked my necklace out of the way and tucked the beads in the best I could. I asked, "Do I need to take my necklace off?"

"No. Keep it on."

I nodded and tucked the necklace back in my shirt.

I looked at all the other charms hanging from the mirror. "Hey, if it's so safe in here, can I just stay in here until Monday? I'd have to go back inside to grab my and Fuzzy's stuff. But right now, I'm scared enough that I'm willing to pee in a bottle for a day if that's what it takes."

"That was more information than I needed."

"Well? Would I be safe in here?"

"You might be…Do you really want to give up your chance to make a choice for yourself and hide instead?"

I felt queasy. "No," I said, while I looked down and toed the floor mat.

Zo was quiet for a long moment. "This is about choices. Yours and the house's. The position of housekeeper is truly a great honor. There's nothing and nowhere else on the planet quite like this place. The housekeeper wields a tremendous amount of power—magical and political."

"But?"

"No prize this big comes without a hefty price."

Zo opened the door and climbed out of Babs, saying, "Keep

the beads with you. Think about the information I gave you. Take what help you can from Nor and Wil. And talk to the house. That should see you through to Monday."

She turned to close the door, and as she stood framed in the doorway I had a sudden thought, "Hey, do you know if the house has a name, and what it is?" I don't know why I asked, but I suddenly felt like Zo would know.

Zo gave me another of her long looks and said, "The fact that you even thought to ask that question—that, in a nutshell, is why you need to seriously consider being the housekeeper."

Chapter Thirty

I watched Zo disappear into the trees. It occurred to me that her house was too far away for her to have walked here so quickly, and I hadn't seen or heard her drive up. Huh.

Wondering about Zo only distracted me for a minute. Then our conversation sank in, and I slumped my head back onto the headrest.

"What am I going to do?" I said to the ceiling. I realized I had a death grip on the steering wheel. I choked out a laugh. An apt metaphor: white-knuckling the wheel but going absolutely nowhere.

Fuzzy climbed out of the backseat and curled up in my lap, purring softly.

"Thanks," I said, concentrating on the feel of his soft fur under my fingers until I could take a deep breath again.

If I wanted the job, I had to stay here. Forever.

Just the thought sent my heart racing, my stomach clenching, and my foot edging toward the gas pedal.

If only it were that easy.

Okay, pros and cons. I could do a list of pros and cons.

I looked down. Well, if I stayed here, I could keep Fuzzy. That was a huge pro.

My gaze shifted over to the house. Pro. Like the biggest pro of all time, but not for the reasons these people thought. I didn't give a soggy hairball about all their power and politics. I'd found my own version of a mermaid, right here on dry land. Imagine what I could do with that! There was so much to study, I couldn't begin to wrap my brain around it. I could study the house's history, habits, and personality. Then there was language development—just how far did its communication skills extend? And I couldn't even begin to conceive how the magic angle would play into my daily existence with the house.

Which led to the overwhelming cons: giving up my plans and getting stuck here for the rest of my life.

I had to spend another few minutes taking deep, slow breaths and petting Fuzzy before I could return to that thought.

I forced myself to think it through. If I took the job, I'd have a guaranteed home for the rest of my life. And certainly money wouldn't be a problem. With the salary Sarah had mentioned, I'd probably have trouble spending it all. Those were pros.

But I just couldn't see it. I'd spent all this time cooped up in our tiny diner, watching travelers come and go, hanging on every word they said about the places they had gone. I was so tired of my same four walls that places like El Paso and Victorville seemed exotic to me. Now I was on the eve of finally achieving my jailbreak, and the universe was throwing this wrench at me?

I said out loud, "Dick move universe. Like orphaning me and burning down the diner weren't bad enough, now you're going to throw this shit at me. You suck. This is old news, granted. But still. You. Suck." I gave the universe the finger for added emphasis.

Alright, what else was on the con list? I looked at the house, saw the door open, watched Tango and Cash exit, and sighed.

Another huge con: my extended family. Well, fine, Nor and Wil seemed okay. But if the rest of the council was like Sarah, Meg, and Doug, then I was not going to enjoy dealing with them. Worse, my contact would be strictly limited to Fosters—not a good thing.

As Tango and Cash approached my window, I realized with a sinking feeling that my con list was definitely outweighing my pro list.

They'd taken off their jackets, and I could see that both of them were armed. I wondered what had been happening inside that they'd just tossed the whole assistants pretense out the window.

I didn't want to contemplate what it said about the way my day was going that I didn't freak out when I saw the guns. Sure, they were holstered, and it's not like the guys were waving them at me. Still, I should have been alarmed. Instead, my prevailing feeling was "Told you so."

Well if they were going for the full-on, merc-looking body-guard thing, I couldn't give them action-hero names like Tango and Cash. Looking at the two of them, new names for them clicked in my head.

By the time they got to my window I was smiling. Tango reached me first and knocked on my window. Cash, long blond hair blowing in the breeze, took up position behind Cash and slightly to the left.

At the rap on my window, I rolled it down an inch. "Yes?"

"What are you doing out here?"

"Teaching my kitten how to drive."

He looked at Fuzzy in my lap, sighed, and tried again. "Seriously, why are you out here?"

"I fail to see how that's any business of yours, Lars."

"Lars? I thought I was Heimdahl."

I shook my head.

"Okay, I'll bite. If I'm Lars now, then who's he?" Lars jerked a thumb behind him.

I looked behind Lars and my grin spread. "The Real Girl."

Lars just raised an eyebrow, but the Real Girl put both hands on his hips. "How come he gets to be Lars?"

"Have you seen your hair?" I asked, just as the Real Girl did a hair toss.

Lars looked over his shoulder at the Real Girl and shrugged. "She's got a point." Lars looked back at me, "You want to come on out of there?"

"Not really."

"How about you do it anyway."

I thought about testing Babs's defensive capabilities, but decided I couldn't take the risk of something harming her. I was still planning on driving out of here in another day, and I needed her in one piece.

I sighed and rolled the window back up. Clutching Fuzzy to my chest, I climbed out, gave Babs a pat on the roof, and followed the men back toward the house. But I took my sweet time, forcing both men to slow to a snail's pace.

"I don't suppose you have any interest in learning our actual names?" the Real Girl said.

"What fun is that? Your name's going to be something totally normal, like Kevin."

Lars snorted and I looked over in time to see the Real Girl doing an eye roll.

"What?" I asked. "Oh no, your name's not actually Kevin is it?"

Lars was failing to suppress a smile.

The Real Girl said, "No."

"Oh phew."

"But my snake's is."

I stopped short. Fuzzy and I looked at him. "You have a snake named Kevin?"

"Yeah."

I shook my head. "Of course you do." I started walking again. "Well, I'm glad I didn't go with any *Conan the Barbarian* names as an option. If I'd have named you after that snake guy Thulsa Doom, it'd have been a little too on the nose."

The Real Girl perked up. "Thulsa Doom. Now *that's* a good name."

"Not gonna happen," I said.

I reached the porch and stepped up on the first stair. The house let out a loud squeak. I dashed up the remaining steps and gave the porch post a huge, one-armed hug. "You're okay! Oh thank whatever kinds of gods magical houses believe in! I'm so glad you're okay!"

I stood clutching the post with one arm, Fuzzy in the other, bouncing on my toes a bit. The porch flooring made happy, grunting sounds under my feet.

Lars and the Real Girl stood at the foot of the steps, stone-faced. Well, they worked for Sarah, so they probably weren't excited to see me buddying up to the house. And they were going to report everything I was doing to Sarah, so I whispered to the house, "We'll talk later," and let go of the post.

As I walked across the porch to the front door, I heard the guys coming up the steps behind me. Every time they took a step, the stairs made a fart sound. It was like they were walking on whoopie cushions. I was snickering when I walked in the front door.

Lars and the Real Girl intercepted me as I stepped inside.

"In here," Lars said. He gestured me into the sitting room on the left. The Real Girl slipped around us to stand so that he was blocking me from going either up the stairs or down the hall.

I opened the door and found Nor and Wil hovering near the window.

When I stepped into the room, Lars shut the door behind me.

I stared at the closed door, opened it, and found Lars had taken up position outside the door, blocking us from leaving. I shut the door again.

Turning to face Nor and Wil, I said, "Hi guys."

"How are you feeling?" asked Nor.

At the same time, Wil asked, "What happened? What did they say?"

"Okay, I think, and not much," I said, as I walked over to a couch and flopped down. I put Fuzzy on the floor, and he immediately began exploring the room.

"How come we're in here?" I asked as Nor and Wil seated themselves. Nor took the armchair, and Wil took the couch across from me.

Nor said, "Sarah sequestered us in here. While we were talking with her in the kitchen, she somehow signaled Doug to sneak around us and go check your room. He came back and reported you weren't there, and we wouldn't tell her where you'd gone, so she stuck us in here while they located you."

Wil said, "What were you doing outside?"

"Sitting in my car, until Lars and the Real Girl came and got me." Well, that was the partial truth.

Nor laughed. "Lars and the Real Girl? Tell me the Real Girl is the one with the hair."

I grinned and nodded.

"Oh, that's perfect."

Wil just shook his head.

Nor said, "I don't know how much time we've got, so we need to tell you some stuff, fast."

Wil leaned forward, elbows on his knees, hands clasped. His face looked drawn as he said, "Sarah moved up the next round of the test." He glanced at Nor, then back at me. "We haven't been able to figure out a way to force her to give you tonight to rest. It's normal to do the last test on Sunday morning."

"How come you look like you swallowed an eel?"

"Uh, given how drained you were after the last test—"

"Wil's worried—we're both worried—about you using any magic so soon after a burnout."

Wil rubbed his nose under his glasses. "It's just not done. I don't know what she's thinking."

"Do you know what the test is?"

They both shook their heads, and Wil said, "The whole process is supposed to be super secret. But enough people make it through the first rounds of tests that, over the years, people have talked. Very few people make it to the third test, by the way."

"Lucky me. I feel so privileged."

Wil said, "And almost no one makes it to the final test. Given how few people have taken it—and that nearly all of them became the housekeeper—they've been able to keep the details of that test under wraps."

"Well given how fun the last test was, that sounds super peachy."

"There's more," said Nor. "In case you make it through the last test, it's crucial that you know the, uh, fine print involved in being housekeeper before you make your final decision."

"I'm listening."

Nor said, "The housekeeper is a lifetime position."

"Okay."

Wil said, "I don't think you understand. The housekeeper

does a bonding ritual with the house. Once you're bonded, it's for life."

I grimaced. "Okay. So it's not like I delay school, work here for a year, and then leave."

"No," said Wil.

"What if I go through with it, and then I change my mind someday, and I just say 'screw it' and leave?"

"No one's ever done it, but the common consensus is you'd die."

Before I had a chance to start to process that little nugget, Nor said, "Moreover—"

I said, "Really? 'Leave and you die' wasn't enough? Now you're going to hit me with 'moreover'? Because you know nothing good ever follows when a lawyer says 'moreover.'"

Nor gave me a tight smile, "Finn, try and take this seriously. If you take the position—"

"The and-we-are-so-not-kidding-about-this *lifetime* position," I said.

She nodded, "Yes the lifetime position—that even I couldn't get you out of, by the way—there's another major caveat. You also can't leave the property. Ever."

Well, I knew that from Zo. But now that I was with actual Fosters, maybe I could get some details. "Just to clarify, the housekeeper can't leave the house or can't leave the property?"

Wil said, "The property. Which is huge, so it's not as confining as it sounds."

"Uh huh." I thought for a minute. "What about groceries? Medical care? What if Fuzzy needs a vet?"

Wil asked, "Are you considering taking the job, then?"

I said, "Hell if I know. But before I do another damn thing, I want all the cards on the table. No more of this stumbling around crap."

Wil said, "Well, everything you could possibly need is provided by the Fosters. And, of course, there's the Internet—"

"I'll have access to the Internet?"

Wil said, "The housekeeper always has the latest technology. So, you'd have full cable and Internet, etc., along with whatever new gadgets come down the pike."

I didn't even have cable or reliable Internet when I lived in the desert, so that would be a welcome change. I said, "Back up a minute. Talk to me about the whole 'provided by the Fosters' thing. You guys said only Fosters are allowed in the house. Is that a hard and fast rule?"

Nor said, "Yes."

Wil didn't say anything, and he was looking at the floor.

Nor fixed him with a hard stare. "Wil?"

"Um." Wil hopped up and started pacing.

"Wil…" said Nor. The look she was giving him would have made me pace, too.

Wil lowered his voice, "Look, this can't leave the room. And if I divulge this, you're both going to owe me one. A big one."

Nor stared at him, assessing, then crossed her arms and said, "I'm good for it."

Technically, I was a homeless, one-suitcase-owning, college-bound orphan. I had no idea what kind of big one of anything I could deliver. But at this point, the more information I had, the better, so I said, "Sure."

"I may have gotten a look at some notes about the circumstances surrounding the original spell."

Nor said, "Private, classified *council* notes?"

Wil ignored her. "The point is that the central component of the spell is the part about the Foster bonding with the house and staying on the premises. The primary purpose of the housekeeper is to keep the spell intact so the house remains in Foster possession. There is nothing about only Fosters being allowed in the actual house—it doesn't matter with the housekeeper here."

To me, this just seemed like more of the bullshit I'd been dealing with since I got here. But this must've been truly stunning news because Nor dropped her lawyer face and looked shocked. Like open-mouthed, wide-eyed shocked.

I rubbed my eyes and tried to focus. "So, all this time, the Fosters have been isolating the house and the housekeeper because they're paranoid. Terrific. Did anyone ask the house how it felt about only ever seeing the Fosters?"

They both looked blank.

I shook my head at them and sighed. "Jeez, you guys. Okay, let me ask you this. Since the Fosters have spent all these years alone with the house, what's its name?" I held up my hand. "I know, I'm a jerk for not thinking to ask sooner. In my defense, I've been a little bit overwhelmed with all this…well, everything. Still, it's inexcusable. And obviously, you can't go around just calling it 'the house' all the time. So…?"

Wil clasped his hands in front of him and didn't meet my eyes, "It does have a name. Did have a name. It was…lost."

"Whaddya mean it was lost?"

Nor said, "That's professor code for 'We totally forgot it.'"

I just blinked at them for a minute. "You *forgot* it."

Wil pushed his glasses up his nose and said, "Not me, personally, but our family. Yes. A long time ago, in fact. It's so thoroughly lost that even I haven't been able to track it down." He started pacing again.

Now I was the one staring at him with my mouth open. "That's just…" I sputtered and threw up my hands. "The house has been helping the Fosters for, like, ever. You guys keep telling me how it's such a big deal and so unique, and it's got all this extra special magic. And they forgot its name? The least they can do is give the house the courtesy of referring to it by name. What is wrong with these people!" I thunked my head against the back of the couch and took a few deep breaths until I was sure I could talk without yelling. Staring at the ceiling, I said, "So, let me get this straight. The Fosters lost the house's name. But then no one bothered to ever give it a new one? Or at least a nickname?"

Wil sat down. "The convention for as far back as I've been able to research has been to simply refer to the house as, well, the house. To be honest, I don't think anyone but the housekeeper really talks with the house, so it hasn't been an issue."

I said, "So, to sum up: The Fosters bonded with the house so they could have the house and its special magic all to themselves. Then, they totally isolated the house, basically to make extra triple double sure that nobody else gets to play with the house, too. As a result, most of the time, the only contact the house has is with the housekeeper."

"Yes."

"The housekeeper who is the only one who ever talks to it."

"Yes."

"And who doesn't even know its name."

"Yes."

I felt a little sick. "And that doesn't strike you as wrong? Or cruel?"

Obviously it didn't because Wil gave me a blank look and said, "Uh…"

"You said the house has been getting weaker for some time now?"

"Yes."

"Did anyone think that it might be because the house was being mistreated, and it was tired and lonely?" Nor and Wil traded looks. I grimaced, "Don't answer that. Of course they didn't."

I didn't have Wil's background in the Fosters, but from what I'd learned so far, I was thinking they were horrible caretakers and very undeserving of the house, bond or no bond.

I lay down on the couch and stroked the floor with one hand. "I'm so sorry, buddy," I said.

Chapter Thirty-One

I'd apparently rendered Nor and Wil speechless, because they didn't say anything after that. We all sort of spaced out for a few minutes, each lost in our own thoughts. Then we went to our corners and did our own thing.

Nor and Wil each wound up doing stuff on their phones. I was still feeling like my limbs each weighed an extra 50 pounds, so I stayed lying down on the sofa, idly tracing the wood grain on the floor. Fuzzy hopped up and curled himself into a ball next to me. I'd just started to doze off when the door opened.

Lars loomed in the doorway and said, "Let's go."

"Lars, you do not have the authority to order us around," said Nor, continuing to tap away on her phone.

"It's not an order. It's a request."

Nor continued to tap away. "And if we refuse?"

Lars said, "Do you really want to go down that road?"

Nor looked up. "So it is an order then." But she didn't get up. Instead she looked over at me. "Finn, do you feel up to following Lars?"

I eyeballed Lars. "While the idea of making him carry me has some merits, I suppose I can drag myself off the couch. I need a bathroom break anyway."

Nor looked at Wil. "Wil, are you in agreement that we should go?"

"Sure." Wil stood up.

Lars said, "Great. Now can we get moving?"

Nor remained seated, attention back on her phone. "Not until you tell us where we're going and for what purpose."

I smirked. I couldn't help it. I know it's not wise to poke the big guy with the gun, but it felt so good to have some backup.

Lars crossed his arms. I wondered if he did it just to make his muscles bulge to try and intimidate Nor.

If so, he failed.

He said, "We're just going down the hallway to the kitchen. Sarah wants to see you."

"And she can't come in here because…?"

Lars said, "Don't know. Don't care. Let's go." Nor still didn't move, so he said, "Now."

Nor sighed. She took her time standing up, did a long, slow stretch, then sauntered over to me rather than walking toward Lars.

I'd hiked myself into a sitting position. Nor offered me her hand and helped pull me up off the couch.

I turned around and scooped up Fuzzy, then followed Wil across the room toward Lars. Nor took up the rear. A glance back at her made me grin. She looked like a warrior going into battle—head held high, shoulders squared, and a look that said she was looking forward to kicking someone's ass.

"Glad you're on my side," I whispered.

One corner of her mouth quirked up and she shot me a wink, then resumed her badassness as we passed by Lars.

The Real Girl was in the hallway. He walked in front of us, while Lars followed behind Nor. I felt like we were prisoners on the march.

They stopped almost immediately in front of the bathroom under the stairs. It'd have gone much quicker if they'd let us dash to our rooms, but they didn't. They made us stand there and take turns like we were school kids on a field trip.

No one spoke. The longer we stood there, the more awkward and weird it felt.

When we'd all had a turn, Lars and the Real Girl walked us the remaining few feet toward the kitchen.

But then they stopped us again, outside the kitchen door.

"Why are we stopping here?" Wil asked.

"Just wait," said the Real Girl. He looked at Lars, who

nodded, and then the Real Girl went to the back door, opened it, said, "We're ready," and closed it again.

Ready for what? I wondered.

I glanced behind me and stiffened. We were standing near the weird door—the one I'd seen all the people clustered around last night when the house hid me.

The back door opened and Sarah, Meg, and Doug strolled into the house. Sarah took up position in the kitchen doorway with Meg and Doug in the kitchen behind her. Lars moved down the hallway, effectively blocking us from moving toward the front of the house. The Real Girl stood so he was blocking access to the back door and mudroom.

The message was clear. We weren't going anywhere until they allowed us to.

Nor, Wil, and I bunched up in front of Sarah.

Wil said, "Sarah, Meg, Doug," nodding to each of them. He looked at Sarah and asked, "What's happening?"

Sarah said, "Final test."

Nor shouldered her way to the front, placing herself between me and Sarah. To my surprise, Wil shifted so he was standing shoulder-to-shoulder with her. I realized I was grinning.

I glanced at Lars. He was eying Nor and Wil, assessing whether he needed to intervene. I caught his eye, and though I knew I shouldn't, I stuck my tongue out at him.

I nearly bit my tongue when he stuck his tongue out at me in return. He yanked it back in so quickly I wondered if I imagined it. I glanced around me but no one else seemed to have noticed.

My attention switched to Nor, when she started talking.

"Not acceptable. The final test is always held on a Sunday. I checked."

Sarah said, "If you'll check your watch, you'll see it's after midnight. That makes it Sunday."

Nor looked unperturbed. "Forcing a participant to undergo a test while recovering from a big magic expenditure is also a violation of family law, as well as of the rules of the selection."

Sarah's smile widened. I did my best not to cringe. She spread her arms, palms up, "I'm not forcing anyone to do anything. Finn is free to drop out and refuse the final test."

Nor looked like she was about to make another rebuttal, but Sarah held up a hand and said, "Meg took her final test at 12:01, while you were waiting in the other room. Once the final round of testing has begun, it must continue until all candidates have had a chance to complete it…or forfeit."

Sarah looked toward me, "I told you that we were both bound by the rules of selection once you began testing. I also told you that when you got to the final round, you would have a choice whether to continue or not. So here we are, it's the last test. Choose. Continue or decline, it's totally up to you."

Nor looked at Wil. He nodded slowly, "Those are the rules, yes."

Nor said, "A moment," and walked back to me and nudged me away from them. We couldn't really go very far, so we wound up clustered against the far wall. Right against the damn door.

I eyeballed it. It didn't look like anything special. It just looked like a door.

Nor lowered her voice and said, "I'm out of options. If you want to go through with whatever this test is, then you need to know that you do so at significant risk to your health. I have no idea how much magic she'll try to make you expend, but given the previous test, I have very real concerns. If you want to back out now, there's no harm, no foul."

"Is there any way to find out what the stupid test is actually going to be?"

"No. If there was, Wil would have known."

I sighed. I listened to the house around me. I could feel it waiting. Well, hell. I couldn't let it down. I owed it to at least *try* to get to the end. If I passed this final test, then I could worry about whether I actually wanted to be housekeeper or not. I realized I at least wanted the option to make the decision myself, rather than forfeiting now. And to be honest, a part of me just wanted to give Sarah, Meg, and Doug a hard time. I'd about had it with all three of them.

Nor nodded. "You don't need to say it. I can see it on your face. Okay, you should know that I've put some protections in place to try to minimize whatever fallout occurs."

I nodded and looked at Sarah. Out loud I said, "Okay, let's do it," but my tone was "Bring it on, bitch." I glanced to the right, and I could've sworn that that was admiration I saw flashing across the Real Girl's face.

Wil looked equal parts alarmed, curious, and cautious. Meg looked smug. Doug had a calculating look. And Sarah, well Sarah looked like I had just handed her a victory.

I started to walk over to Sarah, but Nor stepped in front of me again. She said to Sarah, "You should be aware that while we were sequestered, I left word with my office that Finn has sustained a significant magic drain that resulted in unconsciousness and that she has possibly suffered damages that we haven't had a chance to ascertain due to the conditions of the selection process. However, should Finn incur any further harm as part of the process, which, as you know is explicitly against family policy, then my firm is under orders to a) distribute the *detailed* account I sent them of the proceedings thus far to every member of the council and other parties whom I've selected, and b) they are to initiate an investigation with the intent of securing damages and/or filing charges for assault."

Meg looked at Doug. He shrugged. She looked at Sarah, who was having a staring contest with Nor. Sarah broke first.

"I see. You made good use of the time you spent in the sitting room." She turned to Wil. "And you, Wil? I'm assuming you've also made provisions?"

Wil was all innocence when he said, "Of course, I've followed council policy and the protocol you put in place. All my notes, which I've been updating regularly on my phone, upload to the cloud. And, per policy, I have a program in place set to download them to various council members in the event of my disappearance or demise."

She looked at Lars. "You were right. I should have taken away their phones." She sighed. "Well, what's done is done." She looked at Nor. "What do you want?"

"We want to act as witnesses. Whatever you have planned next, if Finn decides to go through with it, Wil and I will act as witnesses."

I was feeling pretty good until Sarah smiled. "No problem," she said. "In fact, I'll even let you both participate."

Meg jostled Sarah, saying, "Sarah—"

Sarah put up an arm and blocked Meg from pushing forward. "Stay where you are. It will be fine." She looked at Nor. "Agreed?"

Nor turned to Wil. "Wil?"

"I'm in. But it's up to Finn."

Nor walked the few steps to me and said, "Finn?"

I nodded. "I'm in, too."

She looked at me intently and then gave me a tight smile and a nod. She turned to Sarah and said, "Agreed."

Sarah said, "Excellent. Let's proceed."

Behind her, Meg looked like she was mentally rubbing her hands together. Doug looked satisfied. Did they really want me to fail that badly?

I stepped forward with Nor and said, "Alrighty then. Let's get this party started. What's the test?"

Sarah gave me a smile. "It's simple really. I just want you to open that door." She pointed to the door behind me.

If I hadn't already known that there was something unusual about the door, the look of joy on Meg's face would've tipped me off.

Nor murmured, "Are you all right?"

I said, "I need a minute with Nor," and grabbed her arm.

We scooted as far away from them as we could get. I said, "I'm really sorry, I should have told you before. The door. It's not what you think."

Nor said, "Short version?"

I said, "I saw something. The door…it's…something's up."

I could see the wheels turning in Nor's head, "So this is rigged."

I said, "Yeah, I think so."

Nor said, "I figured it must be, that's why I hedged your bets the best I could." She looked grim, "Look, bottom line…if you refuse, you're out. If you stay, it could get ugly. Your choice.

We'll back you either way."

I rubbed my eyes. Well, I couldn't abandon the house now. I turned to Sarah. "How far do I have to open it?"

Sarah gave me a magnanimous smile. "Just a crack is fine."

I looked back at Nor and shrugged. "Yeah okay, let's do it."

I knew that even a crack was going to be a stretch. It'd taken three people to open the door a crack the other night. I looked at Meg. I knew she couldn't have gotten the door open on her own, so either she'd somehow cheated on her test, or Sarah had asked her to do something different. Then I had a really bad thought. What if Sarah hadn't made her take another test at all? What if she was counting on me to fail so that Meg was the only candidate left standing?

Sarah studied Nor and me and said, "You look a little worried. Really, there's no reason to be. Here, I'll show you." She turned to Wil. "Wil, would you please open the door?"

Wil froze. Slowly, he nodded. "Sure."

He walked to the door. He sized it up. Then, he put his hand on the knob.

Beside me, Nor went still.

You could've heard a mouse sneeze, it was so quiet in the hall.

Wil turned the knob and opened the door.

I whooshed out the breath that I'd been holding. The door opened easily. It didn't even squeak.

I peeked past Wil. Inside the door, there was a really dark closet. It extended to the right, under the stairs. Other than being in dire need of a lightbulb, there didn't seem to be anything wrong with it.

I wasn't buying it. I'd seen the whole shenanigans with the damn door the other night.

I shot a glance at Wil. Nothing seemed to be tickling his Spidey sense. On the contrary, from the set of his shoulders, I could tell that he was relieved.

Not Nor, though. A glance at her told me she was still on alert.

Sarah said, "Wil, if you'd shut the door please? Thank you. Now you try, Nor."

Nor frowned, but she stepped forward, and without a pause opened the door.

Same thing as Wil. It opened easily, and we got a glance of the closet. Nor closed the door. When she turned back toward me, a deep frown was marring her face.

She pinned me with a look and said, "I don't think this is a good idea."

I couldn't tell her what I knew, so I just said, "Me neither."

Sarah said, "Nonsense, Nor. You're overreacting. You and Wil have just proved that this test is perfectly safe. Now Finn, if you'd take your turn?"

I did a quick survey. Meg looked tense, while Doug looked vaguely bored. Wil was trying hard to contain his curiosity and failing. Nor's frown had deepened.

Lars and the Real Girl looked like dogs on point.

And then there was Sarah. Sarah brought me up short. She looked polite, but underneath that face there was something hungry swimming, and there was no doubt in my mind that she thought I was going to make a nice snack.

Well, hell. I couldn't make a fuss without revealing what I'd seen, and I had a very strong feeling that I shouldn't play that card.

I handed Fuzzy to Nor. Remembering how he'd behaved the last time he'd seen the door open, I said, "Hold on to him tight."

I waited for Nor's nod, and then I walked over and faced off with the door.

I reached out a finger and gave the door a quick little poke, jerking my hand away as soon as I'd touched the door. Nothing happened.

Behind me, Meg snickered.

I ignored her. I inched toward the door until I could put my hand flat on it. I tuned out everyone else around me as best I could and concentrated on the door.

At first, I didn't feel anything. Then I felt a ghost of a hum, so faint I wasn't sure if I was imagining it.

I turned the door knob, and it turned easily. Too easily. I frowned and let go. Something wasn't right. I was missing something.

I bowed my head. I probably looked like I was praying because more snickering ensued.

Under my breath, I called out to the house, barely moving my lips or making a sound as I said, "Okay house. Please help me open the door in whatever way is the right way to win this test."

The house didn't make a sound, but I still felt it watching us tensely.

Well, there was nothing for it. House help or no house help, I had to get going. I put my hand back on the knob and tried to turn it.

This time, it was a lot harder. My hand ached as I forced the knob to turn. "C'mon," I coaxed under my breath.

Finally, the knob turned all the way to the left. I pulled.

The door didn't budge. It sat there glaring at me, refusing to move. I let go.

Sarah broke the silence. "You get three tries…that was one."

I glared at her. If I'd known I only got three tries, I'd have put a lot more effort into the first one.

I tried again. Using both hands, I turned the knob and tugged hard.

The door let out a little "Mmph" but didn't budge. I did, though. My sweaty hands slipped off the knob, and I stumbled back.

Last try.

Wiping my hands on my pants, I stepped forward again and planted my feet. I grabbed the knob with both hands and turned. Before I started pulling, I reached out to the house, focusing on that tense awareness around me, and muttered, "If you want to, if you can…help me. Please."

Then I pulled.

At first, nothing happened.

But I kept pulling.

I felt a slight give to the door. It didn't really move so much as shift, just a tiny, tiny bit.

But it was enough to have me redouble my efforts and keep on pulling.

Underneath my feet, the floor seemed to soften a bit, allowing my feet to dig in and giving me better traction as I pulled on the door.

I leaned back all the way, using all my body weight to pull on the door.

Under my breath, through my gritted teeth, I chanted "Open, open, open," as I pictured the door opening.

I felt a low vibration, barely a hum, working its way up through the floor into my feet, a gentle tingle tickling the bottom of my toes.

I kept pulling, but concentrated on that tingle, imagined pulling on it, too. I felt the tingle move up my body, until I felt like I was passing through a cloud of feathers.

The feeling made me a little light-headed, but it wasn't unpleasant.

I kept my hands on the knob and pulled harder on both the knob and the tingling feeling.

The tingle switched to a low buzz that traveled up my feet and through me until my whole body was vibrating. Nausea swept through me. I swallowed hard and clung to the door.

I visualized the door swinging open as I whispered, "Please, please open for me," and threw every ounce of strength I had into pulling on the damn door knob. At the same time, I opened myself up to the buzz I was feeling.

Suddenly, the buzz changed to a zapping feeling. There was a crackling in the air. Spots were dancing before my eyes, but I held on.

I heard Fuzzy yowl.

I started swaying. I thought I smelled salt air, but then there was a wet slooshy sensation in my nose, and blood began pouring from it.

"Finn, let go!" Nor shouted.

At least I think that's what she said. It was hard to hear over the rushing sound in my ears.

The door jerked open a foot.

The world around me went black around the edges. As I fell to the floor, I heard myself say, "Is that a tree?"

Chapter Thirty-Two

When I woke up, I was lying on my side on a hard cot in a small, dark room. I could see a toilet and a sink gleaming a few feet away.

My hands were zip-tied in front of me, but I didn't care at the moment. I was too busy panting from the pain knifing through my skull. Tears leaked from my eyes. I realized I was going to throw up and made it to the small toilet next to the cot just in time.

I spent a good while on the floor praying to the porcelain gods. When I looked down, I gagged and nearly vomited again. The chest section of my shirt was soaked in blood. Had I gotten cut? It was hard to think straight, but I forced myself to concentrate.

Last thing I remembered, I was trying to open the door. Oh yeah, blood had been gushing out of my nose. My vision had gone all fuzzy. I thought I might've also been hallucinating a bit because I could swear I'd seen a tree in the darkness on the other side of the door.

Hallucinations and bloody noses aside, the main point was that I'd opened the door. And that meant I'd passed the test.

Maybe that was why my hands were tied?

I realized that there was a warm spot on my chest. It took me a minute to figure out that the charm Zo had insisted I carry felt hot. I guessed that meant it was doing its thing, and I wasn't actually going to die, as much as I felt like it.

When I was pretty sure I wasn't going to hurl anymore, I stumbled to my feet and used the sink to rinse my mouth and drink some water. When I splashed water on my face, it came away clear. Someone must've had cleaned all the blood off my face while I was unconscious. There was no mirror to check, but I was pretty sure that even without a bloody face, I looked awful.

Lurching over to the cot, I sat down on the edge and peered at my surroundings.

The only light came from a night-light. The room was even smaller than I'd thought, the darkness having made the walls look farther away than they actually were. The room contained the cot, toilet, and sink, and nothing else.

A cell. I was in a cell.

I made my way over to the door and tried the handle. As expected, it was locked.

"Hello?" My voice came out weak and raspy, so I cleared my throat and tried again. "Hello?"

No answer.

I trudged back to the cot and slumped down on it. As I started to lose consciousness again, I had a last fleeting thought.

Nothing in the room was made of wood.

When I woke up again, Sarah was sitting on a chair halfway between the cot and the door.

She straightened and said, "Ah. There you are." She turned her head toward the door and called in a louder voice, "She's awake again. Ten minutes."

I wasn't sure I wanted to know what was going to happen in ten minutes, but I was pretty sure I shouldn't be lying down for it. I hoisted myself to a sitting position and shifted so I was sitting on the side of the cot, facing Sarah.

I rested my elbows on my knees and put my head in my hands. I swallowed hard and stifled a moan.

"How are you feeling?" Sarah asked.

Despite my efforts to sound badass, my voice wobbled when I said, "Pretty sure I'm not gonna barf again, but I can't make any promises."

Sarah leaned sideways and retrieved a tall to-go cup. She walked over, handed it to me, then resumed her seat, saying,

"Drink that."

I peered at it. "What is it?"

"Wil sent it." Sarah shrugged. "I have no idea what's in there, but he was quite insistent we give it to you when you woke up."

I took a tentative sip and recognized the concoction Wil had given me the last time I'd passed out. He must've really upped the dose of whatever was in there, or my mom's charm was helping it work better, because just the one sip helped right away. I drank some more.

Sarah watched me closely, saying, "You realize you scared the hell out of us."

"Sorry?"

Sarah sighed and said, "What is *wrong* with you?"

"You want a list? It's kind of long."

"Finn, you could have killed yourself and for what? To get a shot at a job you don't even want. Why didn't you just stop before you went too far?" She scanned me from head to toe and shook her head. "It's a damn miracle you're even sitting up already. I don't know how you're doing as well as you are."

I did. I could feel the heat from my mom's charm radiating against my skin.

I said, "I'm not in the house anymore am I."

"No."

"Where am I?"

"In a council facility."

"Why?"

"To help you heal."

My headache had receded to a throb, but even though I could think more clearly, I couldn't figure out what was happening. "Why am I tied up?"

Sarah sighed. "It was necessary."

"Why?"

"It's for your own protection. Since you don't have control over your magic yet, we're trying to help. We didn't want you sleep-casting while you were unconscious—any use of magic when you were that wiped out would have been...dire. You probably don't know this, but it's much harder to cast spells without the use of your hands. Plus, for added protection, the zip-tie is charmed to suppress magic. And just in case you somehow managed to overcome that, this room is sufficiently isolated to keep you from harming anyone else. If it helps, you won't be here very long."

I couldn't decide if that was supposed to sound ominous or not.

"I passed the test, didn't I?"

Sarah crossed her arms. I took that as a yes.

"I didn't even want to take your stupid tests. You basically forced me. And now that I passed them, you're punishing me?"

"You're not being punished. And as hard as this may be for you to grasp right now, I'm actually trying to help you. I didn't want to make you take the tests any more than you wanted to take them. But like everyone else in our family, I'm bound by the rules governing the selection process. Once you showed up in time, you had to be included."

Sarah clasped her hands tightly. "I tried, Finn, I really tried to keep you out of it as much as possible. This whole time, I've been trying to protect you. We only realized someone had invited you when you RSVP'd. From that moment on, I've been trying to spare you from learning about any of this so you could go on with your life."

"Spare me how?"

"Well, at first, by delaying you on your trip, so that the whole selection process would be over before you even got here."

"Delaying me?"

Sarah brushed at her skirt. "I sent you directions that, had you followed them, would have mired you in travel woes and kept you from arriving on time. But you didn't follow them. So, I was forced to improvise to place some other...obstacles... in your way."

"Obstacles?" My mind raced. I'd thought my journey to the house had seemed like an adventure because I'd never taken a road trip before. But, on reflection, that really was a lot of weird to encounter in one trek. My mind seized on the first wacky thing that had happened. "The sinkhole?"

Sarah nodded, then sighed. "That was a little overzealous in my opinion."

"Overzealous? I could have died."

Sarah waved a hand in a "what can you do" gesture. "This is what happens when one is forced to outsource."

I said slowly, "The tornado—all the crazy weather. That moose. That was all you?"

"It's a mark of how much I wanted to protect you that I even used freelancers from other families. All so you wouldn't have to deal with any of this."

"Wow." Her idea of protecting me was to put life-threatening obstacles in my way to slow me down? I couldn't begin to find the words to respond.

She must've misinterpreted my "wow" and thought I was impressed with her, because she looked pleased. She continued, "Once it was clear you'd be here on time, I instructed Meg to limit what she told you, so we could still shield you, and you'd go on your way unaffected. But you kept questioning things."

She was right about that. I'd pushed for more information.

She continued, "And when it came time to test you, even then I did what I could to make sure that you could still go off to school." Sarah huffed, frustration written all over her face. "I threw tests at you that even a top-level magic user would have trouble passing, but you blew through them all. And there's no way you should have been able to open that door on your own."

She eyed me. "How'd you do it? How'd you cheat? Some kind of amplification spell painted somewhere on your body?"

"Is that how Meg did it?" I asked. Sarah looked down, refusing to meet my eyes. "Or did you just say she did, and she didn't actually open the door at all." I knew I was right when she flinched.

Slowly, it dawned on me. "That's why I'm not in the house. I beat Meg." I swallowed. "Oh no. I'm the top candidate for housekeeper now, aren't I?"

Sarah shook her head and sighed again. "Finn, you may have passed the tests, but that doesn't mean you are in any way suited to be the housekeeper."

She stood up and began stalking around the room. The cell was so small that she couldn't go very far, and she wound up pacing back and forth like a caged animal. "I honestly don't know how to make you understand things in the time we've got."

She stopped behind the chair, gripping the back with both hands. "I've spent my life dedicated to the protection and well-being of our family. Literally, my entire life. I was raised with a singular focus on leading the Foster clan."

"Bully for you," I said.

She ignored me. "And I can tell you that it is honestly not in anyone's best interests—yours or our family's—for you to be housekeeper. Since it's my job to make sure we all thrive—including you, Finn—I'd like to work something out that would be for the good of everyone."

"Okay…"

"You don't really want to be stuck in that house for the rest of your life, do you? You've already spent so much time trapped in that diner in the middle of nowhere—do you really want to spend your entire life confined like that?"

She nodded when I flinched.

Sitting down again, she said, "And being housekeeper is far more confining than being a waitress in that diner. You'll be isolated. No people coming and going all day. Just you and the house, most days."

"At least I'll have cable," I said. But it sounded flat, even to my ears.

Sarah said, "You'll have cable and much more at that school you're planning on attending. I had my people check it out. It's really a top-notch institution."

"Try not to sound so surprised."

She smiled, "You're reading me wrong. Not surprised, delighted. Genuinely glad that you have a real shot at making something special out of your life. As I said, Finn, I like it when my people succeed. If you're doing well, then I'm doing well."

I'd have crossed my arms but my hands were tied. "Do you have a point?"

"My point," she said, leaning forward, "is that I'm not your enemy. In fact, I'm your best ally. I'm the person who can make good things happen for you. Particularly now that you've been brought fully into the family fold. I can think of a number of magical opportunities that would really benefit from the type of education you're about to get."

Carrot. She was offering me a carrot. A vague carrot, but I was betting I could ask for just about anything, and I'd get it. But carrots weren't free. "What do you want in return?" I asked.

"Nothing. You don't have to do anything. Just stay here and rest. Think about what you want to do next and how I might aid in your future endeavors."

"So stay here while you make Meg the housekeeper, is what you're saying." Like I had a choice. I rubbed at my head with my hands. "Tell me this, why do you want Meg to be housekeeper so bad?"

Sarah looked like she was debating with herself. Then she smoothed her hair as she said, "Meg and I share a similar vision for the future of this family, and with her in charge of the house, I can make some much needed changes. I'm sure you'll be relieved to hear that I'm going to see what I can do about changing the rules governing the selection process. I need to be more…forward-thinking, more proactive in shaping how this family moves through the 21st century."

"Like forming an alliance with another family?"

Sarah looked startled. "How did you…?" She grimaced. "I told Gram the hailstorm was a mistake. If you can figure out he's been traipsing around the property, then it's possible others will make the connection."

A little click went off in my brain. "He's Not-Doug."

Sarah looked at me like I was nuts. "Of course he's not." She peered at me for a moment before saying, "You should drink some more of that stuff."

I slugged back some more of Wil's concoction. The more I drank, the cooler the charm became, so I must be edging back from the danger zone.

Sarah crossed her legs and folded her hands in her lap.

"Finn, I'm here to make you a deal."

"And if I say no you'll what…leave me here to rot?"

"You haven't even heard what I have to say, and you're already saying no." She shook her head and gave me a look that said she didn't know if she wanted to throttle me or laugh. "You're really something."

"Uh, thanks?"

"Look, I'm not an arch-villain. I brought you Wil's shake as a gesture of good faith, didn't I?"

I nodded.

"You really don't have any choices when it comes to the house. The bonding will be over soon, and there won't be anything you can do about it. What you need to decide is what you want to happen next. You can go off to school as planned, if you like. As an added bonus, I'll even throw in some tuition assistance. You are a Foster, after all, and a former housekeeper candidate, no less. I make sure that we take care of our own."

"It's as easy as that?"

"Not quite," said Sarah. "You will, of course, have to submit to a memory wipe. Given your current state, you'll have to remain here at least a few days before we proceed. We wouldn't want to cause you any harm."

I choked back the "Are you kidding me?" that tried to come flying out of my mouth. Instead I nodded and tried my best to look like I was considering what she said.

I must've still looked pretty doubtful because she said, "Finn, I'm sorry, but you don't belong here. I don't care how powerful you are, you weren't raised in the Foster traditions, and you just aren't qualified to be a housekeeper. Your path lies elsewhere."

"You're not even giving me a chance to decide if this is something I actually want to do. More than likely, I would've turned down the job and gone on my way."

Sarah shook her head. "That's not the kind of chance I'm willing to take, not with our family's future." She looked at her watch. "The house should be waking by now, fully recovered after its exertions opening the door with you. In three hours,

Meg will have bonded with the house, and you'll be out of the picture."

So there was still time. For what, I wasn't sure, but I felt a small wave of relief. Although the "you'll be out of the picture" thing wasn't sounding too good.

"If you form an alliance with the water family, won't that mess up the balance of power? Won't the rest of your council be mad?"

"They won't be in a position to argue when Meg and I have control of the house. Besides, the kind of power I'm offering them, with earth and water working together, any objections will just be for show."

"What would you want to do with that kind of power? Why do you need it?"

Sarah beamed a big, genuine, excited smile at me. "Family first and always, Finn. And I have big plans for us."

Frankly, I didn't want to think about what Gram and Sarah could accomplish together. The whole idea made me shudder.

Sarah stood, folded her chair, and walked with it to the door. She knocked, there was the sound of clicking locks, and the door swung open partway. Sarah handed the chair through the doorway, but I couldn't see who was on the other side.

Sarah paused in the half-open doorway and said, "Get some rest Finn. I'll be back later when everything is all settled, and we can discuss your next steps." And then she was gone.

The door closed, the locks clicked, and I was left alone in my cell.

Chapter Thirty-Three

I finished off Wil's miracle-cure slurpee then lay down on the cot. My head was spinning, though this time not from a headache.

I had so many thoughts jumping around that I didn't know where to start. I grabbed onto the first thing that popped up: Gram. I shook my head. I didn't know why it hadn't occurred to me before that he might be the one helping Meg open the door. When he was leaving, he'd told Meg he'd be hanging around nearby. He must've seen me go walking the next morning and followed me, then taken advantage of the opportunity when I'd accidentally presented him with one by wandering over to a weak spot on the border. He'd seemed familiar at the diner, but I hadn't put it together. It seemed pretty obvious now.

So the posse at the diner had been right to be worried. With the Fosters and the water family making an alliance, the rest of the families would be at a severe disadvantage. This was the kind of stuff that led from cold wars to bloody, ongoing feuds. Family feuds were horrifying enough when conventional weapons were involved. I couldn't even begin to imagine what kind of havoc magical feuding would wreak, not to mention the kinds of innocent casualties that would be involved.

I stood up and started prowling around. I had to get out of there. I at least needed to warn Zo and the others what Sarah had planned. Ya know, before they mind-wiped me…and didn't that sound like fun.

I searched my pockets the best I could with my tied hands

and quickly realized that there was no cell phone on me. A scout around the room told me they hadn't brought along my purse with me, either. No surprise there.

So I was alone with no tools. The cot was bolted to the floor. Sarah'd taken the chair, so I couldn't even beat at the door with that.

I sat down on the cot and tried to think. Out of habit, I reached for my necklace. I had to peel my blood-soaked shirt away from chest to get to it, but the need for comfort outweighed the ick factor. When I pried the necklace free, I realized it was covered in blood.

Wow, that nose bleed must've been truly spectacular. Like Monty Python "just a flesh wound," blood-spurting spectacular. No wonder Sarah had looked so worried.

I walked over to the sink and set about cleaning the necklace off. When I opened the pendant up to clean the scissors, I stopped short. Scissors. I was carrying scissors! Duh!

I flipped the scissors around so they were facing the zip-tie. I frowned. If I held the scissors the usual way, the scissors didn't reach. They were much too small.

After some fiddling, I figured it out. I slid the zip-tie as close to my hands as possible. Next, I cupped the scissors sideways between my palms, with one of the finger holes sticking out from my hands and the cutting part of the scissors placed on either side of the zip-tie. Then I used my mouth to open and close the scissors.

By the time I'd managed to saw through the zip-tie, I'd bruised the hell out of my mouth and somehow managed to bite my tongue. But I was free. Unfortunately, I had lost precious minutes.

I hurried over to the door to see if I could use the scissors there somehow. A quick survey had my shoulders slumping. There was no lock. My best guess was that there was some kind of electronic lock on the outside. Not that I knew how to pick a lock, but at least I could've tried. The hinges were also on the outside of the door, so I couldn't even try prying at them.

I banged on the door. "Hey! Anyone there? Hello?"

Nothing.

I banged harder and yelled louder. "Hey, let me out! I need to talk to Sarah!"

I listened but I couldn't hear a thing from the other side of the door. I didn't think anyone was out there. And with a sinking feeling, I decided it was likely that no one was coming until after Meg was housekeeper.

I leaned my forehead against the cold metal of the door and placed both hands flat against the door. The scissors were still clasped in my hand so they rested against the door under my palm.

"I need to get out of here and get back to the house," I said.

I heard a yawn followed by, "I can help you with that."

My heart stuttered. I whipped around to face the room behind me. No one was there.

"Over here," said the sleepy voice.

I turned back to the door. I felt like an idiot, but I said, "Uh door, are you talking to me?"

I heard laughing. "The door? You think the door is talking?"

I put my hand on my hip. "If a house can talk to me, why not a door?"

The laughing tapered off as the voice said, "You have a point."

"Look, I don't have time for games. I've got to get out of here. Who are you, where are you, and can you help me or not?"

All humor was gone when the voice said, "Okay, okay. Don't get your knickers in a twist. I'm here. No, not over there. Here. In your hand. Oh for the love…your *other* hand, the one with the necklace."

I looked at the pendant and jumped a little when I saw that the seed on the front was glowing blue. "Uh, is my pendant talking to me?"

"Not the pendant, exactly. Well, not the pendant itself at all. I'm sort of…attached. For the sake of brevity, let's just say the pendant is my current home."

"Have you been in there the whole time?"

"If by the whole time, you mean the entire time I've been in your family's possession, then yes."

"Why didn't you say anything before?"

"I was asleep. Mostly. Look, we can talk about this later. Right now, we've got to get you out of here."

It said something about the way my weekend had gone that I was totally unfazed by the fact that my pendant was possessed. I just sort of went with it and asked, "Okay. How?"

"Where do you want to go?"

"Out of here."

"I understand that," the voice said, "but let's make the best use of our time, shall we? Once you leave, what then? Where do you want to go?"

I hissed in frustration. "I hadn't thought about it. Uh... okay. The diner and the doc's are too public. So is that pub where I first met Lou and Pete. That leaves Zo's place or the house." I paused. "I want to go back to the house. I'll have the most options there. And...well, I need to check on the house. And Fuzzy. I'm worried about them."

"Where in the house do you want to go?"

I thought about it for a moment. "My room. No one should be in there, except maybe Fuzzy. Oh jeez, poor Fuzzy. I hope he's not freaking out."

The tone of the voice changed to a brisk, commanding tone. "Walk over to the cell door. Take the pendant off the chain."

I did as instructed and put the chain in my pocket.

The voice instructed, "Hold the blades of the scissors in your—you're left handed?"

"Yes."

"Of course you are. Why make anything easy," it muttered. "Hold the scissors in your left hand. Slide the cover with the seed on it so that it covers the left-side finger hole in the scissors. You should have the cover on the left, the other empty finger hole on the right, and the closed blades facing down."

"Like this?"

"Good, now place the pendant against the door. Flat against the door, with the blades of the scissors pointing down. Not like that. Flip it over, so that the seed side is up. Mm, more to the left, so it's left of center. Good. Now concentrate. Tell it where you want to go."

Feeling foolish, I said, "Could you pl—"

"Don't ask! Tell."

"Uh, hi, er, take me to my room. In the house. Please."

"Let's try that once more, like you have a spine."

I closed my eyes. I could feel the seed pressing into my palm, and it calmed me. I took a slow, deep breath and said, "Take me to my room in the house. Please."

"Open your eyes."

A pale blue light was pouring out from under my fingers.

"You can let go."

Slowly, I took my hand away, expecting the pendant to fall to the floor. But it stayed where it was, suspended against the door. Instead of softly glowing, the seed was now pouring blue light around the pendant.

I gasped and took an involuntary step back.

The seed sprouted a blue tendril that grew sideways until it passed through the finger hole on the right side of the scissors and disappeared into the door.

From the middle of that vine, another tendril sprouted and shot vertically down the scissors, until it implanted itself into the door right below where the scissor blades ended.

It looked like a glowing, blue capital T.

At the bottom of the T, two more tendrils sprouted, one going left and one going right, each disappearing into the door. Now it looked like a blue, glowing capital I.

The vertical part of the "I" grew outward some more, forming an arch that was big enough for me to fit my hand around.

The whole thing took less than a minute.

I gaped at it. "That looks like a—" I said.

"Door handle? That's because it is. Now pull."

I tentatively slipped my hand around the handle. It felt warm, and it pulsed softly. It wasn't icky, just odd.

I hesitated. The last time I'd tried to open a door, it hadn't gone so well.

"Oh, will you stop waffling. This isn't your magic you're using, so stop worrying and give it a decent pull."

I took a firmer grasp and tugged.

There was a pause, then the edges of the door turned bright blue.

The door began opening—from the hinge side.

I blinked at it, then looked at the right side of the door. Somehow, the door had become, well, bendy.

I shifted my gaze to see what was on the other side of the door.

My gaze caught on my suitcase.

I was staring through the door into my room in the house.

Fuzzy was standing on the bed, staring back at me.

With a "MEOW!" he launched himself off the bed and scampered through the door and into the cell with me, where he began clawing his way up my legs.

"Ow! Crap, ow!" I pried him off my pant leg and held him close. He was purring so hard his whole body was shaking. "Hey buddy. I missed you, too."

Well, Fuzzy had come through with no problem. I held onto him and stepped through the door into the house. I had a brief moment of vertigo and then I was through.

The floor under me let out series of squeals and I heard *Ding, ding, ding, ding, ding* chime from my bathroom.

I was startled by the flood of relief that poured through me. "Hi house! Oh I'm so glad to see you. Are you okay?"

Ding!

"Oh thank the house gods. I was worried opening that door might've wiped you out as badly as it did me."

Ding. Then a pause. Then, *ding ding.*

Yes and no. Huh. Well it seemed all right now, so I clung onto that. "Phew. Glad you're okay. Uh, hey, you might want to keep it down, so they don't realize I'm here and come drag me away again."

A quieter *ding* came from the bathroom.

"Thanks."

I turned to face the door and nearly dropped Fuzzy as I

watched my pendant-turned-magic-door-handle pop out of my side of the door.

The voice said, "You're not done yet. Close the door."

I put Fuzzy down on the bed and then walked back to the door. With a last shuddering glance at the dark cell, I pulled on the handle. The door closed.

But where the door to my room in the house should have been, the door to the cell remained. And my pendant was still stuck there playing door handle.

"Now what?" I asked. "How do I, uh, turn it off?"

"Use your words."

I rested the flat of my palm lightly on top of the door handle and said, "Thank you for your help. Please close the door all the way now and go back to being my necklace," and imagined the pendant the way it was when we started.

I yanked my hand away as I felt the handle start to sink.

As the arch in the handle sank back into a straight, flat tendril, the cell door began to disappear. It was like the current door was overwriting it from the edges inward, the wooden boards growing over the metal surface of the cell door, moving inward toward the pendant.

It took only a few moments until the door to my room looked as it always had, except that stuck to the door was my pendant, its glowing, blue tendrils forming the shape of a capital I again.

But then as I watched, the tendrils unsprouted from the door in the reverse order that they had appeared. Within a few seconds, all that remained was the original pendant, scissors pointed down, pendant cover on the left, with only the seed softly glowing blue.

I reached out and pulled at the pendant. The light in the seed went out, and the pendant came away from the door easily.

I looked at the scissors in my hand. I'd been wearing this pendant for years, and I'd had no idea what it could do.

"I need a nap," said the voice.

And I'd had no idea what was in the pendant, either. Not that I really knew now.

I glared at the pendant. "What do you mean you need a nap? You just woke up! And I have questions for you. Lots of questions."

The voice sounded sleepy. "We can talk later."

"Not later, now."

It sounded half asleep already when it said, "You get one. And ask it fast."

"I don't know where to start. Hell, I don't even know what to call you. Do you even have a name?"

"Yes."

"Great. What is it? And what are you? Why are you living in the pendant? And why did you wake up now? Hello? Oh for Pete's sake."

Apparently it had gone to sleep because it wasn't answering.

Chapter Thirty-Four

I sat down on the edge of the bed and stared at the pendant.

Fuzzy meowed his way across the bed, climbing into my lap when he reached me and giving me a head-butt.

"Oh Fuzzy. What a mess," I said and petted him with one hand.

I stared at the necklace. Some part of my brain knew I should be fascinated by what had just happened. But I wasn't feeling curious or excited at all.

Instead, I found myself fighting back tears. My heart ached at the thought that one of the only things that I had left in my life that made me feel safe had now become...well, *this*. Whatever this was.

What was I going to do now? I supposed I could stuff the necklace in my suitcase. Not wear it anymore. But just the thought made me feel so naked and vulnerable that I felt even worse.

That decided me. I may not like what the necklace had become—I'd have to wait and see. But for now, there was no way I was going to leave it behind. I folded the scissors back up. Then, I pulled the chain out of my pocket, strung the pendant back on, and placed it back around my neck. Despite the fact that I now knew that something was living in there, the familiar weight was comforting.

As opposed to my blood-encrusted shirt, which was fifty shades of gross. And starting to itch. I peeled it off, crammed it into my dirty laundry bag, and put on a clean one. After a moment's debate, I decided to leave the charm in my bra, since I promised Zo I'd hang onto it till Monday.

Next, I looked for my purse, but it and my cell phone were missing. Well, that narrowed my choices.

"Okay, house. As quietly as you can, please answer my questions. Remember, it's one for yes, two for no. Ready?"

A *ding* came from the bathroom.

"Have you bonded with Meg yet?"

A loud *ding ding* followed by the floorboards groaning.

I felt relieved. I knew I shouldn't, but I did.

"Okay, is Nor in the house?"

Ding.

"Is Wil?"

Ding.

"Hot damn! Are they upstairs?"

Ding.

"In their rooms?"

No response.

"Huh. In Wil's room?"

Ding ding.

"Nor's room?"

Ding.

"Even better. Anyone else up here?"

Ding ding.

"As long as I stay upstairs for now, is it safe for me to leave my room?"

A pause. *Ding.*

"Okay, thanks."

I put Fuzzy down and tried to leave the room without him, but he glued himself to my legs, tripping me as I walked.

"Okay, okay. You can come, too, for now," I said, picking him up.

I cracked open the door, saw that the coast was clear, and tiptoed across and down the hall to Nor's room, where I knocked quietly on the door. "Nor?" I whispered.

The door whipped open. Nor stared at me for half a second, then grabbed my elbow and yanked me inside. She grabbed me by the shoulders, scanned me from head to toe, then gave me and Fuzzy a brief hard hug.

"Holy shit." That came from Wil.

Nor released me as Wil came over.

They talked over each other with Nor saying, "Are you alright? Where have you been?" while Wil said, "How'd you get back here?"

"I'm doing okay—thanks for the slurpee, Wil. As for where I've been…" I plunked myself in a chair, with Fuzzy on my lap, and explained about the cell and Sarah's visit. "As for how I got here, I, uh, had some help. I'll explain more later." I took in the circles under Nor's eyes and the general haggardness of both their faces. "Are you guys alright?"

"We didn't sleep much," Nor said.

"We've been trying to figure out a way to find you and get you back here," said Wil.

Nor said, "Sarah took our phones and computers, so our options have been limited. She's been offering us every bribe she can come up with not to cause problems now or to make a fuss once this is over."

"But we've been plotting anyway," said Wil with a grin and a wink.

"Well thanks, I appreciate it. If I hadn't've gotten out on my own, I sure would have needed the help getting out of that place. Hey, is that food?"

Nor and Wil turned to the tray behind them, loaded with fruit and sandwiches. Nor waved at the tray and said, "Help yourself. We've basically been locked up, too, just under house arrest instead of in an actual cell." She compressed her lips and frowned. "I can't believe she put you in a council facility." She looked at Wil.

He shook his head, "We're so far off the map for a usual selection that I have no clue what's happening at this point."

I put Fuzzy down and let him explore while I raided the tray. Around a mouthful of sandwich I said, "Speaking of things not going according to schedule, I have a question. Is there any way to buy some time here, so we have a chance to figure things out?"

"As long as Sarah is here in charge, they're not going to delay," said Nor.

Wil said, "The bonding is due to start in an hour. But even if we could somehow convince Sarah to delay, it would have to be a short delay. The bonding must take place today."

"Okay, so I have an hour to break this up."

Nor and Wil traded a look. Nor cleared her throat and sat down in a chair next to mine. "Not to be a wet blanket, Finn, but why? Have you changed your mind about becoming housekeeper?"

My mouth went dry, and I had a hard time swallowing. "No," I said.

I must not have sounded very convincing because Nor raised an eyebrow at me.

I put down my sandwich. "I just, well, I need a minute to think. I, just, I need breathing room!" I got up and walked to the window, staring out at the woods.

I could feel Nor and Wil having a silent exchange behind my back.

"What?" I said, without turning around.

Nor said, "If you're having doubts, any doubts, about leaving, then you need to give the housekeeper position serious and full consideration."

Wil said, "Nor and I were talking. There's no doubt in either of our minds that you would be the best housekeeper this place has had in a long, long time." He sighed. "I thought about what you said. You're right. The family hasn't treated the house very well. And nobody noticed. Nobody cared. But you did—you do. That says something."

I leaned my forehead on the window, letting the cool glass soothe the headache that was threatening to return. "I just need time. Quiet time. Freedom to think."

Wil said, "Well, until the bonding is over, we're not going to get much freedom. And there's not a lot we can do about stalling, either. The housekeeper can only be temporary for a limited amount of time—"

I turned around, "Wait, wait, wait. I think I have an idea."

I noticed Fuzzy stalking the sandwich platter and pulled him onto my lap as I sat down. "Meg's temporary, right?"

"Right," said Wil.

"As in not permanent, not bonded, just a placeholder?"

"Er, yes?"

"Can we switch temps? I mean in the real world, temps come and go all the time—that's why they're called temps. So can't someone else be the temporary housekeeper?"

Nor stood up. "I see where you're going. Wil? Put that photographic memory to good use. Is there anything in the archives about switching temps?"

Wil leaned against a wall and stared into space. After about five minutes he said, "Yes. It happened once that I can remember reading about, back in the late 1700s. The temp got pneumonia and wasn't going to survive long enough for them to complete the selection process. But the temp was being stubborn, insisted he was fine, and refused to give up the bond. So they forced a switch, took the temporary bond off the old temp, and transferred the power to a new temporary housekeeper."

"Great. How?"

Wil frowned and shook his head. "I'm sorry, Finn. It won't help us. You need the house's permission."

"Well, I have no problem at least asking."

Wil was still shaking his head. "You don't understand. You have to petition the house by name."

Okay. That was a problem.

However, before I could think of a way around it, I heard footsteps coming down the hallway.

Chapter Thirty-Five

I jumped up, clutching Fuzzy, and dashed into Nor's bathroom. I made it around the corner just as the door to her room banged against the wall.

While Nor was saying, "You really want to add forced entry to the list?" I whispered, "Hide me. Please," to the house.

The wall between the tub and the sink silently split open. I stepped into the back of the closet in the adjacent room. In the few moments it took me to step in and turn around, the wall had already closed behind me.

I heard a heavy tread enter the bathroom. It walked right past where I'd just been standing. A swish-clinkty-clink told me the shower curtain was being opened.

Fuzzy became a ball of coiled tension, eyes fixated on whoever was on the other side of the wall. If he'd had laser vision, whoever was out there would've been nothing but a puff of smoke by now.

The thumping footsteps went back into the main room.

"All clear in here," the Real Girl called.

I heard a door close in the distance and footsteps approaching Nor's room.

"She's not in her room, either." That was Lars.

Oh crap. They knew I was out. That was so not good.

Lars reached Nor's room and added, "But her cat's gone."

I looked down at Fuzzy. Maybe taking him with me wasn't a good idea.

"Have you seen Finn?" Lars asked.

Nor said, "Finn? You mean Finn that you dragged out of

here, bloody and unconscious?" There was a pause. "Do you see a bloody, unconscious body anywhere?"

Wil said, "Did you guys decide to bring her back here, after all? You should let me see her. Is she awake? Did you give her the shake I sent? She really needs to drink that whole thing."

Lars ignored Wil's questions and asked, "What about the cat?"

"Off wandering, I imagine. If you'd let me hang onto him instead of insisting I put him in her room, he probably wouldn't have gotten bored and wandered off. Why the sudden concern about her kitten?" asked Nor.

"Sarah wants him," says Lars.

I looked down at Fuzzy again. Okay, taking him was a great idea.

"No kitten here," said Wil.

I assumed Nor was slapping them with one of her lawyer looks because I could hear Lars's sigh through the wall. "Stay here," he said.

I heard them clomp out, and the door close. The muffled sound of them talking made its way through the wall, but I couldn't hear what they were saying. I heard footsteps tromp away.

"Finn?" Nor was in the bathroom whispering.

"You can let me out. Please," I said to the house. The wall opened, and I found myself facing a startled Nor.

Her look of surprise changed to a smile. "Well done."

"Why are you whispering?"

"One of them is outside the door, standing guard."

Wil came around the corner, caught sight of me standing in the open wall, and laughed softly. "Nice."

Nor and Wil started whispering back and forth, trying to figure out what we should do next.

I tuned them out, thinking furiously. The thought that kept hammering at me over and over was *I need more time.* I needed to sit still and really think with no drama swirling around me. So how could I buy myself some breathing room? I realized I was alternately patting Fuzzy and the wall as I was thinking.

Staring at the wall, I got an idea.

I interrupted Nor and Wil with, "Look, I'm not staying."

Wil asked, "What? Where are you going?"

"I'm not sure. You guys sit tight for now."

Nor frowned but didn't argue. She said, "Be careful."

With a nod, I said, "Close it up please," and the house closed the wall.

I turned around and opened the closet door a crack. The room on the other side was empty.

I closed the closet door again and put the hand that wasn't holding Fuzzy against the door.

"House," I whispered, "can you hear me? If you can, please signal me as quietly as possible."

The lightbulb in the closet blinked on and off.

I smiled. "Speaking of lightbulbs," I said, then whispered my idea. I finished by saying, "I want to be really clear that I'm not making any promises here. I'm just trying to buy us time to consider our options. And, most importantly, this is only if you want to do it. You get to make a choice here, too. If you just want to go ahead with the bond with Meg and get it over with, I totally understand."

There was a pause in which I assumed the house was mulling over my proposition. Even though I could feel the sands leaking from the hourglass, I waited patiently. Even Fuzzy was holding still.

The closet door in front of me swung open.

As I tiptoed into the room, the wall on the far side split open. The house was directing me somewhere, so I followed its lead.

I hurried through the hole in the wall and found myself in Wil's room. He had books, papers, and clothes strewn everywhere. I tried to pick my way through it, but I bumped into something, and it fell to the floor with a thud.

I froze. Fuzzy froze in my arms. I think both of us were holding our breath, hoping maybe no one had heard anything.

The clomp, clomp, clomp heading in my direction told me I wasn't going to have any such luck.

The house opened the wall in front of me just as I heard the door to the room between Nor and Wil's whomp open. The boots went inside.

If they were going room by room, they'd check Wil's room next. I ran through the opening in the wall, into the next room, trying desperately not to make any noise as I went.

The wall had just closed behind me when the door to Wil's room slammed open, and I heard the heavy tread go inside.

My heart was pounding, and my sweaty palms were sticking to Fuzzy's fur. The room I'd entered was at the end of the hall. There was nowhere else for me to go.

The house opened a much smaller segment of the wall in the front, right corner of the room, to the right of the door.

"I can't go out into the hallway, he'll see me," I hissed to the house, as I skittered over to the hole in the wall.

When I reached it, I realized that I was looking at an enclosed staircase, not the hallway. My brain churned. I remembered it was the stairwell to the attic. It smelled kind of musty, but right then I didn't care. Footsteps were approaching the room.

I put Fuzzy on a stair and squeezed myself through the narrow hole in the wall and joined him. I whipped around to see the hole snap shut just as the door to the room opened.

I held still. Stairs headed up to my left, but I paid more attention to the door to my right, terrified he would open it. My heart was doing its best impression of a bass drum at a death-metal concert, and I was panting quietly.

The footsteps moved around the room, then paused in the doorway. Too close to me. Too close to the attic door.

I heard another set of footsteps coming up the back stairs from the mudroom.

Fuzzy was already halfway up the attic stairs. He came back down a stair, swishing his tail at me. He went up a stair, looked over his shoulder at me, and flicked his tail again.

Right. Up the stairs, into the dark. Sarah had said there was tons of junk in the attic. Maybe we could hide there.

While I crept up the attic staircase, the footsteps reached

the top of the back stairs.

From right outside the attic door, Lars said, "Problem?"

"Thought I heard something. Might be nothing but…" the Real Girl said.

"But nothing is going the way it should today," Lars said. In a lower voice he added, "I told them they should have taken Finn farther away. It was stupid to put her at the facility right in town."

I paused. Well, that explained how they thought I'd be able to get back to the house already. I hadn't been that far away to begin with.

"Did you check in here?" Lars asked.

"Not yet," said the Real Girl.

I felt the stairs vibrating under me and took that as my cue. It sounded like the door was sticking, which gave me the extra few seconds I needed. I hurried up the remainder of the steps and made it around the corner just as I heard the door at the bottom of the steps open.

A beam of light flashed up the staircase, but both Fuzzy and I were well out of its reach.

"Look at that layer of dust," said the Real Girl. "No one's been up here in a while."

"Fine, but leave the door open. In fact, let's leave all the doors open. I don't trust the house not to cover for her if she does show up. And it'll be easier to keep an eye out for the cat this way."

"What's Sarah want it for anyway?"

"My understanding is she'll use it for leverage if Finn shows up."

I swallowed the snarl that I felt rising.

As they wandered off down the hallway, the Real Girl gave a soft whistle. "Dude, that's harsh. I'll be glad when this job is over."

Lars said, "With you there. Now focus."

Then they were out of hearing range.

I turned my attention to the attic. A few randomly-spaced, dirty windows let a dim, gray light into the space, but I couldn't see all the way to the other end. Dust motes drifted and settled on shrouded hulks that were strewn willy-nilly throughout the space. In the immediate vicinity, I saw a couple of steamer trunks, a sheet-covered thing that I was betting was a couch of some kind, a floor lamp that was missing its shade, and a precarious stack of old magazines. I bet Wil would have a field day up there.

I followed Fuzzy a bit farther into the room, picking my way around the various obstacles. I was dying of curiosity and had to force myself not to snoop. I stopped and whispered, "House? What now?"

I felt the floor vibrate softly. At first, I couldn't figure out what was happening. Then I saw Fuzzy's and my footprints disappear, and I realized the dust was shifting. Within a few seconds, a clear spot appeared on the floor in front of me. Then it spread, the dust parting to form a nice, clean walkway. A path. It was a path.

Fuzzy figured it out before I did. He stepped onto the clean floor, shook a paw, gave the dust a dirty look, then proceeded along the path, tail in the air. He paused at the first bend to look back at me.

"Yeah, yeah, yeah. You're smarter than I am. Everyone knows this. No need to rub it in," I whispered. I followed after him down the path.

I came around the first bend and found myself facing one of the windows. It was nearly opaque with dust, but I realized I was looking down at the left side of the house. I hadn't walked around this side of the house yet, so I paused to look. With my bird's-eye view, I could see parts of a path that wound through the woods and a circular clearing with a bunch of big rocks in it.

Then it dawned on me. Those weren't rocks. They were gravestones. That was the graveyard.

A knot formed in my stomach as I watched a blurry Sarah and Meg emerge into the clearing. They toured around it, talking. Sarah was gesturing to the headstones, and from her body language, I was pretty sure Meg was laughing.

In a soft voice, I did a voiceover of their conversation.

In my Sarah voice, I said, "And this, Meg, is where you'll be buried."

In my Meg voice, I said, "Gee, Sarah, I can't wait! How about over here? Over here looks great."

I shook my head and shuddered.

Turning back to the attic, I followed the path, trying to keep quiet but moving much more quickly now. There was so much stuff everywhere that there was no direct route through the junk, and I had to trust that the house knew what it was doing.

I rounded an enormous armoire and found Fuzzy sitting in the darkest corner of the attic in front of a pile of miscellaneous junk. I had to squint hard to make out a trunk, a croquet set, a shovel, and some pieces of wood stacked in a pile on the floor.

Kneeling on the floor, I opened the trunk. My heart sank as I realized that the entire thing was crammed with papers and books. It was too dark to read in this corner, and the trunk must weigh a ton. Even if I could manage to drag it over to a window, and somehow not make a ton of noise, no way did I have time to read through everything in there.

I looked up at the ceiling. "Please tell me it's not in a book," I whispered.

I heard the house sigh around me.

The floor jiggled, and the stack of wood fell over, disgorging an annoyed spider that scurried away. I froze. No one came to investigate the noise, so I scrambled over to take a look.

While Fuzzy chased after the spider, I rapidly searched through the pile. It looked like a bunch of wooden planks that someone had used for building at some point. By the time I reached the bottom of the pile I was huffing in frustration. I grabbed the last plank and was considering hurling it into the dark when I realized that it had something carved into it.

I squinted, but I couldn't see well enough to read. I ran my fingers across the surface. That felt like…letters? And something else.

I hopped up and headed for the nearest window. Fuzzy followed after me.

I held up the wooden plank in the pool of light. The hole in each corner tipped me off to what I was looking at. It was a weathered sign, the type of placard I'd noticed hanging on lots of the older New England houses, proclaiming things like "Built in 1790" and "McInerny Family."

The light from the window was just bright enough that I could see the carvings more clearly. There were two trees. And in between them was lettering.

"Is this it?" I asked. "Is this your name?"

From somewhere deep in the attic, I heard a soft *ding*.

"It's perfect. I'm so very pleased to be able to call you by name, Bayley."

Chapter Thirty-Six

I hugged the placard to me with one arm and scooped up Fuzzy with the other.

"Bayley, I need to talk to Wil and Nor. Can you please lead me to the space over Nor's bathroom?"

I hurried along the path the house laid out for me until the path dead-ended.

"Okay, can you please open a hole in the floor?"

As a manhole-sized opening appeared, I put Fuzzy and the plank down and lay on my stomach next to the hole.

I was looking into the tub. I could hear Nor and Wil talking in the other room.

"Nor?" I whispered.

Nothing.

I was trying to figure out how I was going to reach them when Fuzzy leapt through the hole, onto the edge of the tub, and then down to the floor. While I choked back my cry of dismay, he slinked his way across the bathroom and out the door.

A few seconds later I heard Wil falter mid-sentence, cough, and then resume speaking, albeit in a more strained tone.

Nor said, "Hold that thought. I need to use the loo."

A few seconds later, Nor entered the bathroom carrying Fuzzy. She shut the door behind her.

"Up here," I whispered.

Nor looked in the direction of the door to her room and whispered, "R.G. is out in the hall, and the door is open."

I nodded. "I need Wil."

Nor put Fuzzy down, flushed the toilet and ran the water

for the sink, winking at me as she said, "For verisimilitude." Then she went into the other room.

I didn't hear anything for a moment and then Wil said, "Now I have to go. Be right back."

He entered the bathroom, shut the door, and swept the room with his gaze. I waved, and he looked up.

"Got the name. How do we do this?"

Wil blinked a few times. Then he crossed his arms and paced back and forth a bit before asking, "You sure you want to do this?"

"Yes. And I'm running out of time, so could you hurry it up?"

Wil ran a hand through his hair, then rubbed his nose under his glasses. "You remember our deal, right? You're not going to back out?"

"Wil, this is only temporary, remember? But yeah, I remember the deal. Now give."

Wil whispered the instructions to me. They were actually simple, if unpleasant.

"Great, thanks. I'll be back when it's over," I said. I was about to tell him to hang onto Fuzzy for me when the edge of the hole sprouted downward, forming a ramp to the edge of the tub.

Fuzzy leapt up onto the ramp and scurried up into the attic with me, the ramp retracting behind him as he went. I caught a last glimpse of Wil looking bewildered before the hole closed up.

I looked at Fuzzy. "What, did you make some kind of deal with the house while I was gone?"

Fuzzy decided this would be an excellent time to groom the fur on his chest.

"Uh huh. We'll talk about this later."

Now I needed Meg. Wil had said she'd have to change before the ceremony, so my best bet was to wait for her in her room.

"Show me where Meg's bathroom is," I said to the house.

I picked up the name plank and followed the path that the

house laid out through the attic toward the front of the house.

I looked around me until I spotted a clear surface. I put the placard down on a table and said, "I'll be back for you later."

Then I returned to the spot where Meg's bathroom should be and said, "Can I have a small peephole please?"

Fuzzy and I peered into Meg's bathroom. It was empty. I listened, but I didn't hear anything coming from the other room.

"Okay, let me in there."

The hole opened wider and a set of stairs grew down into the bathroom.

"Oh man, that's cool. Hey, uh, I'm really sorry if all this crazy architecture shifting is causing any kind of strain. This must take a lot of effort."

The floorboards around me let out a muted volley of deep grunts that sounded a lot like…

"Are you giggling?"

I heard one clear grunt.

I looked around me in amazement. "Wait, are you having fun?"

Grunt.

"Well, that's, uh, actually that's good to hear. Glad I'm not, you know, sucking the life, er, magic out of you or anything."

Grunt grunt. Pause. *Grunt grunt grunt grunt grunt.*

I smiled and patted the edge of the hole as I walked down the stairs, Fuzzy at my heels.

Once I hit the floor, the stairs retracted and the hole closed up.

The bathroom was bigger than my bedroom.

I froze and listened. All quiet.

I peered out into Meg's room, then yanked my head back in, eyes watering. After the dimness of the attic, the brightness of Meg's bedroom was nearly blinding.

I gave my eyes a few seconds to adjust and looked again.

The room appeared to be empty. It spanned the front of the house and was flooded with light from the windows in the front and side walls.

Unfortunately, the door to the hallway was open, and R.G.

was pacing up and down the corridor.

I jerked my head back in before he turned around and saw me.

Well, that complicated things.

I stayed in the bathroom, fretting, until I heard Meg coming up the back stairs.

"I'll be back in a few minutes," Meg called to someone, "and then we can finally get this over with."

Her footsteps stopped somewhere down the hallway.

Meg said, "Nor, Wil, it's time. You two go with him. He'll take you outside to the ceremony. I'll be there in a few minutes."

Without waiting for a response, Meg started walking in my direction. I heard a bunch of other footsteps receding toward the back of the house, so I guessed that Wil, Nor, and R.G. were following Meg's instructions and heading outside.

Meg entered her room and shut the door.

I stepped out of the bathroom. "Hi, Meg."

She spun around, took me in, and then smiled at me. "There you are. I figured you'd turn up."

She didn't look worried. In fact, she looked pleased.

I frowned.

"Hold her," she said.

Two wooden hands sprouted from the floorboards and grabbed my ankles. I struggled, but I couldn't budge. Worse, she was standing too far away for me to touch her.

I crossed my arms and glared at her. "Really? This again? Is there some kind of foot fetish thing that runs in our family?" I looked at my feet and sighed. "Well, last time I got mud in my shoes. I suppose I should be grateful that I don't have splinters."

Meg talked as she bustled around the room, laying out a simple shift dress and a sparkly, beaded robe, and then removing her jewelry.

She said, "The way I see it, you have two choices. You can officially cede your spot as housekeeper, and I can go on with the bonding ceremony. Or you can continue to be a stubborn pain in the ass, I can banish you from the property, and I can go on with the bonding ceremony. Your choice."

"Have you been watching Disney movies all morning?"

Meg gave me a long-suffering look. "Why?"

"Because you're perky enough to make Cinderella cringe. And also, it looks like your fairy godmother barfed glitter all over your robe thingy."

She laughed. "That's pretty funny. Doug would think that's hilarious. I'll have to remember to tell him you said that when this is all over." She put her hands on her hips. "So, what's it going to be?"

"Before I cede anything, I want to make sure the house is going to be okay."

"So you, what, expect me to prove myself to you?"

I squirmed a little. "I wouldn't put it that way…"

"Screw you, Finn. I don't have to justify myself to you."

"Meg—"

"No really. Screw. You. Who do you think you are? You show up out of the blue, you're here all of like two minutes, and you decide you can sit in judgment on me, on us, on our family traditions?"

"I'm not judging anyone—"

"Aren't you?"

She stared me down until I dropped my gaze and looked at the floor.

"I don't get you," she said. "You've got a whole future mapped out, just waiting for you. You don't need this job. You don't even really want to be here. But instead of doing the reasonable thing and stepping aside, you're trying to take away my home—"

"I am not!"

"This isn't just some house. It's my home, Finn. I grew up here. You're trying to take my home, my career—basically my entire life—away from me. And what for? Because you can?"

I couldn't meet her eyes. An answering ache came from the place in me that longed for the home I'd lost. My cheeks heated, and I felt ashamed that it hadn't even occurred to me that Meg might have more than one reason for wanting to be housekeeper. I'd been painting her as a cartoon villain, all heartless greed. But the thing is, people are never simple. The map to a person's personality isn't a straight road to a single destination. It's loaded with back roads, switchbacks, and dead-ends leading to all sorts of weird places. It should have dawned on me that Meg, though ambitious, could have other motivations feeding into her reasoning.

It also hadn't occurred to me that in her version of this story, I was the villain. I wasn't used to thinking of myself as the bad guy, and I didn't like the way it felt.

I said, "Look, Meg, I'm not trying to ruin your life, I swear. I just want some time to think things through, to make sure the house is going to be okay."

Meg said, "Well, you're out of time. And the house is not your responsibility. It's mine. C'mon, Finn. Don't force me to make you leave. I can, and I will, if necessary. But that'll just make things…messy…politically. Make things easier on everyone and cede your position."

She had some reasonable points. Maybe I should just let this whole thing go. I frowned and tried to consider what she said.

But she must've taken my frown as me digging my heels in, because she sighed and said, "Fine. I'll give you a little taste of my plans, so you can put your mind at ease, and we can get on with things. Ok?"

I nodded slowly. "Thanks, I'd appreciate that."

"No problem. As housekeeper, it's my job to help my fellow Fosters." Meg gave me a magnanimous smile, then glanced at the clock. "I've got to finish getting ready while we chat, though."

I nodded.

As Meg began undressing, she said, "With my mom as the last housekeeper, I had no choice but to stay here. And I used that time wisely. I watched her, and I learned, and I planned. So that when the time came, it would be obvious that I'd already *earned* my place as housekeeper." In her bra and underwear, she walked over to the bed and slipped the shift dress on. "And now I'm going to make this place really work for the family." She looked around as she added, "In the past, we've barely tapped its potential. But I'm going to change all that. I'll be the one to help the house really show what it can do, really give its all."

I said, "What about the house, Meg? What about what it wants and how it feels?"

"It's a house."

"It's a living being."

"Don't worry, Finn. The house will get what it needs to survive. It's not like I'm going to starve it. But we all have to earn our keep, one way or another, the house included."

"Meg…I don't think you're being fair to the house—"

"And I don't think you know what you're talking about. You're new to magic, so I get why you'd be impressed with the house. And it is impressive. But in the end, it's not a person, and you can't expect to treat it like one."

Oh yes I could, but I didn't say that out loud.

She glanced at the clock again. "Time's up. Last chance. Cede or leave."

Closer. I needed her to step closer.

Time to play dirty.

"Bet you're glad your momma isn't here for this," I said.

Her eyes narrowed and she said, "I wouldn't."

"Wouldn't what? Say that you haven't changed at all since the last time I saw you, not really? That it's all about you and what you want? When we were kids, you wanted more—more money, more clothes, more attention. More control. And it's the same thing now." I shook my head and gave her my best pitying look. "It's almost a mercy your mom's not here. You'd be breaking her heart."

I saw it coming. I saw her take two steps forward and raise her arm to slap me. I braced and got ready to grab her.

But she stopped. She lowered her arm slowly. And she smiled.

I flinched.

And she was still just out of reach.

"Door number two it is, then. And Finn, just so you know, for that last remark, I'm making your banishment permanent. House—"

Fuzzy streaked into the room, growling like he was four times his actual size. He dashed behind Meg and launched himself at the back her legs, claws out.

"Ow!" Meg yelled as she staggered forward.

I reached out and grabbed one of her flailing arms. It was easy to pull her all the way off balance because she was already halfway there.

She fell to ground, and I bent my knees to follow her down, wrenching my ankle in the process.

As we fell, I called, "Splinters."

Sharp splinters of wood sprouted from the floor and as Meg hit her knees, I said, "Sorry about this," and slammed both our arms onto the splinters.

Meg yelped and tried to pry her arm from mine. But I gritted my teeth and held on.

Blood from both our arms mixed and smeared on the floor.

In a rush, I said, "Bayley, I, Finn of the Fosters, petition you to claim the housekeeper bond. Release Meg—"

Meg talked over me, saying, "What? What are you doing? Let me go—" as she struggled harder to pull free of my grip. When I held on and kept talking, she rained punches at me with her free arm, landing a solid blow on my mouth.

But I didn't stop. I ignored her and the blood dripping from my lip and kept going with the words Wil had taught me.

"—Bayley, with your permission, I freely accept the bond. As I will it, so will it be."

Meg and I both froze. I don't know if she felt anything. I felt tingly and lightheaded, but that might have been because she'd been beating on me.

She said to me, "What did you do?"

I looked at the floor and said, "Release me."

The wooden hands released my ankles and disappeared back into the floor.

Meg looked horrified. "No," she said.

"House remove Meg from the property—"

"You can't do this! House, stop her. House, silence her. House!"

"—and don't let her reenter until I say so. Do it now."

From the bathroom I heard a loud, cheery *ding*. Then, one of the windows opened. Vines of ivy came snaking through the window, twined around Meg until she was wrapped up like a mummy, and whisked her outside. Though muffled, she continued yelling all the way out the window.

I went to the window to watch and saw that the ivy was dragging Meg down the driveway toward the road.

"Don't hurt her," I said when I noticed the ivy bouncing Meg more than necessary.

I got a much less enthusiastic *ding* this time. But the ivy slowed down and carried Meg off down the driveway much more smoothly.

"Okay house, you up for a little more?"

Loud *ding*.

I smiled and shook my head. "Leave Nor and Wil alone. Remove from the property Sarah, Doug…any guests they brought along, including bodyguards. Actually, belay that. Bring Lars and R.G. to the front porch, but everyone else can go. Don't hurt anybody, but don't allow any of them back until I say so."

I didn't even have to add the "now" this time.

From overhead, I heard a shriek and a "What the f—" followed by muffled sounds.

The laughter that floated down to me I was pretty sure belonged to Nor. Several people must've been up on the roof because, as I watched, a bunch of ivy-wrapped bodies flowed down the side of the house, up the driveway, and out of sight. More followed from various spots in the woods. Huh. That was a lot of ivy mummies. Apparently there were a lot more people here than I knew about.

The last two ivy mummies detoured and stopped on the front porch.

"Anyone else I need to worry about? Nor and Wil are fine. But any water family, or any of Sarah, Meg, or Doug's peeps, anyone at all I need to worry about?"

Ding ding.

"Great." I leaned against the cool glass. "Great job, Bayley. Seriously. Well done."

The curtains on the window swished back and forth.

"Is that your happy dance?"

The swishing increased and a staccato crunchy groaning sound came from the floorboards. It sounded like chortling.

I smiled, then winced as it pulled at my split lip. "I'm gonna go get some ice."

I limped my way downstairs. I was going to have huge bruises on my legs from where the house had clamped me in place, and my twisted ankle was sore. I could feel my lip swelling, too.

All in all, I really wanted this day to be over.

I'd just made it into the kitchen when Wil and Nor came banging in through the front door.

"Finn? Finn!" called Nor.

"In the kitchen."

Nor and Wil pulled up short when they caught sight of me. "Jesus," said Wil.

"I don't suppose either of you know any healing spells?"

Chapter Thirty-Seven

It turned out we didn't have the ingredients for any healing spells, but Nor was surprisingly good at first aid.

I kept a bag of frozen peas on my lip as we tromped out front to where Lars and R.G. were bound on the porch. To their credit, they weren't wasting a lot of effort struggling. They were waiting, eyes watchful when they saw us come out the front door.

They were covered head-to-toe in ivy, but I could see their eyes. Fuzzy sniffed at them then hopped up on a porch railing to watch.

"Hey, could you please unwrap their heads?" I asked.

The house sighed, but it complied. The ivy made a slithering sound as it unwound, revealing a very irritated R.G. and an impassive Lars.

"Gee, this must make you miss Kevin," I said to R.G.

He frowned and tossed his hair. I glanced at Lars, and I could've sworn he was trying not smile.

"Okay guys. I'll send you on your way in a minute. But first, where's our stuff?"

Lars raised an eyebrow and said, "Your stuff?"

"Our phones, my purse—"

"—my laptop," added Nor.

"Her laptop. Where's our stuff?"

"What incentive do we have to help you?"

I shrugged. "None. You know I'm not going to hurt you. That's not my style. But we're going to find it anyway, so you might as well hand it over and save us some time."

Lars said, "Let us leave under our own power—we'll take our SUV and go—and you've got a deal."

I looked at Nor, who nodded. I looked back at the guys and said, "Fine. But no side trips or back in the ivy you go."

"Deal," said Lars. "Your stuff is locked in the SUV."

"Let them go," I said.

"Weapons," said Nor.

I held up a finger, "But take away all their weapons."

Lars grimaced, and R.G. rolled his eyes, but neither said anything.

The ivy unwound. Tendrils poked into the bodyguards' clothing, searching for and retrieving various weapons.

R.G. yelped. "Hey, at least buy a guy dinner first."

I snickered and said to the gun-waving ivy, "Uh hey, you can put the weapons over there," and pointed to the wall next to the door, well out of the bodyguards' reach.

The amount of clattering and clanking had me turning my head to look at what the ivy was dumping. "Are you kidding me?" I said. I walked over to survey the pile. There were guns, knives, mace, a stun gun, some kind of baton, and even a pair of brass knuckles. The pile was knee high.

I looked at the bodyguards. "How do you even walk carrying this much stuff?"

R.G. grinned. Lars just gave me his usual flat look.

"Alright you two, let's go."

The group of us walked over to the SUV. Lars typed in a code on a keypad on the door. Sure enough, there was a pile of our stuff inside. Lars and R.G. climbed into the front while Nor, Wil, and I grabbed our things out of the back.

When we had our stuff, we went back to the porch and watched them drive off.

I put a hand on the railing. "Tell me when they leave the property."

A short time later, the floor board under my feet grunted.

"Gone?"

Grunt.

"Any problems? Any unnecessary side trips?"

Grunt grunt.

My shoulders sagged, and I let a breath. "Okay good. Thanks." I looked at Nor and Wil. "Alone at last."

Wil said, "Finn, I don't mean to be a wet blanket, but we haven't solved anything. We still need to do the bonding. Today."

"I bought us time."

"But—" Wil's phone rang, interrupting him. He glanced at the number, then at me and Nor. "It's Sarah."

Nor nodded. "Makes sense she'd reach out to you. You're the one with council ties."

He looked at me. "What do you want me to do?"

"If you're up for it, try to calm her down. You can tell her I'll talk to her about the final bonding soon."

Wil stayed on the porch talking with Sarah while Nor, Fuzzy, and I went inside.

When we were out of earshot, Nor said, "You sure you don't want me to keep an eye on him?"

"Yup. He can make any deals he wants. I have what I need for now, which is time."

Nor studied me as we walked to the kitchen.

I sat down at the table with a moan.

Nor took my bag of peas and put it back in the freezer as she said, "I can see the wheels turning. What are you thinking?"

"I'm thinking I have to get out of here. Go somewhere and think."

Nor sat down next to me. "You can't. You're bonded to the house, so you can't leave the property. And even if you could, you have to know that Sarah's going to have the exits to this place blockaded. They're not going to let anyone just leave here. They're not going to let anyone enter, either, so if you were thinking of calling in reinforcements, that's not going work."

I waved a hand at her. "Don't worry. I've got it covered. But I need a favor from you. A big one."

"Okay…?"

"I need you take the bond from me. Just for a little while."

Nor blinked at me. "You're leaving, aren't you."

"I'll be back. I just…" I stood up and started pacing around the kitchen. "I need to go think."

Nor leaned back and gazed off into space, contemplating. For a few minutes, the only sounds in the kitchen were me pacing, and Fuzzy grooming. "Okay."

I stopped. "Okay?"

Nor sat up straighter. "You said you're coming back. I believe you. So okay."

I did a little happy dance.

Nor gave me an evil grin. "Besides, if you screw me over and take off, my girlfriend will not be happy. You think I'm a badass? Trust me, you do *not* want to mess with that girl."

"Er, good to know," I said. The thought of someone who could out-Nor Nor was too terrifying to contemplate, so I put it aside.

I sat down next to Nor again and explained to her what to do. She didn't even flinch. She got up, got a knife, cut her arm, and did it.

I felt a weird sort of emptiness when the bond switched, but nothing too overwhelming.

Nor said, "Bayley, would you please sprout a chair?"

The house complied immediately.

"Well, this seems to be working fine. You're free to go, Finn. Bayley, let Finn leave."

The house sighed around us and groaned.

"Please, Bayley?" I asked.

The floorboards near me let out a single, disgruntled sounding grunt.

"Thanks. I'll be back soon."

Nor pulled open her laptop, and I walked out of the kitchen.

"Finn?" Nor called after me.

I paused in the doorway. "Yeah?"

"Don't take too long."

"I won't," I said. I left her typing away on her keyboard.

Chapter Thirty-Eight

Fuzzy followed me up the back stairs. On the way, I slung my purse bandolier-style across my torso. We entered my bedroom, then I shut the door behind us and turned around to face it.

Fuzzy sat by my feet, facing the door, too.

I hauled my necklace out from under my shirt and dangled the pendant at eye level.

"Hey. Hey! You in there?" I gave the necklace a shake. "Dammit, wake up. I need a door."

"There's no need to yell. And you're standing in front of a perfectly good door."

"Hah hah. How long have you been awake? Are you aware of what's been going on?"

"I'm aware."

"Good, then I don't need to waste time explaining. Can you open me a door or not?"

"Yes. Do you know where you want to go?"

"I do." I unfolded the scissors and placed the pendant on the door as I told the thing where I wanted to go.

As before, the handle sprouted from the door. I tugged on the handle, and the door swung open from the hinge side.

Tears sprang to my eyes as I looked through the doorway.

"Thank you," I whispered.

I turned around and said to the house, "See you soon," and then Fuzzy and I walked through the door.

I sucked in a deep breath of salty air as I stepped out onto rocks that were slick with sea spray. The wind grabbed my hair and swirled it around me as I turned and shut the door behind me. After I retrieved my pendant, I took a moment to gaze up at the lighthouse towering over me. Then I donned my necklace and faced the ocean.

It was so much more than I'd imagined. Seeing it on a screen or in a picture just didn't do it justice.

The ocean sang to me as it shushed in and out along the shoreline and boom-boomed against the rocks. Briny air filled my lungs, and I tasted salt on my lips. I watched as the waves frolicked. They reminded me of cancan dancers, lifting their frothy-edged skirts, flouncing them back down to meet the sand, then dancing back out to sea to do it all over again.

I didn't even try to stop the tears trailing down my face.

Fuzzy snagged my attention as he climbed down the rocks toward the sandy crescent of beach on our left. He got impatient halfway down, leapt to the ground, and dashed after the seabirds waddling at the edge of the water.

Climbing down after him, I laughed as I watched him scatter the flock, the birds cursing at him as they flapped into the sky.

I reached the sand and surveyed my surroundings. The tiny beach was lined with bulky rocks, craggy from tide and time. Looking back at the lighthouse, this place looked just like the picture I'd had pinned to my wall for years. My mom had promised to bring me here someday, and I felt her near me as I let her favorite childhood place envelop me.

I turned back to watch Fuzzy playing with the waves. He was dashing up to them as they went out to sea, then running away as they came back in. I dumped my purse in the sand, took off my shoes and socks, and ran over to play with him.

After a few minutes, he got bored and went off to pounce and play farther back along the sand. He couldn't go very far, so I let him be.

I waded out a little ways and stood looking out to sea. The tide tugged at my legs, urging me to go with it, out there, toward the horizon.

I dug my toes in the sand and held my ground.

"Meow," Fuzzy called.

270   MATTESON WYNN

With a sigh, I headed back into shore. Fuzzy was sitting by my purse, staring at me.

I plopped down next to him and pulled him into my arms.

He snuggled into my chest, his head under my chin, and purred.

I listened to Fuzzy purring, the siren sea singing, and the wind whispering until, finally, for the first time in a long, long time, I felt centered and focused.

"Are you leaving?"

Somehow it didn't surprise me to find Zo standing next to the rocks near the lighthouse.

"I'm not sure yet."

She walked over to me. "May I join you?"

I nodded, and she sat down, setting her huge beach bag beside her. She looked at Fuzzy, then dug in the bag and pulled out a bottle. She handed it to me.

I shook my head. Of course the bottle was warm.

While Fuzzy ate, I looked out at the ocean some more. It was late afternoon, and the light would start to fade soon.

"I have a lot of good reasons to stay," I said. "First, there's the house. I can't stand the idea of it being chained to Meg and Sarah—they're pretty awful. Not to mention the whole balance of power thing and whatever shenanigans those two are going to get up to once they get control of the house. And Nor and Wil can't do it. Shouldn't do it. Neither of them actually wants to be housekeeper, and neither would be right for the house anyway. Then there's the fact that the house seems to like me. Also, Fuzzy here sure needs a good home. So, yeah, lots of reasons to stay."

Zo harrumphed. "You're really not very good at this."

"No kidding."

Zo rolled her eyes. "What I mean is that, once again, you're not asking the right questions. Don't give me that blank look. You haven't mentioned once what *you* want. You. Not the house. Not Sarah or Meg or Nor or Wil. Not even Fuzzy. If ever there was a time for you to be selfish, Finn, this is it. So, what do you want?"

Fuzzy finished eating and curled up in my lap. I handed the bottle back to Zo. Then I went back to staring at the sea. "I thought I wanted to travel the world, sail the oceans, study."

"But?"

I doodled in the sand while I tried to sort through my thoughts. In a quiet voice I said, "I miss having a home. A place that's mine. Being at the house is making me realize that. And a home is not something I'll get traipsing around the world." I sighed. "But I'm worried I'll feel trapped."

"You want to be tethered, not shackled."

"Yes! Exactly. And if I stay here, I'm worried I'll miss out on all the adventure I've been craving, all the excitement. That I won't get to meet interesting people and see interesting things."

"Have you had a lack of interesting people or things so far?"

I snorted. "No."

"Well then, why does that have to change?"

"They keep the house really isolated."

"They have, yes."

A light went off in my brain. "But I don't have to."

Zo raised an eyebrow at me. "Oh?"

"Meg and Sarah were going to make changes—that means I could, too." I thought for a while before I said, "If I were to stay, I'd have to change the rules. A lot. Starting with letting people into the house."

Zo nodded. "I see."

I looked out at the ocean. "Still, I'm not sure how this doesn't wind up feeling like the diner...only with fewer people and more trees. And, you know, with magic."

In my peripheral vision, I could see Zo tilt her head, but she kept her gaze on the ocean. "What if I told you I can pretty much guarantee you won't be bored—that your universe will expand, not contract...that you won't lack for...interesting things?"

I turned to stare at her, my thoughts racing.

She watched me think then nodded. "That's what I thought," she said. She smiled at me and gestured to my lap. "And besides, don't you want to stay and find out what Fuzzy is?"

Chapter Thirty-Nine

Fuzzy and I came back to the house just as the day was edging toward twilight.

I closed the door and took in the quiet in my room. I could feel the house waiting.

Sitting on the edge of my bed, I talked with Bayley. I explained my thought process and what I wanted for the future. When I finished, I said, "I'll work with you, of course, and you will get to make choices, too. But that's my plan. So, knowing all that, I have to ask you: Bayley, would you like me to be your new housekeeper?"

A loud *ding* reverberated through me as the curtains started swishing madly. Then two branches sprouted from the floor, reached up, and gently wrapped around me, enfolding me. I hugged Bayley back for a long moment before the branches withdrew.

I went downstairs with Fuzzy and found Nor and Wil in the kitchen. They both stood up as I walked in.

"Okay, let's do this."

Nor looked me over and said, "You're staying."

"Yup."

"Okay."

Wil said, "Really?"

"Yes."

"What changed your mind? And why are you covered in sand?"

"Later, Wil. Let's just get this done. Do we need Sarah for the ceremony?"

"Actually, no."

Nor said, "While you were gone, I asked the house if there was a copy of the binding spell anywhere on the premises. Bayley led us right to it."

"It was in the attic," said Wil. "You should see all the stuff up there. Who knows what else is lying around in a trunk, waiting to be found."

"Focus, Wil. So we can do this?"

"Yes."

"Great, let's go."

Wil and Nor exchanged looks. "It's, uh, it's pretty intense, Finn."

"I figured," I said. Still, I flinched when Wil grabbed a wicked-looking knife from the butcher block.

Nor said, "We planned ahead, just in case, so we have everything ready." She handed a bag to Wil, who grabbed a sheaf of yellowing pages in his other hand. Nor plunked a second bag on the table and pulled out a tank top and shorts.

"Go put these on," she said, handing them to me.

"Why?"

"So you don't ruin your clothes."

And didn't that sound fun. I didn't argue though. I quickly changed in the bathroom and met Nor, Wil, and Fuzzy at the back door.

Nor said, "What do you want to do about Fuzzy?"

"He comes with us," I said.

When I stepped out on the porch, I came to an abrupt halt. "That wasn't there before," I said, looking at the staircase spiraling up the back of the house.

"We're going to the roof," said Wil.

Fuzzy and I followed him and Nor up the stairs.

When I reached the roof, I paused to look around me.

A raised platform in the shape of a large, flat circle dominated the middle of the roof. A walkway led from the stairs to it. As we crossed the roof, a rectangular slab sprouted up from the center of the circle.

I swallowed hard, my throat suddenly dry. It looked like

one of those sacrificial altars I'd seen in horror movies, except this one was made of wood instead of stone.

Wil said, "Lie down on the table."

I did as he instructed. While I was lying down, he and Nor went to work around me.

Wil walked around the edge of the circle, muttering while he scattered something from a pouch. When he'd made a complete circle, my ears popped. He stopped and came back over to me.

While Wil did his thing, Nor laid out bowls: one each of water, sand, fur, a stick of incense, and a small candle. She set them at particular spots in the circle and then went from item to item, muttering to each. The incense and candle ignited when she spoke to them.

When she was done, she and Wil came over to me. Fuzzy stood nearby but didn't attempt to leap up on me.

Nor said, "We're ready."

"Do you have to give me the temporary bond first, or do we just do the whole thing at once?" I asked.

"Whole thing." She caught my gaze and said, "This is going to hurt."

I swallowed hard. "Knife?"

"Knife."

"Fine. Let's just do it."

Nor slashed the knife across my palm. I hissed at the sharp sting.

Wil said, "Keep your palm flat on the table."

I did, and I could feel my blood sinking into the wood. The house hummed under me.

Nor and Wil circled around me as they chanted. Wil stopped at my head, and Nor stopped at my feet.

The air crackled and pressure built, like it was about to thunder.

Underneath me, the slab writhed. Wooden shoots sprouted and covered me, pinning me to the slab. Then the shoots began tunneling into the skin on my arms and legs. I yelled, in terror and in pain.

Things got hazy after that.

The one clear memory I had was of Nor placing her hands on either side of my head, forcing me to look at her as she asked, "Finn, do you agree to accept the permanent housekeeper bond?"

I said, "Yes, I do." Then I'd giggled and said something about shouldn't I be wearing a wedding dress if I was gonna get married?

Things got foggy again after that.

When I fully came back to myself, twilight had deepened into night.

I was still lying on top of the slab. Fuzzy was kneading my lap, purring. I lifted my head and looked down at my body. The wooden shoots were gone. I blinked a few times. There were no marks on me, and there was no blood anywhere. When I raised my hand, the cut on my palm was gone, too.

I turned my head to see Nor was putting the bowls back in the bag she'd brought them in. Wil was walking counterclockwise around the edge of the circle.

"Are we done?" I asked.

They both looked very pale and drawn as they approached me.

"Yes. How do you feel?" asked Nor, concern wrinkling her face.

"Uh," I thought about it. "Fine? Actually, better than I should. Nothing hurts."

Wil didn't look surprised. He said, "Try sitting up."

I put a hand on Fuzzy to keep him steady and sat up slowly. As soon as I was upright, the slab underneath me flowed into a chair, so that I could lean back comfortably.

And suddenly, I felt my connection to the house. It was like an extra presence in my mind. I could feel its joy and something that I thought might be hope radiating toward me.

"Hi, Bayley. You doing okay?" I asked. I heard a single grunt from a nearby plank, but I didn't need it because I could feel Bayley's "yes."

I closed my eyes briefly and tried to sort through the information that was knocking at my consciousness. This was much different than the temporary bond. Not only could I sense all sorts of things coming from Bayley, but I could feel the property around us. I couldn't quite sort through it all yet, but I felt like I could reach out to the trees around us. I stretched my mind and realized I could clearly feel the edges of the property.

Opening my eyes, I stared at the forest around me. I gasped as all the trees in my sight bobbed in unison, as though they were nodding hello to me.

"Whoa," said Wil.

Nor looked awed.

I wondered if my sense of connection would get stronger and what kind of effects it would have. Well, I was going to find out. For now, I tried to shut everything into a corner of my mind so I could think clearly.

I hugged Fuzzy in my arms and stood, wobbling a bit.

A rumbling, rustling, creaking sound made me pause. As we watched, tree-shaped posts popped up along the wooden walkway, continuing all the way into the circle, ending right in front of me. The branches of the trees wove together to form a rail to help me across the roof to the stairs.

The tree post closest to me reached out one branch. I held out my hand to it, and it gently wrapped around my outstretched hand.

"Well," I said. "I think this is going to be the beginning of a very interesting friendship."

Chapter Forty

I sat in the treehouse Bayley and Libby had built for me, sipping a cup of coffee while Fuzzy napped beside me. From up here at the top of Libby, I could see the ocean in the distance.

Nor and Wil had gone back home, but I video chatted with Nor online nearly every day, and she and her girlfriend were planning to visit soon. Wil was also due back for a visit next week. As official liaison between me and the council, he had a lot of work ahead of him.

Once Wil and Nor had informed Sarah, Meg, and Doug about the bonding, they'd taken off for parts unknown. Wil took care of making sure that Meg's and Doug's things were packed and carted off, so now the house was officially mine. Bayley and I were in discussions on how we'd like to redecorate.

I'd gotten a text from a number I didn't recognize yesterday. I nearly fell off my chair when I'd realized it was from Lars. He said he works for some kind of mercenary outfit that caters exclusively to the magical families. I guess I must've made an impression because he told me to keep his number. He seemed to think I was going to need it.

He was probably right. But I wasn't without allies. With Bayley's enthusiastic approval, I was planning on hosting the first multi-magic dinner in, well, forever. Pete, Lou, Eagan, Zo, and the doc were all coming. I hadn't invited Gram. I was still mad at him. But there had to be a less douchey member of the water family somewhere, and I looked forward to meeting them eventually.

Reportedly, the council was horrified.

Bayley and I found that hilarious.

Despite their disapproval, the council had stuck to its part of the housekeeper bargain and set up a generous account for me. But they were withholding in other ways. They refused to tell me what the big deal was with the door until they'd decided what they were going to do about me. I'd only gotten up the courage to try to open it again once. It'd opened easily. To the closet. For now, I'd decided to leave it alone. But I knew I was going to have to figure it out sometime soon.

I'd also epically failed in figuring out my necklace. Whatever was living in there refused to talk to me about who or what it was. But I still couldn't bear to take the necklace off. Wil was setting me up with a magic tutor and hopefully I'd learn enough to be able to figure it out eventually.

Fuzzy yawned, stretched, and stood up. When Dr. Meriwether had called about collecting him, I'd told him not to bother. He'd laughed in a way that said my response was exactly what he'd been expecting. I looked at Fuzzy. He stared back at me. I shook my head and smiled. Nothing about him was expected, and that was just fine by me.

I stood and looked out over the property, my property. A deep sense of peace filled me, edged with excitement. There was so much to explore here. It was going to take me weeks just to walk the entire property. And then, of course, there were the secrets that the house was hiding.

"C'mon, Fuzzy. Let's go find some magic."

Acknowledgements

I've been very fortunate to have a lot of support along this book writing adventure.

First and foremost, my deep and heartfelt thanks to Michael Tangent for outstanding editing and design, and for your unwavering friendship. Years before I finally sat down at the keyboard, you told me I could do this. Unfortunately for you, in the six years it took me to finally release this book into the wild, you had to *keep* reminding me. Daily. Sometimes hourly. You did so with humor and kindness, not to mention a whole ton of cello/sax/flute/trumpet/oboe/French horn/euphonium. You've helped make this book better with your clever insight and ninja-level attention to detail, and I love the cover so much I grin every time I see it. Thank you for the hours of plot noodling and patient hand-holding as I stumbled my way through this process. I'm so fortunate to have you with me on this journey.

This book started as a NaNoWriMo novel. Thank you, NaNoWriMo! At the time, I was recovering from a serious illness and literally staggered into the Austin Java Writing Company's NaNoWriMo meetup. They didn't bat an eye at my wonky, wobbly state and, in fact, welcomed me and made me part of the group. My sincere thanks to my Austin Java Writing cohorts: Hannah Baumann, Emily Bristow, Casi Clarkson, Audrey Coulthurst, Ivy Crawford, Delia Davila, Enrique Gomez, Amber Jonker, Kurt Korfmacher, Rebecca Leach, Deanna Roy, Lori Thomas, Zabe Truesdell, and Helen Wiley. Thank you for all the laughter and support. In particular, thank you to Deanna Roy and Audrey Coulthurst for sharing your advanced authoring knowledge with me. I'm lucky to have such excellent author models to learn from.

Being friends with an author takes a special kind of endurance, and I'm very grateful to have some really patient friends and family. Thank you all!

In particular, thank you to Morgan Miars and Derek Koger. For all the dinners I hijacked with book talk and all the nights I kept you standing in your kitchen discussing magical theory, I thank you. Also, Morgan, my sincere thanks for the excellent styling and make-up artistry. If I'd done it myself, in all my photos I'd have looked like a four-year-old who got into Mom's makeup. Instead, thanks to your skills, I actually look like an author. And Derek, thank you for the hours you've spent helping me with my website and for not once asking me if I've tried turning it off and on again.

Thank you to my excellent advanced reading team: Amanda Barboza, Mary DeNatale, Michael Duhan, Steven Elliott, Tina Giakoumis, Alesha Howe, Francis Jesch, Mary Jesch, Shauna McQuade, and George Moromisato. My peeps, your enthusiasm and support has meant the world to me.

In his book *On Writing*, Stephen King talks about having one, specific reader that you write for. For me, that person is my alpha reader, Moira DeNatale. If you want to know what above-and-beyond support looks like, look no further than Moira. She read the chapters in this book as I completed them, giving me feedback and encouragement that kept me writing. Even though it was torture for her to read a tiny bit, then have to wait however many weeks it took me to get the next bit done, she hung in there, cheerleading me the whole way.

Thank you, Mo. Words are not adequate for how thankful I am for all you do.

And last, but by no means least, thank you to my readers. I'm very grateful to you for joining me and Finn as we adventure forth. My goal in these books is to bring some laughter and a little magic into your day, and I hope I'm sending you on your way with a smile.

And guess what? There's more magic to come.

97748193R00170

Made in the USA
Middletown, DE
06 November 2018